BRAIN WAVES

BRAIN WAVES

A NOVEL
BY SHULI MENSH

THE JUDAICA PRESS, INC.

Brain Waves

© 2008 by Shuli Mensh

ISBN: 978-1-932443-92-9

Editor: Roberta Chester
Proofreader: Hadassa Goldsmith

THE JUDAICA PRESS, INC.
123 Ditmas Avenue / Brooklyn, NY 11218
718-972-6200 / 800-972-6201
info@judaicapress.com
www.judaicapress.com

DEDICATION

*This one is dedicated to my wonderful parents
Rabbi and Mrs. Chaim and Basya Goldman of Chicago*

whose boundless enthusiasm and
constant encouragement mean
so much to me ... thank you for
being my #1 fans!

I'd also like to mention my
special Bubby, Mrs. Esther Frank
of Yerushalayim, whose Rosh
Chodesh phone calls I always look
forward to ...

And to Ashira, Meira, Shoshana
and of course Alan, with much
love and gratitude ...

ACKNOWLEDGMENTS

I would like to thank . . .

Roberta Chester for editing this
novel in a most professional and
pleasant manner. It was a pleasure
to work with you and I look forward to
future projects.

I would also like to thank
Nachum Shapiro and everyone at
Judaica Press for turning this novel
into a reality. Your dedication and
professionalism were apparent from the
start and very much appreciated.

I'd also like to mention my
amazing sisters, Ahuva Wainhaus
and Tirza Wealcatch, who could
always be counted on for helpful ideas
and insightful advice ... thank you!

"What existed is elusive;
it is so very deep.
Who can fathom it?"

– ECCLESIASTES 7:24

"*Mom?*"

"Yes, Jacob?" she asked eagerly, thrilled that her son was calling her. His phone calls had dwindled from occasional to sporadic to very infrequent, so naturally she wondered what prompted his call. They hadn't always been on the best of terms, occasionally clashing over his life choices. Still, he was her son. Her only son.

"Ma, I thought we've been through that." He clearly sounded annoyed. "It's Jack, remember? The name's Jack."

"I'm sorry, son," she answered quietly. "I guess I forgot. It's just that your grandfather, Jacob, was such an upright man ... a G-d-fearing man ...."

His voice rose. "Well, that's all very nice and good, but let's face it. He's dead and I'm very much alive. You really need to let the past go, Ma. Just let it go."

It was the old argument, and Pearl Morgenstern no longer had the strength to quarrel anymore. Besides, what could she say? Deep down she knew she was guilty of not having set much of an example. Not that she hadn't tried to impress upon him the importance of their Jewish faith; she'd tried, repeatedly, and failed.

She'd simply lacked basic knowledge about Jewish observance, never having learned much about her heritage. Still, she regretted the fact that her son had shown no interest in Judaism, never attending synagogue with her, preferring instead the company of his friends.

Her husband also hadn't been knowledgeable about Judaism, and after he died, her son had ignored her attempts to introduce what he considered to be foreign concepts into their lives. Then he'd left for college. He returned only once or twice a year, each time more antagonistic toward her efforts.

He'd even mocked her each Friday evening when she lit two candles in the lovely silver candlesticks she had inherited from her mother, a ritual she had kept ever since she'd been a young bride, as her mother had before her.

And as he grew older, long after he graduated college and embarked on a successful career, Pearl's heart ached. She often found herself contemplating what she could have done differently. She found herself constantly wondering what she could possibly say to make him understand that a Jewish life should be infused with some meaning, but she'd lacked the proper words.

It was hard to verbalize why these seemingly old-fashioned rituals were so important to her, yet she was aware that she carried a spark within her that even she couldn't quite comprehend. But since her son was so disdainful of what he considered to be her strange obsession, over the years she'd gradually refrained from mentioning Judaism to him altogether.

Time passed, and several years earlier Jacob had married. Though his bride had been cold and distant from the start, Pearl had tried to forge a relationship with her, taking solace in the fact that at least she was a Jewish girl.

Pearl had been overjoyed when six months ago they'd been blessed with a child, a daughter, and she had generously offered to baby-sit any time at all. They had never before accepted her offers, so she was completely surprised by what her son was now saying.

"... so, anyway, I have this interview in Oakland, and Fran has an audition in San Francisco, so we figured it would be best if you could come here for the weekend to watch the baby. What do you say?"

Pearl was so excited that for several seconds she could hardly speak.

"Oh, that would be wonderful!" she exclaimed. "It'll give me a chance to get to know my precious little Sarala."

"Her name is Sarah," he sighed. "Let's not confuse her. You practically insisted on it, remember? The very least you could do is call her by her given name."

"Of course, son, of course," she replied, hastily. "A beautiful name ... and my mother would've been so proud ..."

He chuckled, though he didn't seem at all amused. "Yeah, whatever. Are you sure you're up to the challenge? She's six months already, and quite a handful. The nanny is on vacation, so I figured ..."

Pearl immediately said, "Of course, son. Don't worry, she'll be in good hands."

"So we'll see you Friday, okay?"

"Sure, I'll be there."

Pearl hung up, too ecstatic to feel hurt by the cold, hard edge in his voice. Now she would have a chance to bond with her granddaughter, and she could hardly wait.

"Jack's number is written on the pad of paper on the counter," her daughter-in-law called over her shoulder as she climbed into her car. "I won't be able to take any calls."

"All right, that's fine," Pearl answered. "Good luck on your –"

The car was already backing out down the driveway, the gravel crunching under the tires.

Her son hadn't been there to greet her, and his wife had been terse and hurried. She was pursuing a career as an actress, and though this didn't please Pearl, she was in too good a mood to dwell on it.

She had only been in their home a few times, and each time the invitations had seemed begrudgingly extended. Therefore, she was still a bit stunned that her son had acquiesced to have her stay at his house all weekend.

Just her and Sarala.

She closed the mahogany doors and surveyed the room around her. The living area was very spacious with soaring ceilings and floor-to-ceiling windows. The house was built high in the hills, and the view was spectacular. Her son was obviously doing quite well, but to Pearl, none of that mattered.

All that mattered to her was the precious baby who was sound asleep in her bassinet, her tiny hand close to her sweet little mouth.

She wasn't aware how long she stood gazing lovingly at her adorable granddaughter. She was content to just stand there, admiring the baby's long dark eyelashes, her pudgy cheeks and the steady, even breathing that seemed so peaceful.

The sun was dipping lower in the sky ... she knew it would soon be the Sabbath.

She walked over to her suitcase and withdrew the two shining candlesticks, which she reverently placed on the table.

She was rummaging through a kitchen drawer, hoping to find some matches, when she heard the sound.

It was her granddaughter, beginning to stir.

She rushed to the bassinet and cradled the child in her arms.

"Shh, don't cry, Sarala, dear," she murmured. "Bubbie is here, isn't that wonderful?"

Though the baby didn't recognize Pearl, she seemed quite content in her arms, nonetheless.

"I knew we'd get along just fine," she crooned. "What a delicious girl you are! What a big girl!"

She carried her granddaughter into the kitchen, to resume her search. Finally, she found a book of matches, and she placed the baby gently into her high chair.

"It's time for me to light the *Shabbos* candles, my precious. See what I'm doing? I am going to light one candle, and then the next ... here we go ...."

And then Pearl recited in a loud, clear voice the only blessing that she knew, the blessing on the candles.

The lit candles cast a glow that was reflected in the baby's enormous blue eyes. Mesmerized by the flames, the baby stared. An innocent smile formed on her little face as she looked from the candles to Pearl, and then back again.

"You like the candles, right, Sarala, my sweet? Of course,

you do," she soothed. "And when you're older, you'll light the *Shabbos* candles, too."

It was more than just wistful words, she realized. It was more like a prayer. She silently mouthed her heartfelt hope … that this child should indeed grow up to live a fulfilling Jewish life … to respect her heritage … to rekindle that Jewish spark ….

"You'll be like Sarah, our Matriarch. Isn't that right, precious? I know you will … you'll see, you will …."

And the baby stared at the candles and smiled.

Thirty-six years later . . .

CHAPTER 1

The day was mild and breezy, and the sunlight felt warm and invigorating. Lifting her face upwards and basking in the bright glow of the new day, she walked quickly across the crowded parking lot to her car.

She was glad that she'd gone ahead and purchased the sleek, new convertible, even though Michael was less than enthusiastic. Today, the silvery blue color was almost blindingly bright in the sun, and she paused to admire its aerodynamic, streamlined design and its supple leather interior. This was her dream car. Sure, it was a little extravagant, but after all, she'd earned it day after day, year after year, working endless hours, and through sheer determination, courageously forging a new firm all her own.

The car was only a symbol; still, when she was behind the steering wheel, her amber hair blowing in the wind, the car was a statement to the world that she, Sarah Morgan, had made it!

As if Mother Nature herself had declared a celebration, it was a perfect February day. Unusual for downtown Los Angeles, the cloudless sky was blue and clear, and the hazy smog that usually hovered over the city was nowhere in sight.

She found herself singing along to the radio, for the first time in ages.

At every traffic light, she couldn't help admiring the sparkling new ring that encircled the finger on her left hand. It was exactly as she'd pictured it from Michael's description. The brilliant faceted diamond was so spectacular, it almost distracted her from the proposal that accompanied it, she thought wistfully. Gazing at the ring, Sarah couldn't help but wonder, even now, whether Michael had felt pressured into finally proposing. Not that Michael hadn't been sincere; he had, of course, but she still didn't know if marriage was what he really desired.

What had been his exact words? She wished she could recall them … the proposal itself had seemed surreal … perhaps because she'd longed to hear it for so long …

Always precise and detail-oriented, Michael had cleared his throat, as he was wont to do, and very seriously and properly asked for her hand in marriage … and with unflinching certainty, she'd said yes.

She would be the future Mrs. Michael Sloane.

Her cell phone beeped, and touching the speaker pad, she answered, "Hello?"

"Sarah, it's me."

"Michael, I'm finding it difficult to drive."

"Really? The traffic's bad this early?"

"No, the traffic is fine. It's the glare from my ring that's blinding me!"

He gave a wry laugh. "Try not to get into an accident, okay?"

"I'll try not to," she answered.

His tone became a bit more serious as he asked, "Did you call your grandmother?"

She could not answer the question.

"Sarah, we've been through this …"

"I know. Don't worry, I'll call her from the airport."

"I think we both know that's not going to happen. I think you're going to have to deal with this, Sarah. We both need to deal with this."

"I'll only be away for three days … can't we do this when I get back?"

"I can't help but feel this just isn't your top priority," he replied sharply.

"Don't be upset with me, Michael," she pleaded. "Please, I just need to do this in my own way. You can understand that, can't you?"

"I suppose so. I just can't see procrastinating the inevitable … why not just get it over with?"

"Speaking of not procrastinating, have you mentioned our engagement to your brother?" she challenged.

Michael had only one half-brother, the mysterious Robert who worked in the Midwest, whom she'd never met in all the years of their courtship. She used to tease Michael about him, insinuating that Robert didn't even exist and he'd conjured up an imaginary friend to allay his loneliness.

He had humored her until one day, finally exasperated, he showed her Robert's picture, and that had ended the mock argument. Although they only shared the same mother, the resemblance was unmistakable with their blonde hair and similar eyes.

"Of course I told Robert. In fact, he was the very first person I told," he said defensively.

"That's the difference between us, Michael. I know you like it when everything is definite and clear … but when it comes to my family, everything is so much more complicated … you just have to trust me on this one, okay? I promise to work things out when I return."

"All right, whatever," he responded curtly. "Listen, the Henderson clients just came in the office, I need to go …."

She chose to ignore his last, clipped remark. "Good. Just go over the numbers we spoke about, okay? They deserve to take this to trial, with a stunning verdict. I want MeadowLane to pay for what they did."

"Sure, boss," he said. "Have a safe trip, okay?"

"I'll call you when I land in Chicago."

"Bye."

She hesitated before she pressed the "END" button. She knew Michael was annoyed with her whenever he called her *boss,* but she just couldn't seem to muster the strength to make that long overdue call ….

What would she say? How would her grandmother react?

As she drove, she allowed herself the luxury of remembering … something that she didn't do very often. She absentmindedly fingered the faded gold chain that she'd worn around her neck, ever since she'd been twelve years old. A gift from her grandmother, it was in the shape of a *Magen David,* a Jewish star. Sentimental at heart, she'd never removed it from around her neck.

She could still recall how insecure she'd felt that day, over twenty years earlier. Her father, together with his new wife, had thrown an enormous party at their country club in honor of her *bat mitzvah.* No expense had been spared, and it had been lavish in the extreme. All of her friends had been impressed, but she'd had the maturity, even at that young age, to realize that her existence was not enviable.

Her parents' divorce had been vicious; so brutal, in fact, that she'd been court-ordered to live with her grandmother until the judge could work out a settlement agreement. Custody was not the issue in their dispute. It had been agreed early on that her father would have sole custody of Sarah. Her mother's dream of pursuing a career as an actress left little time for motherhood, and so she had not fought for her. The legal battles had been purely mercenary.

It had taken three years. She was only nine years old when she'd moved into her grandmother's cozy, cluttered apartment, and twelve years old when she'd left. Those three years had been the happiest of her childhood, and on the day of the *bat mitzvah* party, her happiness had been bittersweet; she would be leaving her grandmother's home and moving in with her father and his new wife at their Malibu estate. Their new home was the epitome of modern architecture, with cold steel beams carved out of the craggy mountainside. It was perched directly over the shimmering waters of the Pacific Ocean, and to most girls it would have seemed idyllic, but not to Sarah.

Her grandmother had taken her aside that day, privately, and in her heavily accented voice, she murmured, "Here is a little gift from me, Sarala."

She'd pressed the necklace into her hand.

"You've given me so much already, Bubbie. Thank you."

Those two little words seemed so inadequate, and she'd wanted to say more, but her heart was too full to express her feelings. Her grandmother seemed to understand, though, as she nodded and said, "I don't want you to forget."

"How could I ever forget you, Bubbie?"

"No, Sarala, that's not what I mean. It's *you* I'm talking about. Don't forget who you are, my Sarala. Your father wants you to forget, but I want you to remember. You are Sarah Morgenstern, and now, today, you are a young Jewish woman. Never forget who you are. I am giving you this star so you will always remember."

"Don't worry, Bubbie. I won't forget."

Although she hadn't thought about it for a long time, she could recall that conversation as if it had taken place yesterday.

So much had happened since that day. Her father had changed their last name to Morgan, shortly after his marriage. Sarah, in her childish naiveté, had been puzzled why his new wife had been vehement about the change, but her father had casually explained that it was more convenient for his work. In the end, though, it hadn't mattered.

His second wife divorced him barely five years later, and when Sarah was in her second year of college, her father had passed away.

Sarah had attended the funeral, wondering if she'd be able to catch a glimpse of her mother, with whom she'd had no contact since she'd been a young child. True to form, she never showed, of course.

Sarah felt strangely numb at the memorial service, not having really known her father as a daughter should, and being motherless, as well. Her grandmother had been there, stoically holding her own grief in check as she patted the arm of her only grandchild.

Sarah remembered how they had stood there, each of them only having each other left. Overwhelmed by that memory, she pulled her car into the valet parking area at LAX, knowing she'd have to make the call.

A nervous-looking, freckle-faced, young attendant met her car and swiftly proceeded to take her bags from the trunk.

"Take good care of the Jaguar, please. It's brand new," she told the attendant, and pressed a twenty-dollar bill in his hand.

"Of course," he reassured her. "It sure is a beautiful car. It's in good hands. "

She walked over to the outdoor ticketing counter and was

pleased to find that he had stacked her monogrammed Louis Vuitton luggage neatly at the curb. Another extravagance, of course, but since she traveled so often, she felt it was money well spent.

"Tickets and identification, please."

She handed her tickets to the elderly ticket clerk, and, as she did so, her engagement ring was plainly obvious.

"My congratulations to you, Ms. Morgan. My, that's some sparkler you've got on there …."

She merely smiled.

He handed the tickets back to her. "That'll be Gate 7F. Have a nice flight."

"Thank you."

She made her way toward the gate with her pilot's case containing her wallet, laptop and papers, which she would keep with her on the plane. She had always disliked handbags, no matter how fashionable.

Passing through security, she easily found her gate, when she realized with chagrin that she was rather early. They wouldn't start boarding for at least another hour.

Surely she had enough work to occupy her time.

As she rummaged through her case, she spied her cell phone.

She could ignore it no longer; the call simply had to be made. Picking up the phone, she pressed the number 1 on her speed-dial.

A woman's voice answered, "Beth Shalom Home for the Aged, how may I direct your call?"

"Pearl Morgenstern's room, please."

"One moment, please." There was a long pause, and then her grandmother's familiar voice answered.

"Hello?"

"Hello, Bubbie, it's Sarah."

"Sarala, my precious! How are you? It's been so long since I've heard from you."

"I know. I'm sorry, Bubbie. I've been … busy."

"Of course, of course. I know you're working hard. How is your new company?"

"Oh, fine, fine. It's a law firm that I started, with a … friend of mine. It's been pretty successful, so far."

"*Mazel tov, mazel tov!* All your hard work is paying off. I'm so proud of you."

Sarah was surprised to discover that she was on the verge of tears at these words.

Her grandmother continued, "You must have quite a few people working for you. I hear so much noise in the background."

"Actually, Bubbie, I'm calling from the airport. That's why I wanted to call you … to say good-bye. I'm going to Chicago for a few days. There's a legal conference, and I'm a keynote speaker."

"A speaker at a conference? My, my, how exciting! I wish I could be there to hear you."

"I would like that, too. Maybe one day, Bubbie."

"I know you have to catch the plane. I don't want you to be late. I am so happy to hear your voice!"

Sarah felt a stab of guilt pierce her heart.

"I'd like to come by and visit you, Bubbie, when I return. And, maybe even … bring a friend of mine."

"That would be wonderful. I'm looking forward to it. Have a safe trip. Good-bye, my Sarala."

"Bye, Bubbie."

She put down the cell phone. Suddenly, the day ahead was not nearly as exciting or promising as it was before the short phone call.

When Sarah heard the boarding announcement for first-class passengers, she walked to the flight attendant who took her boarding pass.

Her thoughts were elsewhere as she walked across the tarmac that led her to the plane.

Her grandmother loved her, didn't she?

Her grandmother would be happy for her, wouldn't she?

The flight attendants greeted her with smiles, and she settled herself into her seat, repeating those words to herself as if they were a mantra.

She was placing her pilot's case into the overhead bin when her cell phone rang. She reached into her pocket and flipped it open.

"Michael?"

"Yeah, it's me. The Hendersons are happy with the settlement offer ... really happy. I don't think we have to take this to trial; it's a done deal."

"What?"

She just could not absorb what she'd heard. Twenty-two months of hard work ... there had been so much riding on this case ... the offer wasn't nearly enough. The Henderson case was to be the absolute pinnacle – the crowning achievement of their careers ....

MeadowLane Retirement Village was offering them ten million dollars to walk away. A large sum, to be sure; but to Sarah, it was a mere pittance for the families who were affected by the horrific calamity. If they would take this to trial, as Sarah was inclined to do, the sum would be astronomical. Moreover, Sarah was adamant that MeadowLane not emerge from this travesty with a sparkling clean reputation. It was their negligence that had killed Mrs. Henderson's parents and injured several other vulnerable, elderly residents who would never fully recover. She thought of her own grandmother at the nursing home in which she resided, and she shuddered.

Trying to compose herself, she said, shakily, "I just don't understand. After our fee, that will mean only six million dollars for the Hendersons to split with the other families involved. It's not enough, not even close."

Michael paused. "Apparently, it's enough for them. And I have to tell you, Sarah, I'm inclined to agree. We'll be getting a four million dollar fee. That's nothing to sneeze at. A settlement of ten million dollars will put us right alongside some of the most prestigious law firms in southern California. I say we take it."

"And I say we don't!" Sarah said, bristling. "We worked too hard to just take the first offer. MeadowLane was completely negligent … it's open and shut. Two people lost their lives that day, and at least four others will have to live with their injuries for the rest of their lives. Really, in this day and age when we can and should expect more from our institutions, there's no excuse! Ten million is a slap in the face!"

"Why are you shouting at me?" Michael demanded. "It's not as if I'm unaware of the facts of the case."

"I'm sorry. I didn't mean to shout," she replied, lowering her voice. "But you know as well as I do that if we take this to trial the verdict will be stunning. I can predict this in the tens of millions, Michael. I want MeadowLane to pay. Can you imagine if this had been my grandmother?"

"This wasn't your grandmother. We can't let this get personal, Sarah. And they *will* be paying … ten million dollars. What if the jury views it differently? Are you prepared to walk away with nothing? Because, I'll tell you right now, I'm not.

They were elderly people, let's not forget. Juries don't often award large sums for the elderly."

"That doesn't make any sense!" she said, exasperated. "They didn't deserve to die just because they're old."

"I never said they did."

"I'll speak with them, make them see reason. Charlotte Henderson originally said that she didn't even care about the money – she just wanted to see MeadowLane out of business. And so do I."

"You said that already, boss."

She ignored this. "I really think I should tell them –"

"Sarah, I *told* them," he retorted, his voice rising. "Believe me, I spelled it out quite clearly. Their minds are made up. They want to settle and that's that. Deal with it."

She instinctively knew when to back down. Technically, she *was* Michael's boss, and it was at times like these when she had to tread cautiously. "All right, then. I'm sure you did everything you could. Still, I am going to speak with them the second I get back and try to persuade them to hold out longer. We can always settle on the eve of trial, if it comes to that. The offer will still be on the table."

Another pause. "Sure, boss."

In a deliberate effort to change the subject, Sarah said brightly, "Michael? Speaking of my grandmother, I called her from the airport."

"You're kidding," he said, incredulously. "I thought you wanted to do it when you got back. What made you change your mind?"

"I'm not exactly sure … but I did mention to her that I would be visiting her when I return, with a friend of mine."

"Let me guess. I'm the friend, right?"

"Yes, but —"

"But you couldn't bring yourself to tell her just yet." The annoyance in his voice was unmistakable.

"Michael, we will tell her, together. You and I. Okay? This is not something I could tell her over the phone."

"You've left me with little choice."

Just then, a flight attendant walked by and motioned to Sarah to close her cell phone, as the plane was about to taxi to the runway.

"Michael, I have to go. The flight is about to take off."

"Have a good trip."

As she closed her cell phone, she couldn't help but feel a bit deflated at the tone of his voice. It was plainly clear that his pride had been wounded, once again, and she was determined to rectify the situation as soon as it was possible for her to do so. It just wasn't something she was looking forward to.

She leaned back in her seat and tried to relax. As the aircraft ascended higher and higher in the sky, she looked out the small window on her left. The plane tilted first one way, then the other, and she couldn't help but feel like a winged bird, soaring over Los Angeles. How peaceful it all seemed from her vantage point. She found herself looking high into the Hollywood Hills, imagining the future home that she and Michael would one day build there.

They had much in common, the two of them. They were both undeniably driven and ambitious.

Sometimes it caused friction between them, as with any couple that worked together, she told herself. Whenever a large settlement was about to take place, the tension became blatant, as it had today. Michael had a more cautious nature, jumping at the first offer they received, while Sarah was determined to extract every cent they possibly could. They had worked so hard to achieve results in this case … results that were almost within their grasp ….

She tried not to think of the fact that a trial would cost in the tens of thousands of dollars, and a trial date would likely be at least a year from that point.

It would delay their plans of building their dream home, indefinitely. Her loft in Santa Monica was barely enough room for her. How would it accommodate Michael, as well? They might have to look for a rental until their home was finished.

Still, she was prepared to wait. She was absolutely passionate about taking this particular case to trial. She would have to talk to the Hendersons.

The flight attendant walked by with the drink cart. Sarah declined a soft drink and reclined back, eager to catch up on much needed rest. She had been working non-stop for weeks now, getting maybe two, three hours of sleep a night.

And last night, after Michael had dropped her off, she'd been too excited and restless to sleep. It hadn't come as a surprise; rather, she could hardly believe that Michael had finally acquiesced. She had pressured him for a long time to propose, and he had finally given in.

They'd known each other since law school, and they both had similar goals. To Sarah, it made sense. And when something made sense to her, she pursued it until she won. She was pragmatic, not given to overly sentimental, idealized notions, and Michael was much the same, so they had that in common, as well.

No longer able to fight the sleep that was threatening to overtake her, she closed her eyes and drifted off ….

They were walking down a long corridor ... the room slowly came into view, at the very end of the hallway. Upon entering it, she was saddened to see the figure at the window, staring listlessly at the street below. The old woman's eyes, once alive and vibrant, now appeared dull and lifeless, and her shoulders sagged, as if the burden of living had become almost too much for her to bear ....

"Bubbie," she said softly.

Her grandmother slowly turned to her.

"Sarala, my precious. You've come to visit me." Her grandmother looked pleased at first, but then stared at Sarah's left, a puzzled expression upon her aged face.

Avoiding gazing at the companion at her side, Sarah said, "This is my friend, Bubbie. His name is Michael."

Her beloved grandmother's face was crestfallen. "He is so wonderful, Bubbie. Really, he is everything I have been looking for. He is successful, driven ..."

Oddly enough, the man at her side didn't say anything, and she dared not look at him.

Her grandmother replied, "Yes, my precious, but is he Jewish?"

She stood there, as if struck.

"You have forgotten, Sarala, dear. You have forgotten. You promised me you wouldn't forget, but you have. You have forgotten ... you have forgotten ...."

Sarah awoke with a start, her heart pounding. She looked wildly around her. Several passengers were reading, some were asleep, and the hum of the engines brought her back to reality.

It had only been a dream. Nonsense, really ...

But it had seemed so real ...

It had left her feeling shaken. Checking her watch, she was

surprised to discover that nearly three hours had passed. It was unlike her to sleep on a flight. She must have been more fatigued than she'd thought.

She decided to do what she did best when she needed to switch gears; namely, work. Opening her laptop, she began to make subtle changes on the speech she had prepared to give at the conference. She worked the entire flight, not allowing herself the luxury of dozing again.

Lost in the fine points of the speech and the technique of her delivery, she was startled when the pilot's voice came over the loudspeaker, "We are beginning our descent into the Chicago area ... please put away all laptops and electronic equipment."

Sarah closed her computer and stretched, kneading her tense, cramped muscles. Gazing out the small window, she saw the distinctive grid that was unmistakably Chicago below her. She looked at the magnificent Chicago skyline looming in the distance and poised on the shimmering waters of Lake Michigan. She had been in Chicago only once before, years earlier, for a job interview. She could well recall her nervousness and uncertainty at that time.

She experienced a surge of pride as she realized that she had come full circle, returning as a keynote speaker at an influential conference. She could now easily recall the excitement and exhilaration that she'd felt upon first seeing the tall, bold architecture of the many skyscrapers that now lit up the brilliant dusk sky with towers of twinkling lights.

It was already almost evening in Chicago, and Sarah was still on Pacific Time. Nonetheless, she felt a renewed spirit, and an unmistakable feeling of anticipation.

The plane touched down as the flight attendant's voice on the loudspeaker welcomed the travelers to Chicago and gave them a report on the weather. It was clear and cold on the ground, but the next few days would be extremely cold with the probability of snow and sleet and especially hazardous traveling conditions. Accustomed to southern California weather, Sarah had forgotten about Midwestern winters. Suddenly, she felt apprehensive about the possibility of being delayed in Chicago when she had to return immediately to deal with the Henderson case.

After they reached the gate, Sarah grabbed her pilot's case, laptop and belongings, and followed the other passengers off the plane.

O'Hare Airport was teeming with crowds of people, scurrying in every direction. The city's energy was almost palpable in contrast to the more mellow atmosphere of L.A.

She followed the masses of passengers downstairs, toward the baggage claim area, where several chauffeurs were holding up name tags beside the luggage carousels. She hurriedly walked over to an elderly, bewhiskered gentleman whose sign stated clearly, in black letters, *Sarah Morgan*.

"I'm Sarah Morgan," she said.

"Pleased to meet you, Ms. Morgan. My name is Tom Costa, and I'm here to take you to your hotel."

"Excellent. I just have to retrieve my bag."

"Oh, no problem, Ms. Morgan. I'll get it for you."

At that moment, her pager signaled. Checking it, she saw that it was Sharon Pierce, her good-natured, but absentminded, secretary.

She quickly dialed the office number, and Sharon picked it up on the first ring.

"Law Offices of Morgan-Sloane," she said perkily.

"Sharon, it's me. Did you just page me?"

"Is this Ms. Morgan?"

Sarah experienced her usual frustration with Sharon. The middle-aged woman was impossibly scatterbrained, but she'd never had the heart to dismiss her. "Of course it's me, Sharon. Who else would it be?"

Sharon giggled nervously. "Oh, sorry."

Sarah paused. "Well? Why did you page me?"

"Oh, right. Yes, I did, but now I can't remember why ..." she said, vaguely. "Oh, right, now I remember. Mr. Sloane wanted me to make sure that the driver was waiting for you in Chicago."

She sounded pleased with herself.

"Yes, he's here. He's actually getting my bag, and then I'll go straight to the Fairmont."

"Good. I'll tell Mr. Sloane when he returns."

"Okay, I'll touch base later."

She lowered her cell phone with a sigh. Honestly, there were times that Sharon seemed to be completely in a world of her own. She'd had a difficult life, and Sarah had taken pity on her and hired her, although Michael had wanted to terminate her employ almost from the start. Truthfully, for a firm of their stature, Sharon was surprisingly inept. Michael had broached the subject on more than a few occasions, in subtle and not so subtle ways, but she'd vehemently rejected the idea.

"She's a sweet lady," she'd insisted. "Have some pity on her. She gets her work done, more or less."

And so Sharon had stayed for two years, which often seemed interminably longer.

Sarah knew that as her once-fledgling firm would continue to grow, she'd have to hire more competent support staff. Even so, she just didn't welcome the idea.

Mr. Costa hoisted her bag onto his trolley, and she followed him out of the automatic doors that led outside. She was hit with an icy cold wind in the night air and hugged her cashmere pashmina tighter around her shoulders. The chauffeur turned around, the wind whipping his plaid scarf tied around his neck.

"If you don't mind my saying so, Ms. Morgan, you're not dressed right for the Windy City, no Ma'am."

"I'm inclined to agree with you, Tom," she smiled. "I have some warmer things packed in my bags. I'm just going to the hotel. I'll be fine."

He shook his head, grumbled something about *those California people* under his breath, and opened the door of the shiny black limousine.

She got in quickly as he put the bags in the trunk with a thud, and then got behind the wheel. He turned around, and in a thickly-accented Midwestern wheeze asked, "The Fairmont, eh?"

"Yes, thank you."

He sped away from the curb, chatting all the while.

"Ever been here before?"

"Yes, as a matter of fact, many years ago. I was quite taken with the city."

Sarah saw him grinning in the rear view mirror. "Yes, Ma'am, we've got it all right here. You're staying in a great location, too. The Fairmont is just minutes away from business in the Loop, shopping on the Magnificent Mile and nightlife in the theater district."

As the limo approached downtown, and all the glittering lights of Michigan Avenue came into view, Sarah found herself wishing that Michael had accompanied her on the trip. It was a useless wish, of course, since Michael had a fear of flying and so could not join her on this trip, nor any others that required flying.

"We're passing Marshall Field's legendary flagship store on the left, and if you'll look to your right, we'll soon pass over the Chicago River, Ma'am."

The chauffeur then pulled into the winding driveway of the famed Fairmont Hotel, and a bellman, replete with royal blue livery and top hat, nimbly opened the door for her.

"Welcome to the Fairmont, Ma'am."

She thanked the chauffeur, who eagerly piled her luggage onto the gold trolley, and giving him a generous tip, she proceeded to follow the bellman into the brightly lit marble foyer of the hotel.

CHAPTER 2

The alarm clock woke her with a start. Groggily, Sarah reached for it and turned it off. It was only 5:30 A.M., and the room was almost totally dark. For a split second, she was disoriented … and then she recalled that she wasn't in her loft in Santa Monica, but in a heavenly hotel suite in Chicago. Even in the dimness, she could make out the graceful settees and damask wall covering, the plush draperies and the rich mahogany furniture. Fighting off the desire to bury herself further in the comfort of her plush pillows, she threw back the crisp down linens and sat on the edge of the enormous bed, trying to shake off the residue of a troubled sleep.

She hadn't had a recurrence of the dream she'd had on the plane, thankfully. No, it had been nothing like that. Still, it had left her with a vague uneasiness, although its details remained sketchy, at best. In her dream, she'd been speaking at the conference, of that she was sure. Someone had been mocking her, heckling her, and it had rattled her so, that at the podium, she'd found it hard to concentrate on her presentation. He had been tall, blonde, with an athletic build, someone almost like … Michael.

How very silly of her.

Dismissing the confusing dream, she rubbed her eyes vigorously and walked over to the bathroom, where she splashed cold water on her face, before drying it in a warm, soft towel. She smiled at the ingenuity of the towel warmer, wondering, as she was prone to do, whose firm held the patent to such an innovative product, and how they marketed it to a luxury hotel such as the Fairmont. Not that she'd ever been in marketing, of course, but still she admired the person who thought of the idea and had the tenacity to pursue it.

She crossed over to the window and opened the heavy brocade drapes. How very lovely the view was twenty stories above Michigan Avenue! Although it was not yet dawn, there was already some traffic on Lake Shore Drive, and she could see the vast expanse of Lake Michigan to her far right.

Sarah continued to take in the scene long after the first rays of light on the horizon, and then she showered and began to carefully dress for the conference ahead of her. After she dried her hair and brushed it straight, she twisted it into a sleek knot at the nape of her neck, her honey-colored highlights framing her face. Besides a tinted lip-gloss, she wore no makeup, having been blessed with a natural glow and a tan from having lived her entire life in California. The outfit that she'd chosen was definitely business chic, so she decided to add a vibrant, silk Pucci scarf around her shoulders, for a touch of femininity.

Sarah would be speaking at ten o'clock that first day. She debated whether she should order room service for her morning coffee, when she remembered that she had seen a small coffee kiosk in the downstairs lobby.

She quickly scanned the room, gathered her papers, laptop and briefcase, and left a generous tip on the side chest for the maid. As she walked to the waiting elevator, her stride was brisk and confident. Usually an optimist, she was always at her best in the early morning, when the day ahead held the promise of unknown possibilities. Who even knew what could be accomplished on any given day? And, on that day in particular, it was incalculable how many people she'd meet, how many connections she'd make and how profitable it could be for Morgan-Sloane in the future.

Suddenly feeling a rush of adrenaline, she was itching to get started.

Maybe I should order decaf, she thought with a smile, as the elevator doors silently opened.

Sarah rapidly made her way to her left, striding across the shining marble floors toward the coffee kiosk. On her right, a spectacular mural, painted in superb detail over the marble columns that supported the main lobby, captivated her attention.

Though not artistically gifted herself, Sarah had always loved art. She had enjoyed the college art appreciation courses that she had made sure to include in her course curriculum, even though they had nothing to do with her major preparing her for law school. She often wondered what it would be like to devote herself to a pursuit that was totally impractical except for the sheer joy of being creative.

Her classmates had called it her Bohemian side.

After paying for a double shot of espresso at the counter, she walked back to the mural, steaming coffee in hand, to examine the work of art more closely.

It was a breathtaking montage of scenes divided into seven sections and executed with exquisite detail. From the impenetrable blackness of night, her eyes followed the brilliant light … the turquoise, rich waters beneath the cobalt blue sky, then the dusky woods, rich with various trees and foliage, and riotous flowers blooming so vividly, she could swear they were real … the sun, moon, stars and Milky Way, galaxies colliding ….

There was more. The different animals, of all shapes and species, were so lifelike and multidimensional that she had the urge to touch the wall, to be certain. The tranquil waters above her head were teeming with fish and sea life of all kinds. The mural, as she now realized, extended around columns, above skylights and everywhere she looked, each scene more magnificent than the next, blending fantasy and reality so deftly that she could not help but feel totally awed. When Sarah saw the couple, a man and woman dressed only in fig leaves, she realized that she was looking at a rendition of the six days of Creation culminating with Adam and Eve.

She started at the beginning, and there was no mistake about it. The artist had captured the beginning of time majestically and dramatically, and from what she remembered from her days in Hebrew school, it followed the Bible's account in perfect order.

"Beautiful, isn't it?" A voice behind her interrupted her thoughts.

She turned, smiling, to the well-dressed, distinguished man next to her.

"It is, indeed. The six days of Creation, if I'm not mistaken."

"Exactly. As a matter of fact, I've heard that there was quite a scandal when it was first unveiled," he offered.

"Really? How so?"

"Well, you know how it is nowadays with religion. It's a touchy subject all around. Several atheist groups were offended, and some people even protested outside the home of the local artist, in Lincoln Park."

"What a shame. I think it's positively brilliant," Sarah offered.

"So do I, Ms. ... ?" He extended his hand.

"Morgan. Sarah Morgan." She clasped his hand in a firm handshake.

"Nice to meet you. I'm Peter Strauss, from Heller and Strauss. I'm looking forward to your presentation."

"Thank you, Mr. Strauss. It's nice to finally meet you, to put the name with the face, so to speak."

It was true. Sarah had spoken to him on the phone once before, but in person he looked remarkably younger than she'd imagined. True, his dark hair was flecked with silver at the temples, but his face still had a boyish quality about it. She estimated that he was in his mid- to late forties.

"Please call me Peter. I've also spoken with a Michael Sloane, is it? From your firm?"

"Yes, Michael's my partner."

"Oh, I see. Is he here, as well?"

"No, I'm afraid not. He has a fear of flying, so I'm here alone."

"Really ... what a pity. I've heard that hypnosis can be extremely successful ...."

They walked together, engaged in small talk. Before long, more presenters and more representatives of law firms from around the country began to circulate in the lobby. When it was time to convene the conference, there were at least two hundred people in attendance, all of whom began to make their way toward the grand ballroom on the left side of the hotel.

Sarah was still speaking with Peter Strauss when she turned in the direction of the sound of her name.

"Sarah? Sarah Morgan?"

She turned to the young man, replying, "Yes?"

"I'm Rob McCann, the event coordinator. Would you come with me, please?"

She excused herself and followed him through the lobby, toward the massive doors at the end of a long corridor. He held the doors open for her, and she briskly walked into the colossal ballroom. The seats were rapidly filling as the attendees gathered in. He motioned her to the raised platform where several speakers were already seated.

"Thank you, Mr. McCann," she said, as she hurriedly took her place.

She took in every detail of her surroundings, getting her bearings even as she searched for her notes in her briefcase. The glaring lights overhead, the muted hush of the professionals that had gathered to hear her speak, the gravelly voice of the woman who was clearing her throat into the microphone ... all contributed to her mounting anticipation.

On the immediate level, she was conscious of her surroundings, but beyond that she was cognizant of the fact that many years of hard work had begun to come to fruition, as years before she had only dreamed of sitting where she was at that very moment.

Before long, she heard herself being introduced.

"... and I have the pleasure of introducing Ms. Sarah Morgan, founding partner of the Law Offices of Morgan-Sloane. Ms. Morgan has extensive experience in corporate litigation, and she will be speaking today on the very timely topic of mergers and acquisitions ...."

Sarah rose from her seat, amid polite applause, and took her place at the podium. As she looked at the crowd of professionals assembled to hear her speak, she felt a wistfulness that

Michael couldn't be there … he'd surely be proud of her.

Taking a deep breath, she began.

Later that day, a triumphant Sarah returned to her room and made her way to the brocade settee, flinging her high-heeled shoes aside. She dialed Michael on her cell phone while she massaged her aching feet. It rang a few times before his voicemail answered. She smiled at the familiar voice.

Hello, you've reached the voicemail of Michael Sloane. Leave a message and I'll return your call as soon as possible. Thank you.

"Hi, Michael, it's me. The presentation went very well, and I've made a lot of new contacts. I was especially impressed with Peter Strauss, from Heller and Strauss … I think he was impressed with me, as well. With us, I mean. It could prove quite lucrative … call me."

She placed the cell phone next to her on the bedside table and leaned her head back with a contented sigh. The chair was so comfortable, almost *too* comfortable, for she had work to review. Unable to budge, she closed her fatigued eyes for what she resolved would only be a few minutes' rest.

A moment later, she was sound asleep.

The ringing phone startled Sarah from a deep sleep. She answered it, still groggy. "Michael?"

"No, I'm sorry. This is Peter Strauss. Have I, uh … woken you?"

"Oh, Mr. Strauss, that's okay." She fought to regain her composure for a few seconds. "I must have dozed off …."

"I'm sorry to have called at a bad time, then."

"No, it's perfect timing, actually. I have a lot to do."

He continued, "I just wanted to congratulate you on an excellent presentation this morning."

"Thank you, I appreciate that."

"Actually," he continued, "I was wondering if you'd like to join me and a few of my colleagues this evening for dinner. I thought we could further discuss some of the issues you raised."

"I'd be delighted. That's very kind of you to invite me."

"Excellent, then. We'll be at the Seafood Bistro on Michigan, a block from the hotel. Best food in all of Chicagoland, and that's a promise."

"Sounds great, Mr. Strauss. I'll be there."

"Please call me Peter."

"Peter, then."

"Say, around nine o'clock?"

"Perfect. I'll see you then."

She replaced the receiver, a satisfied smile on her face. Stretching her arms, she looked at her watch. It was already almost eight o'clock, which didn't leave her much time to change.

Raucous laughter and the smell of seafood greeted her as she entered the restaurant. It had been a short walk, indeed, from the hotel, and Sarah had enjoyed her little stroll, taking in the fashionable shops and boutiques on the Magnificent Mile.

The restaurant itself was long and narrow, with high ceilings and exposed wooden beams. The dark mahogany paneling on the walls and glittering sconces gave the crowded space the look of an intimate club, and Sarah immediately felt at ease in the upbeat atmosphere.

She spied Peter Strauss immediately. He was standing up at the back of the restaurant and gesturing for her to join their party. Peter and his colleagues all seemed to be in fine spirits, and Sarah smiled as she glanced from face to face, happy to have been invited. It had been much too long since she'd enjoyed an informal evening out. She and Michael were habitually working late, and their schedule left little time for socializing ....

"Glad you could make it, Sarah," Peter Strauss said. "Here, let me pull up a chair for you."

"Thank you," she replied.

Introductions were made all around and Sarah leaned back in her chair, thoroughly enjoying herself and her surroundings. Though they were virtual strangers, she felt comfortable in their presence and began to relax.

Her cell phone rang. Discreetly checking the screen, she saw that it was Michael.

"Excuse me," she said to the group. "I must take this call."

She walked to the side of the restaurant, where there was a restroom and lounge area, to retrieve the call.

"Michael?"

"Yeah, hi. I got your message. How's it going?"

"Oh, wonderful. I'm actually at dinner with Peter Strauss, from Heller and Strauss. He's introduced me to three other people, all from Chicago firms ...."

"That's just great," Michael replied, distractedly. "It sounds like you've accomplished a lot ... more than I can say, I'm afraid."

"Uh-oh. Are you referring to the Hendersons?"

"Yes. Now, don't fly off the handle, but they want to settle, and there's pressure from the other side to get it done, pronto. I say we do it. They're our clients, after all."

Sarah was silent at the news.

"Sarah? You still there?"

"Yes, yes ... I'm still here."

"There's no need to give me the silent treatment, you know," he said, voice rising. "We're talking forty percent, we get a four million dollar fee –"

"I was not giving you the silent treatment!" she retorted. "I was just thinking, that's all."

"Yeah, boss, look … I know you think you can talk them into sweating it out at trial, but believe me, you can't."

His condescending tone annoyed her, and she couldn't help but wonder if perhaps the Hendersons *would* be more inclined to listen to her than to Michael.

"Maybe I should return early," she suggested. "I can fly back first thing tomorrow …."

A short pause. "I don't think that's necessary. Creating connections in Chicago could be invaluable later on … this is just one case, after all."

"That's true, but it's our biggest case yet. And, to me, it's our most important case. It's not just about the money, Michael."

She mulled the situation over, weighing her options. *Should she return early?*

"I was afraid you'd say that," said Michael, a bitter edge to his voice.

"The conference is only two more days. My flight is Wednesday night. What should I do?"

"I think you need to stay there. This could wait until you return. I'll just stall them. Remember, I'm good at doing that."

Her lips turned up at the corners. Michael had stalled their engagement plans for more years than she cared to remember.

"I guess it'll have to wait, then."

"Yeah, we'll discuss this more later."

"All right, I have to go, they'll think I'm being rude …."

"Sure, I wouldn't want your dinner companions to be kept waiting," he said dryly.

Could it be that Michael was a bit jealous?
Good.

She promised to call later that evening, hung up and returned to her table.

The evening proved to be quite enjoyable. The food was fresh and expertly prepared, and her dinner companions turned out to be pleasant conversationalists.

It was after they'd enjoyed a leisurely dessert that Lee Ross, another attorney, leaned back in her chair and asked the question.

"So, Sarah, Peter mentioned that you admired the controversial mural in the hotel lobby."

"Yes, as a matter of fact I did."

A small smile framed her thin lips. "What was it that caught your eye? Was it the artwork itself, or the message it conveyed?"

Sarah swallowed a forkful of pie before answering, "I'm not sure what message it conveyed. I was just taken with the beautiful colors. The artist was very skilled."

Peter smiled. "Lee, just because you're an atheist doesn't mean you can't enjoy beautiful art, right?"

"Of course," she hastily agreed. "I wouldn't dream of forcing my views on others. The artist, on the other hand, seemed to be doing just that, in my opinion."

And so began a lively, occasionally heated debate on the subject of the controversial mural, which led to a discussion on the idea of Intelligent Design. That topic rapidly progressed to the subject of prayer in public schools, politics and other associated issues. Sarah considered herself apolitical; she'd spent so many years pursuing her individual goals, she hadn't had the time, or inclination, for politics. As for religion, she didn't feel adequately knowledgeable to join in the dialogue. Like most people, Sarah enjoyed conversing on topics with which she was familiar.

Religion was an issue that Sarah, admittedly, knew next to nothing about.

It was only after the lengthy dinner was coming to a close, and Sarah stood up to retrieve her wrap, that she realized that Peter Strauss, as well, had been mostly silent throughout the intense exchange.

He turned to her. "Sarah, it's been lovely. Thank you for coming," he said.

"Thank you for inviting me," she responded. "It's been a pleasure meeting all of you."

She exchanged several business cards for future reference and said her good-byes. After exiting the restaurant through a side entrance, she was surprised to find Peter Strauss on the sidewalk just a few steps ahead of her.

"Are you heading in this direction?" he asked.

"Yes, back to the hotel. Would you mind some company?"

"Not at all."

They walked a bit before he cleared his throat and said quietly, "I just wanted to apologize if you were offended by Lee's remarks. She doesn't always think before she speaks, I'm afraid."

"It was fine," she reassured him. "Quite entertaining, in fact."

He chuckled. "Dinner and a show, eh? … I guess I didn't find it all that amusing."

If there seemed to be a slight edge to his voice, Sarah pretended not to notice. Something about the exchange had hit close to home, of that she was sure, and she found herself wondering what it was.

It was Peter Strauss who spoke first. "My daughter seems to have found religion, of late."

He seemed none too pleased about it, so Sarah was unsure as to how to respond. "She'd been searching for answers, I guess, ever since her mother died five years ago," he offered.

"I'm … I'm sorry," said Sarah.

"Oh, that's all right. It's not something I usually talk about. I was just imagining how my daughter would have reacted to the discussion at dinner. She's eighteen, and she's basically informed me that the life we've always led no longer has any spiritual meaning for her."

Sarah's lips turned up at the corners. "It seems that quite a few college kids go through the post-adolescent, idealistic phase. Don't worry, it's probably temporary."

He laughed. "I wish it were true, but actually, she's dropped her plans to even attend college. She went to Israel last summer, and now she only wants to take classes on how to become Orthodox, or something like that."

"Really? I'm Jewish, too. In fact, my grandmother was very traditional. I can remember her lighting two candles every Friday night."

"You know what? I think my grandmother did that, as well," he said, smiling.

Before Sarah knew it, they were walking up the curved driveway of the hotel.

"Thanks again," said Sarah.

"I'm sorry to have burdened you with my problems. I've been keeping all this to myself; I guess it was just all the talk at dinner."

"Not at all," she responded graciously.

And then, almost as an afterthought, he reached into his pocket and drew out his wallet.

"This is Danielle," he said, as he showed her the small picture.

A young, dark-haired girl, the exact image of her father, stared back at her.

"She's lovely," Sarah remarked.

"Thank you. Well, I've taken up enough of your time. See you at the conference tomorrow," Peter responded.

"Yes, it's going to be a full day."

They said good night, and Sarah made her way into the hotel. Noticing the mural once again, she deliberately walked past it, to gaze again at its breathtaking beauty. The colors were so vivid and vibrant they seemed to leap off the columns. Depicting the creation of the universe at the beginning of time, every detail was perfectly defined. Sarah had no doubt that the artist, whatever his religion, was deeply spiritual and wanted to impress the viewer with his vision of the glory and majesty of G-d's creation. The work was nothing short of miraculous.

Sarah suddenly felt a twinge of pity for Lee Ross, for though she knew absolutely nothing of religion, she was confident of one fact.

There most certainly was a G-d.

CHAPTER 3

WEDNESDAY, FEBRUARY 11
5:30 A.M.
CHICAGO, ILLINOIS

Sarah awoke with a start, as she realized that it was Wednesday, the last day of the conference. She felt positively wretched when the events of the previous evening came back to her in a rush. Touching her hand to her throbbing temple, she knew that her eyes were swollen from crying, and her head ached something fierce.

Tuesday, the day before, had not started out badly. In fact, most of it had gone very well, indeed. She had been confident and in her element, and there were many things that had transpired in her favor. She now had a list of contacts from different cities with whom she felt comfortable to call on in the future.

Peter Strauss' name topped the list.

She'd been relaxing in her hotel room; enjoying a moment of quiet solitude late in the evening, reviewing with satisfaction everything that had happened throughout the busy day.

All of those upbeat, positive feelings quickly dissipated when her cell phone rang.

It was Michael. Her happiness at hearing his voice was quickly replaced with annoyance. He'd been in a dour frame of mind, challenging her at every turn. Though she'd become quite adept at handling his volatile disposition, it just hadn't worked the previous evening. Perhaps the distance had been a factor; perhaps she'd been tired. Whatever the reason, the conversation had taken such a nasty turn, she was at a loss as to how to proceed.

She'd argued with Michael in the past, of course, but nothing like this.

She looked at the sparkling ring that encircled the finger on her left hand, and was only able to feel depressed as the conversation played itself repeatedly in her mind. She could remember the entire dialogue word for word ....

"How it did go today?" Michael had asked her.

"Really well," she'd responded. "You wouldn't believe how many people I've met from all over. I've gotten so many ideas —"

"Ideas about what?"

"Oh, all sorts of things. For instance, the diary system in our office is completely outdated. There is so much technology that I've never even been aware of. Our office could run a lot smoother —"

"Smoother than what?"

"I don't know ... smoother than the way it's run until now. Productivity would increase if we'd implement some of the techniques that I've learned. I think that —"

"Whoa, whoa, hold on a second ... you go to a conference, get some ideas and think you can come back and change everything? It's taken us years to establish our system, and everything runs just fine."

"It may be fine, Michael, but who's to say it can't be done better? Even Sharon has mentioned to me that she doesn't think some of our computer programs are effective. As a matter of fact —"

At that Michael bellowed, "Have you lost your mind? You're actually quoting Sharon Pierce, who can hardly remember her own name?"

"You're right, of course, that was a bad example. Seriously, though, I think that we should pursue avenues that could increase our —"

"I really don't have time to listen to this," he interrupted hotly. "Some of us have work to do."

She bristled. "What do you think I've been doing since I got here?"

"You mean, besides going out to dinner, and planning new ways to change our whole office system?"

"What is wrong, Michael? Why are you acting so ... rude?"

His temper was beginning to flare in earnest. "RUDE? I fail to see how I'm the one being rude. I've been working around the clock here on very real, concrete cases. You, on the other hand, have been partying in Chicago and dreaming of abstract, outlandish ways to cost our firm more money. And since when do *you* get to be the one to decide how to run our office?"

"Since it's *my* firm, I think I've earned the right."

The words were out of her mouth before she could stop them.

"I see." His tone was icy. "So that's how it is. Okay, boss, whatever you say."

She drew a deep breath. "I really don't like it when you call me 'boss,' Michael."

"Well, isn't that what you are? You just said —"

"I know what I said, but still —"

"Listen to me, you can't have it both ways. No, really ... I've been thinking this over for a long time now; either we're equal partners, or it just won't work between us."

Her heart seemed to plummet into her stomach at these words. "What are you saying?"

"I'm saying that I've been bending myself over backwards to prove myself to you …. I've literally been pulling an eighty-hour work week for two years straight. I'm tired, I really am. I'm tired of doing all the work and getting none of the perks."

"Perks?" Sarah was incredulous. "Exactly what do you mean by that … trips to Chicago?"

"Do I need to spell it out for you? A four million dollar fee, and I did practically all the work … any time you want to make me a full equity partner, just say the word."

And there it was, out in the open.

Could that be the reason why he'd finally proposed?

Her voice was shaking, "That sounds a little manipulative, if you don't mind my saying so."

"What's your problem, Sarah? We're going to be married, anyway. All of our assets will be shared 50/50, as per California law."

It was difficult for Sarah to stifle the disappointment in her voice. "I see you've thought a lot about this."

Michael's tone was challenging. "I see you haven't. You seem to forget that it's my name on the stationary, too. Morgan-Sloane is in all ways a partnership, really, except in the way that matters most."

A new, even more disturbing notion occurred to Sarah. "Let's not get ahead of ourselves. You're speaking about the settlement like it's money in the bank, and it's just not true. I still fully intend to take this to trial, and who knows, maybe we can collect three times as much!"

"That won't happen." He paused. "I settled the case this afternoon."

Sarah felt as if she'd been punched, and the blow left her feeling breathless. Hot tears of disappointment and rage welled up in her eyes. *Nearly two years of work ... how could he do this to her? She had trusted him. And what hurt her most of all was that she knew she had no one to blame but herself.*

"How could you, Michael?" she managed. "You had no right!"

"Oh, please, I had every right! Four million dollars, Sarah! What is wrong with you? Another firm would be praising me to the sky, making me a full equity partner, but not you. Oh no, not the powerful Sarah Morgan. Nothing is ever good enough for you!"

"That's not true," she whispered.

He continued speaking in the same accusatory manner. "Did you really think we'd just continue on this way? With you owning the firm, and me working as your little lapdog? Forget it, boss."

It was simply too much to bear.

She shouted into the phone, *"STOP CALLING ME 'BOSS!'"*

He snickered. "There's only one way I won't be able to call you boss, and that's if you aren't. My boss, that is. I quit."

"What?!"

"You heard me, Ms. High and Mighty. You'll never make me an equal partner, because you'll never learn to share. I'll take my talents elsewhere. Two words: I QUIT. You can have your firm all to yourself. That's what you've wanted all along, anyway."

"Michael, aren't you taking this a bit too far? I just meant –"

He had already hung up.

She stood, staring in shock at her cell phone. How in the world had the conversation spiraled so completely out of control?

There was no use talking to Michael when he was in

one of his moods; she'd learned that years before. Sarah had perpetually chalked it up to their competitive nature. Not surprisingly, it was a challenge to work together, and the fact that it was she, not Michael, who owned the business didn't help matters. She was well aware of Michael's resentments and petty jealousies, but never before had he threatened to quit the practice. His harsh words and accusations wounded her deeply. Not to mention that he'd gone behind her back and settled the very case that she'd been dreaming of taking to trial ever since Charlotte Henderson had entered her office.

It had been a warm day in May, nearly two years earlier. She could recall every detail, from the lilac scarf that Charlotte Henderson had been wearing, to the dapper handkerchief tucked into the lapel of Martin Henderson's expensively tailored suit. They were a well-to-do couple, married for thirty-odd years, and obviously devoted to each other.

They had unburdened themselves to Sarah when they'd shared their heart-wrenching tale.

MeadowLane Retirement Village was a luxurious gated community in Rancho Mirage, California. It boasted tranquil views overlooking a beautiful golf course, and had on site all the amenities that senior citizens could possibly wish for. It seemed more like a country club than what it truly was, namely, an assisted living facility. Naturally, Charlotte Henderson had been overjoyed to place her elderly parents in such a beautiful place, assuming they were in good hands. That dream became a nightmare one day when the elderly couple was standing on their balcony, admiring the gorgeous vista.

The railing on which they were leaning gave way, and onlookers could only gape in shock as the couple fell twenty-seven feet to their deaths. Several pieces of large masonry rained down with them, resulting in serious injuries to four other residents who had been situated on lower floors.

MeadowLane had balked at first, claiming that the couple exerted undue pressure against the railing, which wasn't built to withstand their combined weight.

After twenty-two months of legal wrangling back and forth and expert medical testimonies, as well as a criminal investigation, they'd finally admitted to prior knowledge that the railing had been installed improperly and they had neglected to get it fixed. The money that they offered to settle out of court was just the tip of the iceberg, Sarah knew. There would be far more when the case went to trial.

The Hendersons had repeatedly told Sarah that they were not in this for mere financial gain. They felt that they needed to speak out on behalf of the victims and their families, and a trial would have been the perfect forum. *Why had they changed their minds?*

And Michael … her feelings were so conflicted. She felt betrayed and found herself in a turmoil just getting her own emotions in order. She'd been overjoyed when he'd finally proposed, thinking, perhaps erroneously, that their problems had been worked through and were finally behind them.

It was obvious, mere days later, how very wrong she'd been.

Had he been serious about quitting? Would he come to his senses and call her? Would he apologize? Should she apologize?

No, she resolutely told herself. *Not this time. Not when I haven't done anything wrong. Not when he's done just about everything wrong.*

Still, the thought of his leaving worried her. How would she be able to run Morgan-Sloane alone? *Wait a minute … it wouldn't even be called by that name if their partnership dissolved ….*

She was getting carried away, she told herself. Surely he would call, apologize and smooth everything over. He always did. Sarah repeated this to herself, over and over again, as she dragged herself out of bed and began to dress for the day's closing brunch.

She looked at the magnificent ring on her left hand. Was it her imagination, or did the diamond seem a bit lackluster, perhaps less glittery than before? She slowly slid it off her finger and placed it in the small pocket of her pilot's case. She couldn't afford to be reminded of the turbulent events of the precious evening, and she just didn't feel like wearing it right now.

She even wondered if she'd ever feel like wearing it again.

She glanced at the bedside clock on her way out. It was almost eight o'clock, and still no word from Michael. No doubt he was still asleep, she told herself. He'd surely call later.

But later never came. Throughout the day she kept checking her cell phone, retrieving her messages, but there was still no word from Michael. And Sharon had called in sick, so even she was unavailable ....

She called him several times, against her better judgment, but he hadn't answered his cell phone.

Fine, she thought. *Let him act like a spoiled child.*

Truthfully, she was almost relieved that he hadn't had the courage to speak with her, for she was far too distraught to converse in a civil manner. She knew that she needed time to figure things out, to sort out her feelings. The trouble was that she had difficulty analyzing what her feelings even were. Actually, she was accustomed to dismissing her innermost feelings for most of her life, never having had a parent in whom she could confide. Consequently, she had learned at a young age that concrete facts were indisputable; she could trust them. But emotions ... they were far too complicated.

Suddenly, it was early afternoon and the conference was over. Everyone was gathered in the lobby, and like the others, Sarah was shaking hands and cementing contacts with new business acquaintances.

Peter Strauss spied her and walked over rapidly.

"It's been a pleasure meeting you," he said. "Here's my card with my private line. Feel free to call anytime, and we can discuss how our firms might be mutually beneficial."

"Excellent, I look forward to it." She paused. "And … best of luck with your daughter."

"Thank you, I'll need it." He leaned forward conspiratorially. "I'm actually leaving tomorrow evening for Israel, to try and reconcile … maybe talk some sense into her."

"I hope it all works out for you."

"I hope so, too," he sighed. "And who knows? You know what they say … if you can't beat 'em, join 'em. I might just find religion myself!"

She chuckled, as he winked and walked reluctantly away.

What a nice man, Sarah thought, *and what a lucky daughter he has.* She then resumed mingling with the crowd and gave her business card to many of the departing guests, albeit halfheartedly. Outwardly, there was no trace of the simmering cauldron that was brewing inside her; yet it was there, and Sarah couldn't deny it. The reality remained that Michael had still not called, and she could not predict her reaction when he did.

She was forced to face the fact that it might always be this way with Michael, for the two of them had strong personalities. When things were good, everything seemed fine; but when they weren't, it was disastrous.

Could she really handle such a volatile relationship? Is it what she really wanted?

There was no easy answer.

Hours later, she hastily finished packing her belongings in her pilot's case and quickly surveyed the room, looking for belongings she might have missed. She wasn't thinking clearly, that much was certain ... her head was throbbing but massaging her aching temples didn't help. Suddenly, the beautiful, spacious room felt claustrophobic, and Sarah knew she needed some fresh air ... she still had plenty of time before the limo would arrive to take her to the airport. She quickly took some cash out of her pilot's case and left the room at a brisk pace.

Crossing through the lobby, she scarcely noticed the magnificent mural now that her mind was otherwise occupied. The icy air, however, hit her with a jolt as she emerged from the hotel and onto Michigan Avenue. The weather had turned menacing in the last twenty-four hours, and Sarah had not even noticed. The sky above looked dark and foreboding, and it had already started sleeting in earnest. Pelted with increasing drops of icy rain, Sarah wrapped herself tighter in her inadequate shawl. Scarcely aware that her high-heeled boots were skidding precariously on the slippery concrete, she walked two blocks toward a pharmacy that she had noticed two nights earlier, for Tylenol and a magazine for the plane ride. Room service could have provided her with both, of course, but she preferred to walk, in spite of the hostile weather. She almost welcomed each freezing drop of rain on her already aching head, as the cumulative effect was a strong dose of reality.

Her relationship with Michael was truly over.

How could she have not seen it earlier? True, she'd experienced much rejection from quite a young age ... had that been the cause of her inexplicable naiveté? *Was her relationship with Michael her chance to rectify the past, to prove that she could be loved?*

The undeniable truth was that her relationship with Michael had ended the day before on the phone. It had ended abruptly and miserably, but there was no going back; not now, not ever. With every step Sarah took, she became more and more certain of it. Her clicking heels on the slushy sidewalk seemed to tap out, *O-ver, O-ver, O-ver.*

She'd met Michael Sloane six years earlier, and theirs had been a roller coaster relationship from the very beginning. There had been times when it had seemed thrilling and exhilarating, especially at first. Over the years, however, the downward spirals and negativity had far surpassed the pleasant times ... culminating in the harsh exchange of words the night before, heralding the end of the long ride.

Michael had claimed to be tired, but as she replayed his words in her mind, she realized in a rush that it was she who was truly exhausted.

She was simply worn out from the heated verbal tango that they'd engaged in over the years ... the power struggles ... agonizing over who was right, and who was wrong ...

Michael's temper tantrums always left her feeling totally fatigued, and she was exhausted from having to walk on eggshells around him, afraid to bruise his fragile, childlike ego.

The two blocks seemed much longer in the harsh wind, and it was with relief that Sarah found the pharmacy on the corner. She hurriedly ran across the busy intersection, bypassing the granite tables and benches that were scattered along the curb, and rapidly opened the door to the store, seeking its warmth.

She roamed through the aisles, searching the shelves for the headache medicine that might relieve her throbbing temples.

She found it quickly and headed toward the counter. As she stood in line to pay the cashier, she glanced at the cover of a magazine whose headlines screamed, *RELIGION: What to do when the two of you aren't on the same page ....*

She thought of Peter Strauss and his daughter, wondering if the rift between them would soon mend. She hoped so, for Peter Strauss seemed like a caring, concerned father, quite unlike what her own father had been.

Immersed again in her own bleak thoughts, she hurriedly paid for the medication and made her way outside.

The light at the corner had turned green and she began to cross the busy intersection, shielding her face from the frigid air with her shawl.

Suddenly, out of the corner of her eye, she noticed a black Mercedes turning the corner with alarming speed, as if the driver did not see her in the foggy sleet. In her haste to reach the curb, she broke into a run, forgetting the icy condition of the pavement. Her high heel caught on the rim of a metal grate. Sarah was pitched forward, careening into the granite benches that lined the corner, hitting the edge of the stone head first with a sickening thud, before landing full force on the concrete sidewalk.

For several seconds, everything in Sarah Morgan's life faded to black.

The first thing she became aware of was the babbling of anxious voices. It was hard to make out all the words they were saying ... they seemed so far away ...

Poor lady, did you see what happened?

Lady, lady, are you okay?

You know, she really shouldn't move ...

Someone call 911 ... does anyone have a cell phone?

Did anyone see what happened?

She took a nasty spill, she's gonna have quite a bump ...

Her eyes seemed leaden; it was difficult to open them ... she literally had to force herself to pry them open. She was laying sprawled on the freezing sidewalk, in the most undignified fashion imaginable. She was further mortified to realize that a small crowd had gathered on the curb, standing over her in a semi-circle, peering at her with concern.

A heavyset man with a kind face leaned over her.

"Lady, are you okay?" he asked. "You okay, lady?"

It took her a while to form the words and respond.

"Okay, yes, I'm okay ..." she mumbled.

She tried to sit up, but as she did, she was overcome by a wave of nausea, and she thought she'd faint. *What was the man saying?*

"Better not move, lady, you took quite a spill ... don't worry, an ambulance is coming ...."

"No, no, no ambulance," she muttered. "I'm fine, really ...."

The people gathered seemed to be swimming, distorted, in front of her ... it was getting a bit darker outside, and the headlights from the cars looked like large, magnified circles ....

The pain in her head was staggering, but she gritted her teeth and tried to breathe. The nausea actually seemed to be receding a bit, and with a Herculean effort, she managed to shakily get to her feet, to a round of applause.

Good for you, lady, that's the ticket!

She'll be okay ... no broken bones ...

Show's over, folks, let's get back to work ...

I've been saying for years that these benches are a menace, but who listens?

The crowd began to disperse, and for that, she was glad. The man, however, was persistent.

"Lady, are you sure you're all right? There's a hospital not three blocks away from here … maybe you should get yourself checked out ….”

“Thank you, sir, but no.” Sarah was pleased to find that her voice had gotten somewhat stronger. “I’m in a bit of a hurry. Thank you for all your help, though.”

“Don’t mention it,” he said, doubtfully.

She walked down the block slowly and shakily. The pain at the top of her head was vicious, and as she reached up to tenderly touch it, she was horrified to feel a lump the size of a baseball.

When she looked down at her hand and saw that it was smeared in sticky blood, she felt nauseous once more.

Breathe, she told herself. *Just breathe.*

She breathed deeply as she walked, the cold air welcome on her painful head. Every few steps, she reached up to touch her head, hoping to find that the bump had receded somewhat. It hadn’t.

She was unaware of how long she’d been walking when she noticed the buildings that loomed over her, stark and forbidding, their lights becoming brighter against the darkening sky. People scurried this way and that, their scarves over their mouths, hoping to seal out the glacial air. So many people … and everyone seemed to be in a hurry …

A feeling of sheer panic and fright began to overwhelm her as she realized she had no idea where she was.

And then … and then …

And then she began to run, with a wobbly, uneven gait, ignoring the hammering in her head, overcome by a terror so fierce and primal, it seemed to seize her very soul … a fright so profound, it was beyond description.

Suddenly, she realized that she had no idea *who* she was.

CHAPTER 4

The room was white, almost blindingly so. Her eyes struggled to open, but the bright light made the effort excruciating.

"Is the light bothering you?" She heard a woman's voice, soothing yet efficient, at her side. "I'll draw the blinds ... that should help."

It did help, somewhat. She was able to open her eyes to mere slits, and peer at the woman, her face blurry, who had seated herself in a chair opposite her bed.

She was in a bed ... how strange ... and this woman, whom she did not recognize, was smiling at her in an encouraging way. For a few minutes, no one spoke, and Sarah simply gazed at the woman, stupidly.

The woman appeared to be in her late fifties and was wearing a white uniform jacket. She appeared to be a doctor of some kind, or perhaps a nurse ... why was she there, staring at her like she was some sort of exotic creature in a zoo?

She seemed to be waiting for her to say something.

"Who are you?" she managed, hearing her voice as if from a distance, garbled and indistinct.

The woman smiled. "I don't expect you to remember me. You were in quite a state when you were brought here last night."

Sarah struggled to look about her. The room was a study in whites, from the faded chair in the corner and the walls and window blinds to the crisp sheets covering the bed. Somehow, she seemed strangely detached from it all; from the room itself, as well as from her own body, almost as if she were floating, as if she were having a kind of out-of-body experience.

The woman seemed to understand her unspoken thoughts, for she said, "You're probably feeling a bit strange ... don't worry, that's just the pain medication, dear ...."

"Where am I?" Again, she noticed that her voice sounded far, far away.

"You're in Northwestern Memorial, dear. You've had a little accident, but you'll be fine ... just fine ...."

She had been in an accident? Funny, she couldn't recall it ... the woman seemed nice ... was she her doctor? Where was her family? Were they worried about her?

Wait a minute ... wait a minute ...

Who were her family members? She couldn't recall them ...

And who was she? She had no idea ...

A hot feeling of dread began to rise like bile in Sarah's throat, and the woman must have recognized the look on her face, for she quickly moved closer and patted her arm reassuringly.

"Don't worry, dear. It's perfectly normal not to remember ... actually, it's better this way. It gives your mind a chance to heal ... try to remain calm ...."

Her voice was a choked whisper. "You don't understand ... I don't remember ..."

"Believe me, I do understand ... try to relax now ... that's it, lay back now ... you should rest for a while now, and I'll be back to talk to you later ...."

She was struggling, fighting from letting herself be coaxed back onto the pillows.

"You don't understand, I don't remember anything …."

"You mean, from the accident? I wouldn't expect you to remember."

Was she not making herself clear? Why wouldn't the woman acknowledge what she was trying to say?

Hot tears began to slide down Sarah's cheeks as she whispered, "I don't remember who I am, don't you understand? I can't remember my name … I don't know where this place is … I don't know who you are … I don't know anything …."

She started crying in earnest now, her shoulders heaving with sobs as her horrifying predicament threatened to overwhelm her.

The woman patted her arm, speaking in reassuring undertones, but Sarah was unaware of what she was saying, trapped in her own frightening world where nothing seemed to make sense.

The woman pressed a buzzer near her bed. She was vaguely aware of her saying, "This is Dr. Lewis. Is Dr. Cooper available? Oh, good … please send him here …."

After several moments, an elderly man, flanked by two orderlies, appeared out of nowhere. Sarah looked back at the woman, wild-eyed with fright.

"Why are they here?" she gasped. "What do they want from me?"

"Don't worry, dear, they're just going to give you some medication."

The elderly doctor regarded her thoughtfully. "My name is Dr. Cooper," he said authoritatively. "Do you remember me? I spoke with you last night, administered some tests."

The tears started afresh. "No, no," she sobbed. "I don't remember anything."

The doctor spoke brusquely to the two aides.

"Nimodipine, 30 mg."

The kindly woman turned to Sarah. "Believe me, you need to try and remain calm. I know that this must be terrifying for you, but please, trust me, it's only temporary."

"All right," said the doctor in clipped tones. "Thank you, Dr. Lewis. I'll take it from here."

He was dismissing her; there was no doubt about that.

She nodded, adding graciously to Sarah, "I'll try to check in on you a bit later."

She left.

"When will I remember?" She couldn't keep the hysteria from her increasingly agitated voice.

"I can't say for sure, but usually these … lapses are resolved rather quickly. Of course, I can't guarantee anything … it'll depend on the nature of the brain injury. We'll know more when all the tests results are returned. As of right now, it doesn't seem to be all that serious, but again, I can't say for certain."

Brain injury? Is that what the man said? This simply could not be happening to her … this was something that happened to someone else, the stuff of which movies were made; in real life, these things couldn't occur … could they?

She reached up and felt the very real bandages that swathed her head.

An orderly held out a gel-like capsule in a small cup for her to swallow. Her hand shook violently as she reached for it, lifted it to her mouth and swallowed it along with a sip of water.

She did not care anymore; everything around her seemed too terrifying to withstand, and she wanted to sleep, to make it all go away. Perhaps, when she woke up, she'd be in her own, real world again. Only she hadn't any inkling as to what that world was.

Suddenly, a thought came to her. She was late … she'd been rushing … she had to be somewhere … didn't she?

The doctor was watching her intently from the doorway, about to exit the room.

"Wait … wait …" her voice called out faintly.

"Yes?" He came closer to the bed. She was all too aware of the starchy whiteness of his lab coat, the shock of thick white hair on his head. His presence was intimidating, and she'd never felt so vulnerable.

"I … I think I remember something …" she whispered, hoping she didn't sound foolish.

"Really?" The man leaned forward. "What do you remember?"

"I'm late … I need to be somewhere … or something like that. Maybe I missed an appointment, I don't know."

He looked at her doubtfully, scribbled something on a pad, and then reiterated, "We'll know more when all the results are in. You'll be pleased to know that the initial CAT scan actually didn't show a lot of damage at all."

"Then why can't I remember?"

"That's what we're trying to find out." And with that, he exited the room, the two aides trailing behind him.

The unrelenting, fiendish throbbing in her head began to subside, while the room around her became fuzzy … the last thought she had before she drifted off was how much she didn't care for that pompous, arrogant doctor … how white he was like everything else in this strange world.

Later in the day, she awoke to find the same kindly woman sitting next to her bed. She was pleased to discover that she was able to recall her earlier visit.

"I'm glad it's you," she heard herself say.

The woman chuckled. "Were you expecting someone else?"

"It's just that I feel more comfortable with you."

"I understand, dear. Dr. Cooper may have a rather … gruff demeanor, but he has a heart of gold. He's the chief neurologist here at the hospital, so you're very fortunate. Truly."

Sarah felt just the opposite but she didn't say it.

The woman continued. "He noted in your chart that several hours ago, you thought you remembered something … having an appointment, perhaps?"

Sarah's mind was still fuzzy, but she was able to recall fragments of what she'd felt before … a feeling of urgency, she'd been rushing, she was quite certain of it.

"All I remember is rushing, not wanting to be late … I think I had to be somewhere, or meet someone … I don't know."

"That's very encouraging, actually." She leaned forward. "An appointment with whom? A doctor's appointment or maybe the dentist?"

"I … I'm not sure."

The woman continued. "Or maybe you're the dentist, who knows? Do you have any recollection about your profession, perhaps? What you do for a living?"

Sarah lay back and tried to think so hard it made her head hurt.

"No." The realization was devastating.

The woman was silent for a moment, as if contemplating whether or not to say something. She nodded to herself, almost imperceptibly, as if coming to a decision.

"Look, I know that it's hard, but it's best to just try and rest for now. I'll be back tomorrow, and we'll talk then. Trust me, okay? We'll get you all better, I promise."

"What's your name?" Sarah whispered.

"I'm Dr. Lewis," she replied. "Anne Lewis, and I'm a psychologist here at Northwestern Memorial, and I also have a private practice. Don't worry, you're in good hands here. We'll help you remember, maybe not today, but very, very soon."

She arose, touched Sarah on the shoulder warmly and was about to leave the room when Sarah called out to her.

"Is there a name to what I have?"

She turned and hesitatingly answered. "I'd rather not give a premature diagnosis, dear. As I said, we'll know more tomorrow."

"Please ... please tell me ... what's it called?"

"We call it traumatic amnesia ... amnesia resulting from direct trauma to the brain. And it seems to be compounded with a form of retrograde amnesia, as well .... I deal more with the emotional side of things, to be perfectly honest with you. Dr. Cooper can better explain the physical ramifications to you. Listen, as I said, these conditions are usually temporary ... we'll talk more later, okay?"

And with that, she left the room, leaving Sarah alone.

Northwestern Memorial ... Anne Lewis ... psychologist ... Northwestern Memorial ... Anne Lewis ... psychologist ...

It seemed vitally important for Sarah to cling to these precious few facts that she did know, feeling that she'd be utterly lost if she suddenly couldn't recall them, as well.

Anne Lewis ... Northwestern Memorial ... psychologist ... brain trauma ... accident ... traumatic amnesia ... what was the name of the medication that she'd been given? She couldn't recall ....

Fighting back the panic, she repeated in her mind the same facts continuously, like a litany, willing herself to remember something, *anything,* about what had happened to her, but to no avail.

She was still mechanically repeating the same phrases, over and over, when at last her eyelids grew heavy and she fell, mercifully, into the black nothingness of sleep.

Maria Ramirez entered the large suite on the sixteenth floor of the hotel and sighed. *Why was it that these wealthy people were forever leaving their belongings behind?*

Although she'd been working at the hotel for only several weeks, she'd noticed that affluent people didn't much seem to care about their property, often leaving their things behind. She'd already been to the Lost and Found room more times than she could recall. She eyed the handsome Louis Vuitton pilot's bag enviously. Why, that bag alone was worth more than what she earned for several months, in all probability. Not to mention the contents ... who knew what treasures were hidden inside?

Suddenly curious, she opened the side pocket, ostensibly just to determine the name of its rightful owner, and withdrew a brilliant, spectacular diamond ring. Astonished, she'd never before seen anything quite like it ....

She found herself in a quandary. Her mama had taught her never to take anything that did not belong to her; it was a mortal sin. Maria was a superstitious young woman, and she feared the evil that could strike her should she take the ring. Still, she had two young children at home to feed. She rationalized that surely the owner didn't care about the contents of the case, or else she would not have left it behind so thoughtlessly.

Holding up the ring, she watched its many facets sparkle in the light. Maria knew that if she'd been the recipient of such a gift, she'd never have let it out of her sight. She weighed her options, and though she was fearful, she couldn't help feeling it served the owner right …. She shakily placed the diamond in the pocket of her starched apron, and then, lifting the piece of luggage onto her trolley, she made her way, once again, to the Fairmont Lost and Found.

1:35 P.M. THAT SAME DAY
LOS ANGELES, CALIFORNIA

Michael Sloane closed the trunk of his sport-utility vehicle with a loud slam. He then bounded to the driver's side of the small truck, got in and dialed the office on his car phone.

"Good afternoon, Law Offices of Morgan-Sloane," answered Sharon Pierce with her usual, nasal drone.

I'll miss that idiot secretary least of all, he thought.

"Sharon? It's Michael," he said, knowing she wouldn't guess his identity unless he mentioned his name.

"Hello, Mr. Sloane, it's Sharon," she responded.

"Yes, I know that," he answered, irritated. "Listen, Sharon, I'm going away for a few days …. I just packed up the surfboard, and I'm heading up to Baja to catch some waves and celebrate the big settlement."

"Good for you, Mr. Sloane. You deserve a little rest and relaxation."

Another thought occurred to him.

"You know, Sharon, you could also use a vacation. Why don't you take the week off?"

She was thrilled. "Thanks ever so much, Mr. Sloane. Will it be all right with Ms. Morgan, do you think?"

He was so *tired* of having his every decision micromanaged by Sarah. He answered, annoyed, "Sure, sure, it's fine."

He knew that, in theory, Sarah would be furious if she came back to find her own secretary on vacation, but to him it no longer mattered. Besides, Sharon Pierce wasn't exactly a boon to the office, and it really was immaterial whether she was physically there or not. His half-brother, Robert, had frequently criticized Sharon's lack of communication skills, wondering why they continued to employ her.

"Sarah feels sorry for her," he'd admitted sheepishly.

"That's ridiculous," Robert had snorted.

Michael was inclined to agree, but he'd decided early on to choose his battles, and Sharon Pierce just didn't seem worth the trouble.

Sharon continued talking. "Nothing like a few days' rest to help you prepare for the Big Day, I say. When will the wedding be, in the summer?"

He'd never before confided in Sharon any details of his personal life and he certainly wasn't about to start now. Of course, she had no idea of recent events, and there was absolutely no reason to inform her.

"Uh, Sharon ... I'm going through the canyon ... you're breaking up ... I'll see you next week ...."

He hung up.

As he swung his car into a big arc that would lead him toward the expressway, he opened the sunroof and sighed with a mixture of anxiety and relief. A curious mixture, to be sure; he'd never before experienced the two feelings simultaneously. Nonetheless, the two conflicting emotions were the culmination of all that had transpired, and not just what happened the last several days.

It had been brewing since he'd begun to work for Sarah. Each day, his deep resentment increased; as of late, it had reached the boiling point. He'd gone to his apartment after the proposal with a sickening, roiling knot in his stomach. He never should have demeaned himself by letting her win, by giving in to what she'd wanted all along. There were easier ways to achieve a modicum of success in the legal field without having to grovel, and paying for that success by chaining himself to her for life.

He didn't need her. He didn't need anyone.

His mild anxiety over his future plans was far outweighed by the profound relief he was experiencing. For him, the day was filled with the intoxicating, unmistakable scent of sweet freedom. The wind felt fresh against his skin, the sunlight shone on his blonde hair, the world was his for the taking. He couldn't ever remember being in such a good mood.

His relationship with Sarah Morgan was over, at long last. Even Sarah's pretty face was no longer attractive to him.

She'd no longer have to agonize about his meeting her grandmother, he thought wryly. *It was a pity she'd worried for nothing about how the old lady would react. It was ironic that she'd thought he wasn't really good enough for her, when the reality was just the opposite.*

She wasn't good enough for him.

A quick getaway to Baja California Sur was just what he needed ... he hadn't taken out his surfboard in ages. He'd been working so hard for such lengthy stretches of time, he'd all but forgotten how to relax. Sarah simply did not know the meaning of the word; her main pleasure in life was work. But what he desired now was complete respite, away from the office, his cell phone and, most of all, *her*. He needed time to sort out the muddle in which he'd mired himself and chart the course for his future.

His vehicle sped onto the ramp that led to the expressway, and as he drove, it seemed as if he was shedding the heavy albatross that had been weighing him down for the better part of two years ... and he began to feel liberated, at long last.

5:00 P.M. THE SAME DAY
CHICAGO, ILLINOIS

"Gilda, where's my passport?"

Peter Strauss stood in the rounded foyer of his attractive home in the prestigious Chicago suburb of Highland Park. He was surrounded by his luggage, searching frantically through his papers and checking his watch.

"Gilda?" he called upstairs.

Gilda Petrakis, his housekeeper, a woman in her early sixties, came rushing down the graceful, mahogany spiral staircase with surprising agility. She smiled solicitously as she handed him his passport.

"Here you go, Mr. Strauss. It was on your dressing table."

"Gilda, what would I do without you?" He took the passport, placed it in his leather reticule together with his tickets and looked around.

Wherever he looked, his beautiful, well-appointed home was polished and spotless; but for the last number of years, this house – which had been his castle – left him feeling hollow and empty inside. His beloved wife was gone; he had not heard her infectious laughter in these rooms for what seemed like ages. And Danielle, his precious daughter, was estranged from him, embracing a culture from which he felt alienated, and about which he knew next to nothing.

He'd often worked late in the evenings just to avoid coming home to an empty house, and the awful, never-ending silence. After Beth had passed away, he'd considered moving, but Danielle had been only thirteen at the time. He'd rejected the idea, fearing that yet another change would be far too disturbing for his daughter. Staying on in the very same rooms without his wife, however, caused him a profound pain of which he'd never spoken, even to Gilda who empathized with his loss every time she looked at his face.

"Mr. Strauss, you'll be late," urged Gilda. "Go now, and maybe you'll avoid some of the Edens Expressway rush hour traffic …."

He checked his watch once more.

"Guess I'm too late for that," he murmured. "I'll call you in a few days to make sure everything's okay."

"Everything will be fine," she reassured him. "My goodness, I've never seen you this jumpy, if you don't mind my saying so. It's not like you've never traveled before."

"True, but I've never been to Israel … it's the other side of the world, after all."

"I can't blame you there, Mr. Strauss. With everything that's happening in the Middle East, you couldn't pay me enough to go."

He grinned. "Glad I never asked you, then. All right, Gilda, thanks for holding down the fort while I'm gone, and all that …."

He gathered his things, took one last look around, and closed the heavy mahogany doors.

Gilda Petrakis stood by the window and watched her employer go, his stride sure and brisk. She genuinely admired him for the decent, good man that he was, and sincerely hoped that he'd be able to bridge the wide chasm between himself and his daughter.

When she saw his car back out of the circular driveway, she prayed silently for his safety before turning from the window to resume her household chores.

Peter Strauss absentmindedly wove through steady traffic, first on the Edens Expressway and then onto the Kennedy, toward O'Hare International Airport.

He was filled with apprehension; not about the problems in the Mideast, as was his housekeeper, but rather about how he'd confront his daughter when he finally saw her after so many months.

How would she react to his being there? What should he say?

He'd negotiated many deals and settlements in his law practice with aplomb and skill, but when it came to his only child, he felt powerless and inadequate because their relationship was more important to him than anything else.

As far as Danielle was concerned, the only thing of which he was certain was his deep, abiding love for her. Those days when they were a family were his best memories. He missed his daughter fiercely, for it had been months since he'd seen her last. In his mind's eye he saw her as she'd looked as a little girl, around four or five years old, her dark hair flowing around her sweet face as she chased butterflies in the backyard with a net that was practically bigger than she was.

Look, Daddy! There's one! It's orange and black, see?
See, Daddy? There it is! Catch it, Daddy! Catch it now!

The memory was so vivid, he could almost hear Beth's contagious laughter as he ran around, flailing the net clumsily, unable to catch the beautiful butterfly for Danielle.

Some things are too beautiful to be trapped, Pumpkin, he told her then. *When you get older, you'll understand.*

It was a memory that seemed to hold some deeper significance, as Danielle was all grown up now, and all he wanted was to catch her, to reestablish that connection, but she was just as elusive as that graceful butterfly ....

He had originally intended to be firm with her, to demand that she return home with him immediately, and yet he was astute enough to realize that in all likelihood, it just wouldn't happen that way. There was no doubt in his mind that she wouldn't follow him that easily, not his Danielle. He'd have to handle this delicate matter in a subtle, understated way, of that he was certain.

Just how he'd get Danielle to board that plane remained to be seen.

He tried to push aside his fears and doubts as he entered the ramp that led toward O'Hare's vast parking garage. He disliked having to leave his car parked there for the better part of his ten day trip, but he had little choice. He smiled as he recalled the reaction he'd received from the partners and staff when he'd told them of his vacation destination.

"Israel? Have you lost your mind?!" his partner, Ray Adams, had roared.

"Ray, it's my daughter. She's there, remember? I'm going to see Danielle."

"Oh, right, she's in some sort of crazy cult," he'd opined.

"Good luck, buddy. Whatever you do, get her home. If you need any help, call me. I'll bust her outta there myself."

It had made him laugh. Ray Adams was a diminutive fellow, but he talked a big game. He was very well connected, and Peter had no doubt that he really *could* "bust her out" if the situation should ever warrant it.

"It's not a cult, Ray."

He'd looked at him sympathetically. "Whatever you say, man."

"Seriously, it's really not like that ..."

Ray had looked at him, shrugged and said, "Whatever. Have a safe trip, buddy. See you when you get back."

Peter had no doubt that he was leaving the firm in extremely capable hands; Ray Adams and Lee Ross would fill him in on every detail when he returned. He had canceled meetings and postponed depositions, but the knowledge that he had such good team support did much to assuage his concerns. Additionally, the world at large had, in actuality, shrunk considerably due to technological advances. Between his PDA and his laptop, he could easily be contacted, if necessary. He parked the car in the enormous garage and walked through the glass walkway that would lead him to the terminal, his luggage in tow.

His heart beat a bit faster as he thought of his Danielle. All he could think was how wonderful it would be to see his precious daughter again.

No matter what.

CHAPTER 5

Daylight found her slowly pacing in the small white room like a caged animal. She'd had a fitful sleep, punctuated by alternate bouts of delirious dreams and moments of conscious lucidity, when she'd awake suddenly, disoriented, only to discover her sad fate had not changed.

She still had no recollection of who she was, or how the accident had occurred. The sharp pounding in her head had receded somewhat since the day before, although she was unsure whether it was due to true healing or just the result of the strong medication she was receiving. Actually, she found walking to be preferable to lying prone. Somehow, it helped ease the pressure in her head.

Her only link to what lay past her door was Anne Lewis. She knew that Dr. Lewis, her psychologist, had been in to see her the day before, in the late afternoon, but she could only recall mere snatches of their conversation ... she'd been so heavily sedated.

Thankfully, she felt a bit clearer this morning, and everything seemed to be in sharper focus. She was glad, almost proud of the fact, that she was able to remember the name of her doctor, and where she was. Northwestern Memorial Hospital. These were, in essence, the only concrete facts that she knew.

She paced the room with increasing urgency ... would Dr.

Lewis check on her? And if so, when? Would she bring good news? Would her family come to visit her today? And, if they did, would that trigger her memories of them?

She looked down at her hands, ignoring the intravenous tube that snaked its way into her right wrist. There were no rings on her fingers, so she didn't think she was married.

Surely, she'd remember *that*.

Wouldn't she?

She glanced at the metal clock on the wall. It was not yet six o'clock in the morning. Surely Dr. Lewis would come soon …

Impulsively, she made her way to the door, dragging her I.V. pole behind her, opened it, and peered out into the long, white corridor. With the exception of an elderly custodian whistling as he mopped the shiny floor, tiny headphones in his ears, the hallway appeared completely deserted.

She quietly closed the door and resumed her pacing in front of the two small windows of the room. She suddenly remembered the many tests that had been administered to her the evening before. Funny, she hadn't recalled them until now.

Dr. Cooper had given her a small ball to squeeze. Another doctor, she couldn't catch his name, had asked her to walk in a straight line. It had been the first time she'd been ambulatory since the accident, and so she'd done the best she could, albeit slowly. When she'd looked down, she'd experienced some dizziness. The doctor had asked her about it, and she'd answered truthfully. She regretted it now; she should've downplayed her symptoms, perhaps she'd be able to leave this place ….

He hadn't said much, just written down notes on his clipboard. There had been more … someone had shined a bright light into her eyes … someone had asked her to lift her arms, first one way, then another ….

She'd had to stand in front of some sort of x-ray or scanning machine for them to take images, to learn the extent of her injuries, she'd been told.

A white hot feeling of dread began to rise up within her.

What if this was all some sort of mistake? What type of a hospital was this? Perhaps she didn't really lose her memory ... perhaps it was the drugs in her system that were purposely making her confused ... maybe these doctors weren't really who they said they were ... maybe she was being held as some sort of hostage against her will ... maybe she had unwittingly fallen into the hands of some strange scientists who were holding her for experiments of some kind ...

As she paced, her thoughts became wild, more fanciful, and her fright only grew more intense. Her mind was racing with escalating thoughts. *But that was plainly ridiculous. A bump on the head that size couldn't be just conjured up ... it was painfully obvious that she'd truly been in some horrific accident and sustained a brain injury serious enough to lose all memory ... she surely wasn't the first person in the world to whom this happened, nor would she be the last ...*

Eager to learn the truth and quiet the troubling voices within her, she stealthily made her way once more to the door. She opened it and peered again into the corridor. Now even the custodian had vanished, and there was no one in sight.

She noticed a plastic container on the wall next to her room, which held a manila folder. Quickly, before she lost her nerve, she grabbed the folder, shutting the door firmly behind her.

She opened it, scanning the contents rapidly, afraid that someone would enter at any moment.

NEUROLOGICAL EXAMINATION
GERALD M. COOPER, M.D.

Patient: Jane Doe

Mental Status: The pt. is awake, alert and attentive. Speech is fluent and spontaneous. Normal speech production, which is voluntary, without stuttering or halting quality. Emotional responses appear in the normal range for post-trauma. Pt. is experiencing acute distress over memory loss. Appears to have well above-average intelligence. Formal I.Q. testing has not been administered, nor is recommended.

Cranial nerve exam: The pupils are equal, round and reactive to light accommodation. Extraocular movements had full range of motility in horizontal and vertical directions. Pt. sensation appears intact. There is no nystagmus. Sternocleidomastoid and trapezius muscles appear normal.

Motor exam: Pt. has normal muscle tone and mass in all extremities, with 5/5 strength in proximal and distal muscles bilaterally. There is no drift. No evidence of atrophy or fasciculation noted. Tremors: none. Pt. is capable of manipulating objects normally in both upper extremities.

Gait: Normal base. Pt. has negative Romberg sign. Tandem gait=normal. No gait limitations.

Sarah scanned farther down, past the medical jargon of which she understood very little, until she located what she was looking for.

> **Diagnosis:** Temporary Disassociative Fugue Amnesia. Pt. appears to have fallen; very slight injury to the hippocampi, temporal lobe region, possible slight injury to cerebral cortex, but not proven.
>
> **Rx:** Nimodipine 30 mg. caplets, daily. Vasopressin 16 IU in form of nasal spray, daily. Rest and fluids are essential.

She stood there, stricken.

How absolutely ludicrous, how perfectly absurd for her to think that she'd been kidnapped by some mad scientists ...

She'd suffered a traumatic brain injury, and it had resulted in a form of amnesia. That much was certain. How she'd received the injury, now that was another matter. The report mentioned that she'd fallen ... but where? But how? She wondered if she'd ever know.

Collecting herself, she quickly put the papers neatly back into the folder, returning them into the rack on the wall, and closed the door behind her once more. Somehow, the heavy door gave her a feeling of security, and a small measure of comfort, acting as a barrier against the vast, unknown world beyond it.

Feeling a bit lightheaded, she slowly crawled back into the bed, pulling the white sheets around her. She felt miserable and helpless as she once again glanced at the large clock on the wall.

There was nothing she could do but wait.

Tears slid down the sides of her face, but she made no

move to wipe them away; actually, she welcomed the salty taste, for they were real, as opposed to everything else about her nightmarish, otherworldly ordeal. To some extent, all she had were her tears to validate her existence. She was an actual person, she was alive … she just had no idea who she was, where she belonged in the world, whether there were family members she'd loved, and whether there was someone, *anyone,* who might be worried about her. She was overcome by feelings of aloneness, isolation and utter abandonment.

Did she have relatives out there looking for her? It surely couldn't be long until someone found her. Would she remember them? Would that trigger her memory?

In the midst of all of her jumbled thoughts, the door opened, and Dr. Lewis entered the room with a confident stride, and an aura of calm. She walked to her bed and patted Sarah's arm in a comforting way.

"Of course, you're frightened now, but things will be better," she murmured, and handed her a tissue.

Sarah took it gratefully and wiped her streaming eyes.

"Do you remember my name?" she said gently.

"Yes. Dr. Lewis," she whispered. "I'm sorry, I can't stop crying. I'm just so scared."

"Of course you are. I understand that, really, I do," she said. "But you've got to try and be positive. You're a very lucky young lady, it could've been a lot worse."

"How could things be any worse?"

Anne Lewis smiled at that. "Well, let's put it this way. You're a whole lot better today than you were yesterday, am I right? Do you even remember much of what went on yesterday?"

"Yes," she said, defensively. "It's a little vague, but I remember the tests a little."

"Really? That's very encouraging." She appeared thoughtful. "Speaking of the tests, I'm sure you'd like to discuss the results. Am I right?"

"Yes, yes, of course." She sat upright and tried to concentrate on what the doctor said.

"Okay, here it is," Dr. Lewis said matter-of-factly. "It seems as if you've had a nasty fall. With the ice storms we've been having, it's hardly surprising. We see a lot of falls this time of year, so it's nothing new to us. I've spoken with Dr. Cooper and it appears as if you're doing quite well. The injury isn't nearly as severe as we originally thought. You could be out of here within the week. Isn't that wonderful news?"

"Yes, but then why can't I remember?"

Anne Lewis nodded reassuringly. "You will, you will. Give it some time."

"What about this I.V.? When can that be removed?"

"Why, is it bothering you?"

"Yes," she answered. "I like to walk around the room, and I hate dragging it with me."

She laughed good-naturedly. "Spoken like someone who's on the mend. I'll see if they could take it out, maybe just leave in a Heparin lock, all right?"

"Thank you."

She nodded to her once more and called over her shoulder, "I'll be back to check on you this afternoon."

She was extremely pleasant, and Sarah felt some measure of gratitude at least for that. The same couldn't be said for the other doctor, who visited her about a half-hour later.

"Feeling better?" Dr. Cooper asked as he walked through the doorway, his tall, bulky frame blocking her view of the corridor.

"A little," she replied.

"Good, good. The results are in, and generally, the news is good," he said. "There was a definite injury, but very slight; nothing that won't heal with time. There's no bleeding on the brain, nothing like that. However, with that said, let me show you this."

He picked up a transparency of what looked to be Sarah's brain and held it up to the light for her to see.

"See this right here? This is the scan that was taken when you first arrived here Wednesday night. I'm sure you don't remember that, and that's perfectly understandable."

"I don't."

"Right. In any case, if you look closely, you can see this area here, the temporal lobe region, was injured slightly … here's what a normal CT scan should resemble."

And he wordlessly handed her another picture.

She looked at the two, trying to find the subtle differences in each.

"Do you see the injury? As I said, it's very slight … believe me, if it had been any worse, we wouldn't be here having this conversation. You were lucky … the impact hit closer to the skull than to the brain itself."

"I … I guess so." She handed them back to the doctor, eager to separate herself from the disturbing images.

"So when will I get better?"

"These things are temporary in nature. I have no doubt that you'll recover completely."

That *was* good news. But the question persisted.

"But when?"

He shrugged. "The mind is complex, and every case is different. In all honesty, your case differs a bit from the others I've seen."

"Really? In what way?"

"Well, in several ways, actually. You're experiencing what is referred to as retrograde amnesia, which means that you're having difficulty recalling events that took place before the trauma. Now, that's typical after the type of injury you've sustained. However, most people suffering from retrograde amnesia also have some form of anterograde amnesia, as well, and so far, that doesn't seem to be the case here."

"What does that mean?"

"Anterograde amnesia is the inability to form new memories from the time of the trauma and onward … let me ask you a question. Do you remember my name?"

She didn't hesitate. "Dr. Cooper."

"See what I'm saying? You're currently able to form memories, which proves to me that your injuries aren't all that serious. You've got a nasty bump on the head, but I think the problem should resolve itself rather quickly."

She was elated to hear it, but her doubts persisted. Still, she said nothing as he scribbled something in her chart, nodded to her and left the room, just as rapidly as he'd entered.

She wanted so badly to remember.

Later that morning, a dour-looking nurse trudged into her room.

"I'm here to change your I.V.," she announced as she reached over, unceremoniously grabbed Sarah's arm and began to remove the tube.

"Ouch!"

"Just a second, hold still." She attached a Heparin lock, flushed it, and snaked the tube away with all the finesse of a pit bull. Still, Sarah was relieved to be free of that dreadful pole.

The nurse then bounded out of the room, leaving Sarah to gape after her.

Was it her imagination, or was everyone here rude in the extreme?

Everyone, save for Anne Lewis. She was kind and gentle, and Sarah experienced profound relief when she came to see her later that afternoon.

"How are you?" she asked.

"Better, I guess. Dr. Cooper said the injury wasn't too serious."

"I know, and it's wonderful news."

"I guess so."

"You don't seem very happy about it," Anne remarked.

"I still don't know my own name. How can I be happy?" she challenged.

"Fair enough. But you remember a lot of other things, right? And that's really encouraging."

"I don't remember anything!" she protested.

"That isn't entirely true," she soothed. "Look, I'm not a neurologist, but I know that short-term memories are stored in the hippocampi, so it couldn't have been that badly hurt. Long term memories, we believe, are stored in the cerebral cortex, and the injury sustained there appears to be very slight in nature. You clearly remember my name, you remember the tests that were administered and so on. Like I've said before, that's very encouraging."

"So, what you're saying is …"

"I'm saying that the fact that you are able to recall short-term memories is a very good sign."

"But it's because I didn't want to forget," she protested. "I kept repeating your name over and over … and the name of the hospital, and everything … so maybe that doesn't count."

"It counts for more than you realize. In any case, you remember that you were repeating my name, right? No, dear. If you had severe short-term memory loss, we'd know it by now. Here, if you don't believe me, I'll prove it to you."

She took a stack of strange-looking cards out of her pocket. "These belong to my little grandson. He lives out of the country, and I'm waiting for him to come visit so I can return them to him. No matter, these will work just fine."

One by one, she held them up for Sarah to see.

On the first, there were two candles, with Hebrew lettering on the top.

On the second, there was a bottle of wine and two loaves of bread.

On the third, there was a pitcher of water.

She then stopped and put them back in the pocket of her white coat.

"Okay, I showed you three pictures. In a few minutes I'll ask you what you saw. In the meantime, we can discuss your medication, okay?"

"Okay."

"Dr. Cooper put you on Nimodipine, which is a calcium channel blocker specific to the central nervous system. It's recommended for head trauma victims. Would you like me to explain how it works?"

"Please." In spite of everything, Sarah couldn't help but find it all a bit fascinating; it made her wonder whether she had some connection to medicine or some related field.

"Okay, Dr. Cooper just explained it to me, and I'll try to keep it simple. It prevents movement of calcium into the cells of the blood vessels, relaxing the vessels and also increasing the supply of blood and oxygen to the brain. It dramatically improves cerebral blood flow."

"Why do I need that?"

"You'll heal quicker."

"Oh."

At least *that* part she understood. She was mentally reviewing all she had been told, when Dr. Lewis chuckled.

"All right, it's time to test your short term memory. What did I show you?"

"Cards."

"Good. What kind of cards were they?"

"One had Hebrew writing on it."

"Excellent!" She paused, a bit surprised. "Do you know any Hebrew?"

"I … I don't think so. I knew it was Hebrew letters, though. I think I might have learned the letters at Hebrew school."

Where had that come from?

The doctor looked as if she was debating with herself whether or not to verbalize something, before saying, "You know, dear, when you arrived here, I knew nothing about you, except that you were Jewish."

She was stunned. "Why did you think that?"

Anne Lewis smiled warmly. "The chain around your neck, dear."

Her hand reached up to her neck, touching the necklace, with its star-shaped pendant. Without thinking, she murmured, "My grandmother gave it to me."

The doctor leaned forward eagerly. "Do you realize that you've just had a memory, dear? Can you picture her in your mind? Might you remember her name?"

Frustratingly enough, she could not. She was quite certain that her necklace had been a gift from her grandmother, but she couldn't remember what she looked like, her name or anything of significance about her whatsoever.

She leaned back against the pillows, her shoulders slumped in defeat.

"Now, don't you worry about it," the doctor said cheerfully. "Since it's typical for a memory to return from your earliest childhood, it's not surprising that you would recall that. The pattern fits. Most likely, you'll be able to remember incidents from your childhood before your adolescence, and then move your way slowly up until the time of the accident. Amazing, no? The mind is the most wonderful machine. Now, what was on the second card I showed you?"

Sarah thought furiously. What *had* been on the second card? She couldn't remember. She swallowed.

"I don't know," she whimpered.

"It's all right," Dr. Lewis said. "Just relax. Do you remember who left the cards on my desk?"

This time she didn't hesitate. "Your grandson."

"Excellent."

There was a question that had been gnawing at her. "Dr. Lewis, what about my family? Has there been anyone asking about me?"

"No, not yet. Don't worry, though. In cases like these, sometimes it takes a while for people to realize that their relative is missing."

"How could they not realize that I'm missing?" she demanded to know.

Anne Lewis laughed. "There could be a thousand reasons, dear. They might not live near here, they might think you're on vacation, or maybe you don't even have any close relatives."

"Oh." She appeared so utterly crestfallen that Dr. Lewis quickly added, "It's also quite possible that a family member is across the street this very minute filing a missing person's report. And when that happens, we're notified straight away."

"Across the street?"

"Yes, at the police station. Chicago's finest. Don't worry, it'll all get sorted out, I promise you. Try not to stress too much about all that, at least for now. If you can try and remain calm, your positive mood will aid in your recovery, I assure you."

It was all so overwhelming. She wanted to ask more questions, eager to keep the nice doctor in the room with her several moments more.

How she hated being alone.

"I have another question. How am I paying for my care? I probably have insurance, but I don't know …"

"Again, not to worry. There are funds for such things. And when your memory returns, as I know it will, we'll present you with a nice, whopping bill. Okay?"

"Okay." She managed a smile.

"That's better." The doctor rose from her chair. "Now, I won't be in tomorrow, but I'll check in with you Sunday morning."

Sarah was alarmed at the news that she wouldn't see Anne Lewis for another two days. Somehow, she was the one person she felt she could trust. She was her only link to the world beyond her door. She found her kind face and gentle demeanor enormously comforting.

"Why – why won't you be here tomorrow?" She tried, albeit unsuccessfully, to keep the panic from her voice.

"I'm Orthodox. Tomorrow is Saturday, the Sabbath. I don't work on the Sabbath. Do you remember anything about that? Perhaps as a child, from your Hebrew school days?"

"Not really …" She was quiet for a moment. "Wait a minute, wait a minute … I remember what was on the card. It was a bottle of wine, and two loaves of bread," she said proudly.

"Good for you," Anne replied encouragingly. "You'll see, you'll start recalling more and more over the next few days ... as Dr. Cooper said, the injury was slight."

"Exactly how slight, would you say?"

"I'll put it this way. On a scale from one to ten, ten being the worst, I would put your injury at no more than a three to four. As I told you before, you're one lucky young lady. Trust me, you'll be good as new before you know it. I'll see you on Sunday morning."

"Thank you," Sarah said simply.

"Here. You can look at these over the weekend, if you'd like. Maybe test yourself." She handed her the cards, patted her affectionately on the shoulder, and walked out of the room with the same brisk confidence that she'd displayed earlier.

How wonderful to walk with such poise, knowing who you are, knowing your place in the world, Sarah thought wistfully. *Had she ever had such self-assurance? Would she ever have it again?*

She looked down at the cards, not really seeing them, just noticing their bright primary colors. *Is that how the doctor thought of her, as a small child?*

The thought depressed her. She almost felt like a baby, wholly unable to fend for herself, dependent on total strangers for her care.

She somehow knew intuitively that it went against her very nature to feel so utterly helpless, although she wasn't sure what her normal nature really was. It was odd in the extreme to not know oneself, but just as she didn't remember her name, she also couldn't be sure of her own personality. She couldn't recall her own likes and dislikes ... or could she?

Thinking hard, she was pretty certain that in the past she'd enjoyed drinking coffee, and actually felt the urge to drink a hot cup at that very moment.

Her excitement quickly subsided when she realized that the rest of the world probably did, too. Certainly, this preference did not make her special or unique in any way.

Suddenly impatient, she once more got out of her bed, with some difficulty, and resumed her pacing in front of the two small windows of her room.

She stopped abruptly, a thought occurring to her. Looking out the window, she took in the scene. Large buildings loomed everywhere, stories high, casting shadows upon the street below. It was downtown Chicago, and it was a busy street, to be sure, with traffic going one way, people another, conveying a general sense of chaotic city life.

She watched for a moment, transfixed. So many people, each charged with a sense of purpose. She felt a bit envious of the normalcy of it all ... ordinary people rushing about, accomplishing everyday tasks ... *did they even know how fortunate they were, knowing where to go home each night?* She was sadly removed from it all, watching life through a glass window, several stories up. It was then that she spied the building diagonally across the street.

Her thoughts were interrupted by a voice behind her.

"Enjoying the view?"

A young blonde nurse approached her. Sarah did not recognize her and didn't know if she'd seen her before or not.

"My name is Marcia and I'll be your nurse today. How are you feeling?"

"All right, I guess. Better, anyway," she replied stiffly. Strangers frightened her, and she had no way of knowing if that had always been the case or if it was a result of her alarming predicament. She supposed it was the latter.

Still, the young nurse seemed pleasant enough. She watered

the plant on the window sill, which Sarah had not even noticed before. "Can I take your vital signs, miss?"

"Yes, yes, of course." She sat down on the bed once more and allowed the nurse to take her blood pressure, pulse, etc. She wrote down all the numbers on a clipboard, the process taking somewhat longer than necessary. Sarah privately thought that the young nurse seemed a bit inexperienced, but she said nothing.

"Okay, your blood pressure is slightly elevated but I would say that's probably normal, considering everything you've been through," she chatted brightly. "I've been a nurse for seven months now, and I've never seen an amnesia case before. Would you mind if I asked you a question?"

"No," she warily replied.

"Do you *really* not remember anything about your past, anything at all?"

"I really don't remember," she answered truthfully. "Not my name, not my family, nothing."

The nurse said in a breezy rush, "That is just the coolest thing …. I've always been fascinated by these things, and as a matter of fact I thought of becoming a psychologist, but there was too much schooling involved, so here I am, a nurse in the psych unit …."

Sarah was disturbed by the fact that this young nurse considered her a curiosity, and was horrified to think of herself as a subject of conversation at the nurses' station. It also came as a bit of a shock for her to hear that she was in a "psych unit." No wonder the corridor had been so empty … where were all the other patients? Were they locked in their rooms, imprisoned in restraints within these very walls?

Oblivious to the fact that she might have upset her, the

nurse went on, "It's a great hospital; you're really in good hands here, if I say so myself … well, I guess I'll check in on you a bit later. If you need anything, just press the buzzer."

She motioned to the button beside the bed, tossed Sarah's chart into the acrylic container at the foot of the bed and bounced out of the room, as quickly as she had entered.

"I highly doubt that," Sarah muttered to herself.

She then laid her head down on the pillow, careful not to put pressure on the bandage. She was so *tired.* She was in a psychiatric unit … and the thought terrified her. *What about the other patients in the ward? Were they dangerous? What if they tried to harm her in some way?*

Her eyelids grew heavy, and although she fought it at first, wanting desperately to stay awake, sleep overcame her.

She awoke several hours later, most likely in the very same position, and allowed herself the luxury of dozing in a dreamlike half-sleep, before she sat upright, remembering where she was. Her muscles were aching, cramped and tight. The incessant throbbing in her head had resumed somewhat, and she lifted a hand to touch the gauzy bandage, wondering what her head looked like beneath it. Slowly rising from her bed, she walked to the windows, and purposefully surveyed what she could see of the outside world.

The scene below her was essentially the same, although the sun was now in the west and she ascertained that it was early afternoon. The street was still congested with traffic and crowds of people, but it was the building diagonally across from her that captured her attention.

It was an older structure, several stories high, a bit shorter than most others around it, with dark, frosted glass columns flanking the entranceway. There was a metal sculpture on the sidewalk directly in front of the building, though it was hard to discern what it was supposed to be. From her vantage point, she was only able to make out the lettering on the sign just above the brick facade.

Chicago Police Department.

She wildly looked around the room for a pen, pencil or some sort of writing utensil, but could find none. Her eyes then fell on the clipboard in the container at the foot of the bed. Sure enough, attached to the board was a small pen, suspended by a slender chain.

Reaching for it determinedly, she grasped the pen.

An idea had begun to form in her mind.

CHAPTER 6

Peter Strauss felt the plane touch down, hitting the ground with precision and skill to a thunderous round of applause. It had been a long flight, and Peter hadn't been able to sleep at all. There had been young children crying, elderly ladies chatting and laughing, men both young and old praying with prayer shawls .... Observing them, he was reminded of his grandfather, who had passed away when he'd been a small boy, five or six years old. He hadn't thought of him in years, but when he saw the men wearing their prayer shawls, black boxes resting on their foreheads, it had awakened a dormant memory. He was sure this was how his grandfather had prayed.

As the plane glided down the runway, slowing a bit, he became aware of the presence of the teenaged boy seated next to him. They hadn't said much to each other during the flight, as the boy had slept through much of it. Peter assumed he was probably seventeen or eighteen years old, around the same age as his Danielle. He appeared to be Israeli. He was also obviously a secular Jew, judging from his clothes and bare head. He had piercings and an outrageous Mohawk hairstyle. Still, he couldn't help but notice the young man's highly emotional response when the plane touched down upon Israeli soil.

Peter was moved, and though he wasn't usually inquisitive, he nevertheless felt compelled to talk to him. He leaned over. "Excuse me, son, can I ask you a question?"

The young man looked at him, tears still streaming unabashedly down his face.

"I'm sorry … but, I'd like to know … why are you crying?"

He looked at him.

"It's because I'm home," he replied, wiping his eyes.

"I see," he said gently, nodding at him to continue.

He continued, his breath raspy and short, "I don't speak English so good, but – I try to explain. I went to America, and it was good. I saw a lot of places, like California, Disney and the big Canyon, how do you say it?"

"The Grand Canyon?"

"Yes. All that. It was good, but it was … just a canyon, you know?"

"Yes, I suppose that's true." Peter smiled.

He continued, "This is my home. And not just mine, but all of us. We are all Jews, and this is our home. I know that He lives here, too." And he pointed his finger heavenward.

Peter felt a curious lump in his throat at these few words, so simply put, yet so heartfelt. The boy looked like a common street hoodlum. But there was such a depth of sincerity to him, he was at a loss as to how to respond, so he asked the boy his name.

"Eden," he replied.

"Like the Garden?"

The boy grinned. "Yes, I guess so."

"And how old are you, Eden?"

"Eighteen … I begin the army next month."

Peter said thoughtfully, "I wish you the best of luck, son."

The boy nodded, silent once more, no doubt contemplating

what the near future held in store for him. Peter realized that most American boys his age did not have to consider such weighty matters, at least not the privileged children of his colleagues with whom he was acquainted. Lee Ross had a son about the same age, and the most pressing thing on his mind was choosing a college that was as far away from his mother as possible. Ray Adams was a father to a teenaged son as well, and Ray often commented that Brandon's chief worry in life was whether he should travel to the West Coast or trek through Europe for his graduation present.

"And what is your name?" the boy's question interrupted his thoughts.

"Oh, sorry. It's Peter. Peter Strauss."

At this, the boy smiled. "Strauss is a famous name, you know. There is a street in Jerusalem named Strauss."

"Yes, my daughter told me that. I don't believe that I'm related to the famous Strauss family, though."

"But you never know, right? Anything is possible."

"I suppose that's true."

The interesting exchange was still on Peter's mind as they deplaned, making their way toward a large bus that would drive them to the airport terminal. Everything was unfamiliar ... the people, the surroundings ... and then, when he was almost at the bus, he spotted an elderly woman who slowly bent down and planted a soft kiss on the ground.

He had never in his life seen that, and it stirred him.

Boarding the bus, he discovered that there were no seats, just poles to grab onto for the short ride to the terminal. And grab onto it he did; the driver drove like he was being chased.

Eden, he noticed, was standing close by, hanging on to a pole of his own with a wide grin on his face.

"Is this your first time?" he asked Peter, practically shouting to be heard over the noise of the bus's engines.

"You mean in Israel? Yes," he shouted back.

"For how long is your stay?" he wanted to know.

"Ten days," he answered.

"You'll see," he said confidently. "You will be different from this trip. Everyone who comes to Israel, his life will change in some way. You'll see."

Peter felt a strange sensation at these words, hoping that if it were true, his life would change for the better ….

Thankfully, the ride ended quickly and Peter exited the bus, feeling a bit queasy. The sign above him said in large letters WELCOME TO ISRAEL.

He entered the building and proceeded to wait with the other passengers in an interminably long line for his turn to show the official his passport. He was relieved when it was finally his turn, and he walked to the small booth, handing the young woman his passport and tickets.

He was unprepared for all the questions she asked.

"Why are you here?" the woman asked him curtly.

"I'm here on vacation, to visit my daughter."

"Does she live here?"

"No, she's a student."

"What is the name of the school?"

"Well, I'm not sure, to be honest …."

She looked at him skeptically, her eyebrows raised a fraction of an inch.

"You don't know the name of the school that your daughter is attending?"

"It's a religious school, that much I know. It's in a suburb of Tel Aviv, she told me. Wait, I have it written down right here."

Peter looked at a crumpled sheet of paper on which he'd hastily scribbled two words. *Bnei Brak.*

"Here it is, Bnei Brak," he said. "That's the name."

The woman smirked. "That's the name of the city, not the school. Do you have an address?"

He colored slightly, not able to recall ever feeling so intimidated by such a young person. He encountered numerous powerful people on a daily basis in the course of negotiating multimillion dollar deals, yet the young Israeli woman he now faced made him feel like a stammering, inept adolescent.

He meekly showed her the crumpled sheet of paper. "Here it is ... Elisha Street, Number Eight. Bnei Brak."

"What is your daughter's name?"

Ordinarily, he would've protested the rude line of questioning, as it was almost as if she was challenging his reason for being there. Still, he held his tongue, knowing full well that Israeli security was, without a doubt, the best the world over.

Considering all the neighboring nations that wanted to destroy it, it simply had to be.

"Her name is Danielle," he answered.

"Same last name?"

"Yes. Danielle Strauss."

"How old is she?"

"Eighteen."

"And when is her birthday?"

"June. June 8th, 1985."

She paused, observed him for a few moments, and then stamped his passport several times.

"All is in order. Enjoy your stay," she said brusquely.

"Thank you," he replied weakly, feeling as if he'd been interrogated.

With much relief, he retrieved his passport and tickets and made his way with the throngs of people toward the luggage carousels.

Eden, he noticed, was already there, swinging the last of his duffle bags onto his cart, appearing to be in his element. He looked to be exactly where he belonged.

Peter, on the other hand, couldn't ever remember feeling so awkward and out of place. He tried to edge his way to the carousel to locate his missing suitcases, somewhat surprised by all the pushing and shoving that seemed to be taken for granted. Many others were already leaving the terminal, having retrieved their belongings, eager, no doubt, to meet their family members.

At last he spotted his handsome luggage looking quite out of place next to the other, shabbier bags piled one on top of another. The bags had obviously been tossed around a bit, as they were now covered in dust, but he didn't care. Loading them onto his trolley cart, he nearly collided with young Eden.

"Eden, I thought you'd left a while ago," Peter panted.

"Not yet. I mean, I was … I wanted to make sure you were okay," he replied, haltingly.

Peter smiled. "That was very thoughtful of you, son. I finally found my luggage and I'm pretty much all set."

"Mr. Strauss, you can't forget to change your dollars … do you know where to go?"

The question stymied him. "Uh, no. I hadn't even thought about it," he remarked, his heart sinking as he saw the long lines at the currency counters.

"Come with me," Eden said assuredly.

Peter followed the boy like a well-behaved child, marveling at how the lines seemed to open to make way for them.

Within several minutes, Peter had made the necessary exchanges, and he turned once more to Eden to thank him for his assistance.

He shrugged it off. "No problem. Do you have a place to stay here?"

"Yes, I'll be staying at a hotel in Tel Aviv."

The young man held out his hand.

Peter shook it warmly.

"Good luck, son. Take care of yourself."

The boy nodded, understanding the depth of meaning in those words, and then walked reluctantly away, exiting through doors on the right.

I'm not a praying man, Peter thought. *But, please, if You are listening, watch over that boy and keep him safe.*

He continued his walk toward the exit doors, burdened with his bulky cart, when yet another official asked to see his passport.

Peter showed it to him, and surprisingly enough, he glanced at it and waved him through. He walked out of the exit doors into a parking lot of sorts, where he saw taxis lined up at the far end of the circular driveway, ready to take passengers to various destinations.

He paused for a moment, contemplating the exact protocol of where he should hail a taxi, when a sudden burst of movement in his peripheral vision caught his eye. Turning his head, he saw a young girl wearing a black jacket with a pink scarf rushing toward him.

Danielle.

All of his fears at seeing her again were forgotten in that very instant. He took the last few steps toward her at a run, and she threw herself into his arms.

"Daddy!"

For several seconds, he could not speak, not trusting his own voice. His eyes filled with tears as he finally drew back, eager to gaze at his daughter, making certain that she was all right.

He quickly took in the long black skirt that she wore and her dark hair, which was worn in a simple ponytail. Her face was all smiles, and without makeup there was a glow about her that he'd never noticed before.

"You look wonderful, Pumpkin," he said in a quavery voice.

"Thank you, Dad," she said as she looped her arm in his, guiding him toward the taxis. "I'm so glad you came!"

"You are?" he asked. Now that *was* a surprise. He'd thought that she'd be irate with him, not wanting him to interfere in her life.

"Of course," she said brightly. "I can't wait to introduce you to Rabbi and Rebbitzen Cohen. You'll stay with us for *Shabbos*, won't you? Rebbitzen Cohen is expecting you."

"Uh, sure ... sure, I'll stay with you, Pumpkin," he quickly agreed, vaguely recalling that Orthodox Jews observed the Sabbath from sundown on Friday until nighttime the next day, or was it the other way around? He wasn't certain but knew he'd soon find out.

Although he'd made reservations at an expensive hotel on the beach in Tel Aviv for the weekend, he was more than willing to forgo his plans. Even it meant losing his payment, he was eager to see the family to whom his daughter had grown so attached, and he was secretly pleased that she'd invited him to stay with her.

Ray Adam's words echoed in his mind as he entered a taxi with Danielle.

She's in some sort of crazy cult …. If you need any help, call me. I'll bust her outta there myself ….

Of course, it wasn't a cult, it couldn't be ….

Could it?

He would soon see for himself just what was going on with his daughter.

The taxi sped off after Danielle gave the driver the address, and Peter found himself peering out the window, taking in the rows of palm trees, the stone buildings and the overall view, which was quite different from what he'd pictured. With such a balmy wind blowing in his face, he could hardly believe it was February.

But the young girl seated beside him was the most surprising of all.

She'd changed so much it was remarkable … not just in her appearance, but in her demeanor and mannerisms. Her very essence appeared somewhat altered, yet he couldn't quite pinpoint just what it was. He'd anticipated that she'd be defiant, or even hostile and defensive about her new lifestyle. But she sat at his side calmly and self-assured. And if he'd secretly expected her to be the meek and glassy-eyed new recruit of some cult, she was quite the opposite, as well.

In fact, she'd never looked more exuberant … more alive.

They didn't say much during the cab ride, allowing Peter to absorb his surroundings and to acclimate himself to the landscape and vegetation that were so totally different from Chicago. Before long, they exited the highway and drove past a surprisingly large, modern facility, with glass walls and a sleek red trim.

"That's the Coca-Cola factory, Dad," Danielle pointed.

They soon turned onto a large boulevard, swarming with traffic. Danielle smiled as she saw her father craning his neck out of the window, unable to fathom the scene that was unfolding all around him.

Smiling to himself about Dorothy who was no longer in Kansas, he was certainly not in Highland Park anymore.

It was if he'd gone back in time, to a world that he'd never known. The old stone buildings loomed above him, clean laundry hanging from crowded porches, small children of every shape and size peering down … and the ever-present noise and energy from the crowded streets. Mothers wearing turbans and scarves pushing infants in strollers, children playing … there was so much to see and so much life and activity, he hardly knew where to look first.

"Welcome to Bnei Brak," Danielle said. "It's unlike anywhere else in the world."

As far as first impressions went, he was inclined to agree. He had never been to a place remotely like it.

"*Rechov Elisha, Mispar Shmoneh*," Danielle told the driver.

"Since when do you speak Hebrew?" Peter asked her.

"I've been practicing since the summer. I don't know all that much, though," she confided. "But my reading has improved a lot."

"You can read Hebrew?" he asked incredulously.

"Yes." She smiled.

"That's pretty impressive, Pumpkin," he murmured, not knowing quite what to say.

The cab veered off the large boulevard, careening up and down several maze-like side streets, finally screeching to a halt in front of a large, stone apartment building.

Peter hastily paid the driver and exited the cab, a bit unsteady on his feet.

"Does everyone here drive like that?" he whispered to his daughter.

She nodded. "Yes, Dad. You get used to it, though."

He lifted the suitcases out of the small trunk, and had barely closed the door when the driver sped off with a squeal of tires ... he was about to comment on it to his daughter when he noticed Danielle standing on the curb, grinning mischievously from ear to ear.

"And just what's so funny?" he wanted to know.

"You," she giggled. "The expression on your face ... it reminds me of when I arrived here in June, not knowing where to go, what to do ... don't worry, Daddy, you'll be just fine."

He hid a smile, and shaking his head, he followed her up the paved path, noticing that the dilapidated looking building was erected on stone pillars, the entranceway open to the street. They had barely gone several feet when a tall, thin man hurried toward them, a broad smile on his face, his hand outstretched.

"Welcome to Israel, Mr. Strauss. It's so nice to meet you," he said warmly, shaking Peter's hand for what seemed like five minutes.

Peter guessed he was in his mid-thirties; his short reddish beard just tinged with a few hairs of gray, his mannerisms animated and youthful.

"Pleased to meet you, Mr. ... ?" Peter inquired.

"Dan Cohen ... we're not formal here. Here, let me have that bag ... we're just thrilled that you'll be spending *Shabbos* with us."

Dan Cohen? So he was the famous Rabbi Cohen so revered by his daughter?

Strange for him, Peter mumbled some sort of unintelligible

response. He couldn't help feeling a bit tongue-tied; his mind was awhirl with so many conflicting thoughts. Rabbi Cohen was so completely unlike the image that he'd envisioned. In fact, he was practically the opposite. For one thing, he appeared much younger than Peter would have expected, and somehow more friendly and down-to-earth.

For the last several months, ever since Danielle had first embarked on her "personal journey to self-discovery," as she referred to it, she'd been waxing rhapsodic over the rabbi's virtues. Sometimes, her hyperbolic description inspired Peter to anticipate the worst, conjuring up visions of some sort of wild-eyed evangelical weirdo with messianic pretensions.

To his profound relief, this young man, with large, guileless brown eyes, who had greeted him so warmly and with such obvious sincerity, was anything but sinister.

Peter felt humbled, shamed even, at the uncharitable and suspicious thoughts he'd originally harbored. He felt the color rise in his cheeks, but Rabbi Cohen seemed unaware as he insisted on carrying Peter's bag, talking all the while as they walked up the narrow flight of steps.

"... I'm sorry that there isn't an elevator," Dan panted apologetically. "We're on the third floor. Our neighbors are in America for a few weeks for a family wedding, so you'll have your own space, with some privacy. You must be exhausted from your trip."

Peter finally found his tongue, saying, "Yes, yes ... I didn't sleep at all, actually."

"Maybe you'd like to rest a while, get some sleep."

He was so keyed-up that he'd never be able to sleep, of that he was certain. Still, it would feel good to put his feet up and have a few quiet moments to himself to gather his thoughts.

They nearly collided in the darkened stairwell with a young, angelic-looking girl of about five rushing toward them, with curly blonde hair and the largest, crystal-clear blue eyes, fringed with the longest lashes Peter had ever seen.

"Abba," the girl said excitedly, "is this Daniella's father?"

"Yes, Rena," he said, as he took his daughter's hand in his own. "Let's go find Ima."

Peter noticed the variation of Danielle's name, but he made no comment.

They reached the third floor landing, and Rabbi Cohen held open a well-worn wooden door in the dimly-lit corridor, calling to his wife. "Esther! We have a visitor!"

The deliciously fragrant smell of freshly baked bread wafted through the small apartment. His own home hadn't smelled like that in ... well, possibly never. Beth, his beloved late wife, had enjoyed many hobbies, but culinary pursuits hadn't been one of them.

And Gilda, as remarkable a housekeeper as she was, wasn't much of a cook.

A petite, pretty woman wearing a blonde wig came rushing out of the kitchen, wiping her hands on a small towel, looking positively elated to greet him.

"Mr. Strauss, welcome to our home," she bubbled effusively.

"Pleased to meet you, Rebbitzen Cohen," he said, automatically extending his hand.

She seemed not to notice his outstretched hand, gushing all the while, "Oh, I see the resemblance, Daniella! You are the very image of your father, just look at that! Can I offer you a cup of tea or coffee? Maybe some cake?"

Peter felt his mouth watering at the suggestion. He hadn't realized how very hungry he was.

"Coffee sounds great," he said weakly. "I … I wouldn't want to trouble you, Rebbitzen."

"Oh, it's no trouble at all! It's my pleasure, Mr. Strauss," she said airily, and he had no doubt that she truly meant those words.

He was quick to notice that Rabbi Cohen went to the small kitchen in the back of the apartment, ostensibly to help his wife. Sure enough, moments later he emerged, carrying a small tray piled with obviously homemade pastries and a large mug of coffee.

"Please, come sit down," he gestured to Peter, placing the delicacies on the long, rectangular dining table that appeared to dominate the entire room. Other than the table and shelves of books lining the walls, he noticed that the room was sparsely furnished.

Peter obediently sat down, soon joined by Danielle, who seated herself to his left. A small boy of around two or three years of age, all blonde curls and chubby cheeks, sidled up to her. She quite effortlessly lifted him onto her lap, where he popped his thumb into his mouth and leaned back into her, looking quite comfortable with the arrangement. Peter found himself a bit disconcerted, for the toddler stared at him with the same enormous blue eyes as his sister, trying to determine if he were friend or foe. And the young rabbi and his wife were hovering about him, appearing as if they had nothing better to do that Friday afternoon than serve him a lovely little repast.

Peter was astounded at their sheer benevolence … he was essentially a stranger to them, but they waited on him as if he were a royal guest.

"Would you like some milk and sugar?" Dan Cohen asked.

"Milk, please, no sugar," Peter managed. "Thank you, Rabbi

... really, I feel terrible bothering you like this, and right before the Sabbath, too."

"Nonsense, it's no bother at all," insisted the young rabbi as he sat down across from him. "And please, call me Dan."

"All right, Dan. Please call me Peter."

"Fair enough. I can't tell you how much we've looked forward to meeting you, to having you at our *Shabbos* table. Your daughter has become such an integral part of our family already. And we've heard so much about you, we feel as if we already know you."

Really? Danielle had mentioned him to them? The day was certainly full of surprises .... It seemed that this couple knew more about him than vice versa .... He hadn't expected that, and he was curious as to what she'd said ....

He had so many questions, he hardly knew where to begin. Yet he remained quiet, absorbing the atmosphere in which he found himself, albeit in small increments, unable to take in too many details at once. Mere hours before, he'd been on a plane thinking that his daughter would be less than thrilled to see him, only to find her at the airport, rushing to greet him. Rabbi Cohen and his wife, so different than what he'd imagined, also seemed delighted to make his acquaintance, and he was at a loss as to how to react.

The answers would come in time, he knew, and for the moment he was content with seeing Danielle so ... at ease and relaxed in her environment.

He bit into a delicious pastry, all flaky dough and smooth chocolate filling. It was by far the most delectable pastry he could ever remember eating.

"Wow, this is incredible," he said earnestly. "What's this called?"

"Rebbitzen Cohen is the greatest baker," Danielle said enthusiastically. "Dad, she makes these from scratch, can you imagine? They're called *rugelach*."

"I had some help in the kitchen, if I remember correctly," Rebbitzen Cohen said brightly. "Daniella rolled up her sleeves and basically made half of the food for *Shabbos*."

"Since when can you cook?" Peter asked incredulously.

Danielle blushed. "Oh, I've picked up some tips here and there .... I find it very relaxing, actually."

Peter couldn't think of any intelligent response. In fact, he was so utterly stupefied and surprised by his daughter and his surroundings, he said very little. Mercifully, Rabbi and Rebbitzen Cohen didn't ask him many questions while he ate, leaving him to his thoughts.

After ten minutes or so, Danielle turned to him, "Dad, your eyelids are starting to close. Why don't I take you next door and get you settled? You'll have the whole apartment to yourself, and maybe you could catch some sleep."

Was this his little girl, Danielle? How well he remembered her tumultuous high school years, trying his best to raise her alone after Beth died .... Thankfully, she'd never been rebellious or difficult, but she'd often been moody and understandably sad, leaving him at a loss as to how to console her when he was trying to deal with his own sadness ....

In contrast, she now appeared to be a well-adjusted, fully grown, mature woman. The changes in her were remarkable, so much so that he felt as if he no longer knew her. It was somehow gratifying and unsettling at the same time.

He thanked the Cohens profusely for the delicious snack and followed his daughter across the narrow hallway to the apartment next door.

She opened the door with a small key and stood back to let him through. The layout reversed, the neighbors' apartment was the exact mirror image of the Cohens'. This apartment, however, had more furnishings, pretty draperies and matching throw pillows on the sofa. Peter noticed that this apartment, like the Cohens', was lined floor to ceiling with bookcases filled with what seemed to be religious books.

Danielle was rushing about stacking fresh linens and towels in the small bedroom located directly off the main room. She seemed oblivious to the fact that her father had remained rooted to the spot, looking around and trying to get a grip on his feelings.

"Daddy?"

He looked up expectantly. "Yes, Pumpkin?"

Danielle glanced at her watch.

"You look like you're sleeping standing up ... there's fresh linens on the bed, why don't you try to sleep for a few hours? I'll wake you in plenty of time for *shul* ... you wouldn't mind going with Rabbi Cohen, would you?"

"You mean to the synagogue, right?"

She nodded with hope-filled eyes, and he didn't want to disappoint her. Besides, he was secretly glad to accompany the young rabbi to the synagogue, if only to assuage the lingering, nagging doubts that still concerned him.

He wanted to see, firsthand, just what this new religion of hers was all about, once and for all.

"Sure, Pumpkin, I'll go with Rabbi Cohen to the synagogue. Are you coming, too?"

"No, it's just for the men tonight .... I'll stay here with Rebbitzen Cohen and the kids. And, Daddy ... can I ask you a favor?" she asked, haltingly.

"What is it?"

"I feel bad asking you, I know you aren't very comfortable with any of this ... but do you think you could wear this while you're here?"

She held out a black velvet *yarmulka*, saying, "I bought it in a small shop down the street. I hope it fits you. You wouldn't mind very much, would you?"

He reached for it, grasped it and stared at it for a while.

His grandfather had worn a faded black *yarmulka* in synagogue, but he couldn't be sure if he'd worn one at other times.

"You mean for the synagogue, right, Pumpkin? Surely I don't have to wear one all the time, like the Rabbi?"

She swallowed. "Actually, I was hoping you'd wear it for the entire trip .... I know it's a lot to ask of you, but it would really, *really* mean a lot to me."

One look at his daughter's earnest face was all he needed.

Danielle hadn't an inkling of the tremendous power that she wielded over him. The love he had for her, his only child ... he was basically incapable of saying "no" to her.

"Well, if you put it that way, how can I refuse?"

Her face lit up as he placed the *yarmulka* on his head.

It fit perfectly.

"Thanks, Dad ... you know why Jewish men wear *yarmulkas*? To remind them that G-d is watching over them. Isn't that neat?"

What could he say? He was reunited with his daughter who was the picture of blooming, robust health, and at that very moment, he indeed felt like G-d *was* watching over him.

"It's very neat, Pumpkin," he murmured, catching his reflection in a small mirror on the wall. *What would Ray Adams say if he saw him now?*

"I'll let you get settled. Try to take a little nap, and I'll wake you in plenty of time."

She was on her way out the door when he called out to her. "Danielle?"

"Yes, Daddy?"

"How do you say the word for synagogue again?"

She smiled. "*Shul.*"

He repeated it to himself, not being familiar with the word. He was self-conscious, aware of his complete lack of knowledge about all things Jewish, and he didn't want to make a complete fool of himself in front of the young rabbi.

"How do you remember everything?" he asked his daughter.

She laughed. "Trust me, that's just the tip of a very large iceberg!"

And with that, she left the apartment, closing the door behind her.

He walked to the bedroom, which was in reality a mere cubicle, partitioned off from the main room by a flimsy wall. Sizing up the tiny space, he noted that the laundry room in his Highland Park home was somewhat larger than this master bedroom.

Still, there were cheerful curtains on the windows, and the place looked spotlessly clean. He sat down on the bed wearily, massaging his temples, and removed the *yarmulka* from his head, placing it on the small bedside table.

The situation in which he found himself was completely unlike anything he possibly could have imagined, and he was unaccustomed to being so mistaken. Here he was, in a cramped apartment with relative strangers across the hallway. Additionally, he was located on the other side of the world, though it could have been a different planet because it was just so … far removed from the lifestyle that he knew.

His daughter, surprisingly, was not hostile or angry ... she had welcomed him with open arms, literally. She had grown close to a family who, unlike his fears, seemed completely genuine and honorable in their intentions.

She'd arrived in Israel in June, a mere nine months prior .... It had been a lark, an adventure, and he remembered acquiescing to the idea readily, knowing how much Beth had wanted to visit Israel during her short lifetime, but never getting the chance. She would have been pleased to have Danielle fulfill that dream.

Danielle, her best friend Kim Silverman and Kim's cousin, Rebecca, had packed their duffel bags with all the excitement and vitality of eighteen-year-olds whose world is a wide open space with infinite possibilities.

The three of them had been friends for years, though inexplicably, Danielle had always been closer to Kim. Now Peter found himself wondering what had happened to Kim and Rebecca, as Danielle hadn't mentioned either of them for quite some time. Did they, like his daughter, find solace in religion? Did they stay to learn about Judaism as well, or had they flown back to America, beginning their college years right on schedule?

Funny how he'd never thought to ask. First and foremost, his concerns were reserved for his daughter, and his daughter alone.

He lay back on the pillow, his eyelids heavy with fatigue.

An instant later, he was sound asleep.

A faint rustling sound, and he was instantly alert. He strained his eyes to see who was there, for he felt someone's presence in the room. The room was brightly lit; so bright, in fact, that it made it difficult to see ....

He had to see, he had to know ...

And then, just as he'd surmised, he was able to see the quiet image standing near the doorway.

"Beth? Beth, is that you?" he whispered.

The image was hazy and surreal ... but in its presence he felt a peace that had evaded him for years ...

"Beth, do you know that I'm here, in Israel?"

She appeared to nod, understandingly.

"Danielle is here, too," he continued, as if the conversation was the most natural thing in the world.

It was then that the powerful truth hit him ... of course, Beth knew.

She had known all along, watching over Danielle, guiding her ... perhaps it was Beth who'd orchestrated this course of events from the beginning ...

Somehow, it was meant to be.

With an inexplicable certainty, he knew.

The image started to weaken ... he tried to get up, but his limbs felt leaden with sleep ... he didn't want her to go ...

"Beth, Beth, come back!" he whispered hoarsely, knowing it was futile. He'd barely made an audible sound.

"Don't go ... please ..." he pleaded, silently.

The image faded into oblivion.

Peter woke abruptly, frantically looking about him. Of course, the room was empty, and he was there alone, with the galloping sound of his beating heart. Closing his hands over his eyes, he tried to remember the details of the dream. It had seemed so real ....

He hadn't dreamed of his late wife in quite a few years,

and it had left him feeling shaken and vulnerable and very much alone.

Yet, oddly enough, the experience had been comforting, as well. Beth would have been pleased with Danielle's religious quest, he knew. Beth had always been a free-spirit. She had always been eager to find and embrace the beauty in all things, whether it was contemporary culture or time-honored traditions, regardless of the prejudices and preconceptions of others.

Danielle, though she resembled him, had her mother's personality. And when she immersed herself in some pursuit, she gave it everything she had.

Although the dream had seemed incredibly vivid, now that he was fully awake, the details were beginning to rapidly recede. Sighing, he slowly swung his legs over the edge of the bed and looked at his watch. He was startled to see that it was late in the day, almost five o'clock. He'd slept for about three hours, when, curiously enough, it had felt like only a few minutes.

He went into the main room and unzipped the garment bag that held his good suit. He was glad that he'd brought it, without even realizing that he'd be attending synagogue that evening. He checked his messages and saw that Ray had tried to reach him several times.

He made the call. Ray picked up on the first ring.

"Ray Adams," he said.

"Ray? It's Peter."

"Dude, how's it going?"

"Pretty well. I guess I'm a little jetlagged, though. I just slept three hours."

"Wow, that sounds good to me. I could use a nap right about now, but no can do, since I'm doing all your work, buddy."

Peter chuckled. "Sorry about that."

"So how's your daughter?"

"She's really well, Ray, much better than I'd even hoped."

"You're sure?" Ray asked doubtfully. "If she needs help, I know a guy who knows a guy ..."

"I'm sure," Peter said definitively. "She's fine."

"That's awesome, man. I'm happy for you. Listen, I know you're on vacation and all that, but I have some questions for you ..."

And he proceeded to fill him in on a few cases that required Peter's input, some scheduling conflicts, etc., and Peter answered each of his queries, happy to be dealing with something familiar for a change. After a few minutes, Ray said, "All right, Peety-boy, that's it for now ... if I need anything else, I can call you at this number, right?"

Peety-boy? That was a new one.

"You got it," Peter answered. "I'll be here."

He hung up, feeling a bit more like himself. He was used to being the one holding the proverbial deck of cards, knowing all the answers and even anticipating the questions. Not knowing how to proceed in this totally new situation unnerved him.

Returning to the bedroom, he unpacked and straightened his personal belongings. He then dressed in his dark gray suit with a crisp white shirt, which he hoped was conservative enough for the synagogue. He felt like a nervous schoolboy, for, in fact, that had been the last time he'd stepped foot in a synagogue. He fingered several ties, undecided, until he finally chose the navy silk that Gilda had bought him for his birthday last autumn.

His eye fell on the velvet *yarmulka* that was resting on the nightstand. He reached for it and tentatively placed it on his head. He then studied himself in the mirror, wondering if it made him look any different.

It certainly made him *feel* different, and more than a little self-conscious.

As if on cue, Danielle peeked her head through the doorway.

"Daddy? Oh, good, you're up …. I didn't want to wake you," she said, eyeing him appreciatively. "You look good."

"Thanks, Pumpkin," he laughed. "I bet you never thought you'd see your old man wearing a *yarmulka*, huh?"

"It looks great on you," she insisted. "It's getting late, almost time for *shul*."

No sooner had the words left her mouth than Peter heard the loud wail of a siren.

"What's that?" Peter demanded, alarmed. "That's not an air-raid siren, is it?"

Looking alarmed, Peter immediately thought of a terror attack, but Danielle only smiled sweetly.

"No, not at all," she reassured him. "It's a special siren that sounds five minutes before the start of *Shabbos*, so everyone will be prepared. Women stop what they're doing and light the special candles. It's the most awesome thing, Daddy. You'll see."

He didn't know quite what to say to that, so after glancing in the mirror, he took a deep breath and followed his daughter out of the apartment.

CHAPTER 7

As he looked around the large room, crammed with worshippers, Peter Strauss was sure he had been transported into a different dimension. He began to imagine the airplane in which he had arrived as a sort of spaceship, transferring him from one time period into another. No doubt, he was in a time warp; though he was dressed in modern clothes, he had been transported into a past era.

Surely this was the re-enactment of old-time Judaism, reminiscent of some photographs he'd seen of the *shtetl*s of pre-WWII Eastern Europe. The only details that connected him to modern life were the electric lights and the fans overhead. In fact, he was so shocked, so completely unprepared for the sights and sounds that greeted him, that he stood still as stone, afraid to move even a fraction of an inch.

Not that he'd have been able to, even if he'd wanted. The room was *that* crowded.

The synagogue was a high-ceilinged space, so totally unlike the plush sanctuary that he'd remembered as a small child. The temple he remembered from his youth resembled a theater of sorts, pictured through the eyes of a small child. He'd only been there on one or two occasions. His father had totally discarded organized religion with a vengeance, declaring himself an atheist at the age of forty, perhaps as a result of his own rebellion. Peter had a dim recollection of arguments over religion between his father and grandfather ....

Peter hadn't even had a *bar mitzvah*, much to his chagrin at the time.

He'd wanted masses of presents, like his friend Jason Brody had received. His father had refused, and by that time, Peter's grandfather had died, so there was no one left in the family who cared much for tradition.

Peter scanned the room. It was as if the tradition of the ages had sprung to life ....

It was a sea of black and white ... there were men wearing black suits, there were men dressed in Hasidic garb, with black satin coats. There were men wearing white shirts rolled at the sleeves, with white *yarmulkas*. There were men wearing magnificent, tall fur hats in the Hasidic style, and those who wore shorter styles. There were black hats of every size, and there were many men who wore knitted *yarmulkas*, as well.

They all had one thing in common.

They prayed with a fervor atypical of anything he'd ever witnessed in his life, seemingly in unison, but individually, as well, all of them speaking and singing words that Peter did not understand .... What he did understand was that theirs was a spiritual experience of devotion to a Higher Being.

It humbled him, and left him feeling awkward and self-conscious.

When the assembled crowd said "Amen" in unison, it stirred him.

He was among strangers, yet inexplicably he wasn't alone. He felt woefully, inadequately out of place, and yet he was a Jew, just like the others. This fact alone offered him a powerful, inexplicable sense of connection, quite unlike anything he'd ever before experienced.

Since he was unfamiliar with any of the prayers and unable to read Hebrew, he just stood among the worshippers, trying to be inconspicuous. He tried to blend in as unobtrusively as possible, grateful that nobody seemed to notice him. Rabbi Cohen very considerately had handed him a prayer book when they'd first arrived, but then had left him to his own devices.

Fascinated by his surroundings, Peter was more than content to observe everything going on around him.

What would Ray Adams say if he saw him now?

You've gone ahead and lost your mind, buddy.

Peter's lips twitched at the image of Lee Ross, atheist that she was, fainting in an unladylike heap at the mere sight of all the worshippers.

The fact was indisputable that in the circle in which he traveled, there was no one who would believe that he, Peter Strauss, Esq., the powerful litigation attorney from Chicago, would ever find himself in these circumstances and in this remote destination.

With people such as these, no less.

And yet ... and yet ...

There was something almost mesmerizing about the ancient melodies, the singing in unison, the feeling of belonging to something infinitely bigger than himself.

And, finally, it was over. He had somehow expected the services to last longer, and he felt a mixture of relief and ...

He wasn't certain. Could it be that he'd wanted it to last longer?

No, surely not. That would be simply absurd.

Suddenly, Rabbi Cohen appeared beside him, led the way

out of the suffocating building and then turned to Peter with an outstretched hand.

"Good *Shabbos*, Peter," he said warmly, extending his hand. Not knowing how to respond, Peter simply said, "Thank you, Rabbi."

Rabbi Cohen leaned forward, whispering conspiratorially, "You know, people may say 'Good *Shabbos*' to you or '*Shabbat Shalom*.' It's customary to return the greetings in the same way."

"You mean, the same words?"

"Exactly. If someone says, 'Good *Shabbos*,' you could respond with a 'Good *Shabbos*.' And if someone says, '*Shabbat Shalom*,' then you can respond in kind."

"Oh," Peter replied. "Thanks for telling me."

"Not a problem."

Peter was able to test out his new knowledge rather quickly, responding to the many passersby who greeted them on the short walk to the Cohens' apartment.

Rabbi Cohen did not pressure him with questions, seemingly content to walk in amiable silence, allowing Peter to absorb the details of his surroundings.

It was the Sabbath, and pedestrians seemed to prefer walking in the streets rather than choosing the stone-paved sidewalks of Bnei Brak. The street was teeming with people – men returning from their synagogues and women gathered in clusters, chatting with friends. There were lots of young people, as well as children playing in the streets, and Peter could not help but feel overwhelmed by the obvious fact that everyone appeared to be in such festive spirits.

He'd never before seen so many people so happy.

It was as if the entire city was on some sort of glorious holiday, and everyone seemed to be having a marvelous time. He found it hard to believe that this was a weekly occurrence. Irresistibly drawn in by all the excitement, Peter's mood was lighter than it had been in weeks as they climbed the old, shadowy stairwell of Rabbi Cohen's apartment building.

The steep climb seemed interminably long, but the incredibly delectable smell that greeted him when they finally reached the landing convinced him that it was well worth the effort.

Rabbi Cohen opened the door with a flourish.

"Good *Shabbos!*" he called out, and was almost toppled over by his two angelic-looking children who rushed into his outstretched arms.

He held the door open for Peter, who entered, looking appreciatively at the beautiful scene that awaited him.

The table, in the center of which was a lovely glass vase filled with bright flowers, was covered with a spotless white tablecloth and set with sparkling tableware. Most beautiful of all was the light from the candles in the silver candelabra shining on the radiant, expectant face of Danielle, who was standing next to Rebbitzen Cohen.

Gaining his composure, Peter swallowed, "My goodness, this is quite a spread. It must have been a lot of work."

"It's in honor of *Shabbos*," Rebbitzen Cohen explained. "And, of course, in honor of our special guests."

"Thank you," Peter said simply, humbled by her sincerity.

He was essentially a stranger to them, and yet this young, vibrant family had welcomed him so graciously that he was truly touched by their kindness.

Danielle ushered him to the seat next to her at the table, which suited him wonderfully. Rabbi Cohen sat to his right, at the head of the table, with his wife facing him on the other end. Their two children sat directly across from Danielle and him.

This promised to be a genuinely festive party, except that it began a little differently than other parties he'd attended.

Rabbi Cohen approached his daughter, placed his right hand over her halo of blonde curls and said a short blessing in Hebrew. When he finished, he leaned over and kissed the top of her head, and her adorable face was wreathed in smiles.

Her little brother, not wanting to be outdone, patted the top of his head, as well, crying, "Me, too! Me, too!"

"Of course, Shmuel. It's your turn."

And he then placed his right hand on his little son, and blessed him, as well. Then he kissed his head, as well, and the little boy looked positively triumphant.

Peter couldn't help but smile. The Cohen children were truly adorable, and exceptionally well-behaved.

Rabbi Cohen suddenly turned to Peter, almost as an afterthought, saying, "It's a custom to bless one's children on Friday night, Peter. Would you want to bless your daughter, as well?"

What could he say?

"Uh, I'm sorry, Rabbi," he said apologetically. "I'm afraid I don't know the words."

"Oh, not to worry," he responded cheerfully. "You can say the blessing in English. Here you go."

He handed him a prayer book and showed him what to say.

Feeling a bit self-conscious, yet eager at the same time, he turned to his daughter. Placing his right hand over her head as he'd seen the Rabbi do minutes beforehand, he recited the short blessing.

May G-d make you like Sarah, Rebecca, Rachel and Leah.

May Hashem bless you and safeguard you.
May Hashem illuminate His countenance for you
and be gracious to you.
May Hashem turn his countenance to you and
establish peace for you.

He couldn't help but feel emotional as he saw the grateful tears that glistened in Danielle's eyes.

"Thank you, Daddy," she whispered.

"My pleasure, Pumpkin."

"Well done, Peter," Dan Cohen exclaimed, clapping him on the shoulder.

"Thanks, Rabbi."

"Please, call me Dan."

"Sorry, that's right. Dan. Can I ask you a question – the word '*Hashem*' – is that another name for G-d?"

"It is the name, indeed. As a matter of fact, in Hebrew, it actually means 'the name.' We use that term because the real name is too holy to utter, so we refer to G-d by the name '*Hashem*.'"

"Oh. That's very interesting."

Dan Cohen then sang the ancient melody of *Shalom Aleichem*, and though Peter was unfamiliar with it, the song and all the rituals that preceded the meal fascinated him.

After the song was completed, the Rabbi sat down and signaled the others to be seated, as well.

After listening to several prayers in Hebrew, Peter, seated next to Danielle, waited expectantly wondering what would come next. It was intriguing to him how Dan Cohen, a young American, could be so well-versed and fluent in his knowledge of Hebrew and this different culture.

Or was it his own culture, of which he was patently unaware?

After several minutes had passed, the rabbi passed Peter a large card with Hebrew words and their English translation.

"Now I'll sing the song *Aishes Chayil*. As you'll see, it is an ode to the wife, the pillar of the family. You can follow the wording, if you'd like."

Peter followed the words in English as Dan Cohen sang the lovely tune in his deep, pleasant voice.

> *An accomplished woman, who can find?*
> *Far beyond pearls is her value.*
> *Her husband's heart relies on her*
>   *and he shall lack no fortune.*
> *She repays his good, but never his harm,*
>   *all the days of her life.*

The lyrics and the tune were so beautiful and moving that Peter felt his eyes welling up with tears.

Even if he knew the Hebrew words, to whom would he sing the song?

He'd had a wife whom he had loved and upon whom he'd once relied, but then she had passed away leaving an emptiness that had never been filled.

As if sensing her father's inner heartache, Danielle leaned over and whispered, "Daddy, this is the song that helped start my whole journey."

He looked at his precious daughter, a bit surprised.

He wanted to know more, but Rabbi Cohen had concluded the song and they all stood, about to begin yet another ritual.

The rabbi poured wine into a silver goblet and began the blessings of the *Kiddush*.

When he finished, he poured some of the wine into little silver cups and passed them around the table. Peter saw his daughter drink the wine offered and followed her example.

He tried hard not to choke on his mouthful, which was sickeningly sweet and syrupy, quite the worst wine that he'd ever tasted. Not that he was a true connoisseur, but still, he enjoyed a fine bottle of Pinot Noir on occasion.

This was unlike anything he'd ever tasted, and he hoped he wouldn't be obliged to drink any more. No one else seemed to mind, and he was relieved when Rabbi Cohen led them all away from the table, toward the kitchen.

"Now we'll wash our hands in the kitchen before the meal is served," he explained.

Peter thought it a bit peculiar for them to all line up in the tiny kitchen, but he didn't say so and instead chose his words diplomatically.

"Is this a custom in your family or do others do this, as well?" he asked Rabbi Cohen.

"Everyone does this. A special blessing is then said on the *challah*, which is the bread. It's symbolic of the double portion of the manna that was received before the *Shabbos*, when the Jews were wandering in the desert."

"Oh, I see." He vaguely recalled the story of the wandering Jews from his childhood, though he wasn't quite sure how he learned about it … perhaps it was later in his World Religions course in college.

Danielle washed her hands before her father, and he carefully observed her movements, noticing that this ritual was performed in a specific manner. When it was his turn, he took the silver washing cup and poured the water twice over his right hand, and then twice over his left.

"You're a fast learner," commented Dan Cohen.

Peter smiled.

"There's a blessing that we say when we wash our hands," continued the rabbi. "You can say it in English, if you'd like."

He handed him a laminated card and Peter said the blessing quietly.

Blessed are you, Hashem, our G-d, King of the Universe, who has sanctified us with His commandments, and commanded us regarding washing the hands.

Rebbitzen Cohen was bustling around the tiny kitchen, checking on food and taking containers out of the refrigerator. Peter was impressed that she managed to cook so expertly in a kitchen that was essentially no bigger than a closet.

Peter followed Danielle back to the table. She motioned to him, with her finger across her lips, signaling him not to talk. Like everything else, this was also odd but Peter assumed that the rabbi would explain this to him, as well.

Dan Cohen made the blessing over the two loaves of *challah* and then cut them into thick, even slices, which he quickly passed around the table. Everyone took a piece, and Peter bit into the warm, sweet, freshly baked bread, which was, by far, the most divine bread he'd ever tasted.

"My wife bakes the best *challah* in Bnei Brak," said Dan Cohen proudly. "Don't you agree?"

Peter asked, hesitatingly, "I'm sorry. Am I allowed to talk now?"

Dan Cohen laughed, as did his children. He turned to Danielle, whose shoulders were shaking with laughter. Also amused, Rebbitzen Cohen did not laugh, but smiled broadly.

Strangely enough, Peter no longer felt self-conscious, realizing they were all laughing good-naturedly.

"We don't speak until after we eat some *challah*," the rabbi explained patiently. "We try not to let any time lapse between the blessing over the hands, the blessing over the *challah* and the actual eating of the bread; that way, each act remains connected."

"I see." Peter didn't really understand, but the simple explanation seemed to make sense, and in any case, the *challah* was so delicious that he was happy to just enjoy eating the *challah* with the delectable hummus spread that was offered to him.

"Were you able to rest this afternoon?" asked Rebbitzen Cohen.

"Yes, thank you," he replied. "I actually took a long nap. The flight was exhausting."

"Of course it is," commented Dan. "We traveled to America last year for my wife's sister's wedding, and I thought the flight would never end."

"It was so much fun, Abba!" exclaimed his small daughter. "I remember the plane ride. Remember me and Shmuel were running down the aisles?"

Both parents groaned simultaneously.

Dan Cohen nodded his head, "How well we remember. Ten hours is a very long time for little ones to stay in their seats."

The Rebbitzen and Danielle got up from the table to serve the meal, as Dan casually asked, "So, is this your first time in Israel?"

"Yes, yes, as a matter of fact, it is."

And so began an easy conversation between the men. Peter's initial awkwardness was rapidly replaced by a comfortable rapport; it seemed as if there was no topic that Dan Cohen was unaware of. They discussed many different matters, including sites of archeological and cultural interest that Peter should be sure to visit on his ten-day trip, several stories from Dan's childhood and Peter's career as an attorney.

They even found that they had something in common; namely, a love of fishing.

Dan confided in Peter that he'd enjoyed fishing since he'd been a kid in Rochester, New York. Peter told him of growing up in the affluent neighborhood of Evanston, Illinois, spending lazy summer days fishing off a pier on the banks of Lake Michigan.

He hadn't had the time for it anymore. In fact, he hadn't gone fishing since Beth's passing.

"Have you ever gone fly fishing?" Peter inquired.

"No," admitted Dan. "I never have. I'd love to learn it one day, though. Fly fishing, if done properly, has almost achieved the status of an art form .... I have a cousin who's an expert fly fisherman. Twice a year he travels to the streams in Kelly Creek."

"Kelly Creek?" he responded. "Where is that?"

"Oh, it's just gorgeous," Dan Cohen replied enthusiastically. "It's a west slope catch-and-release stream in Idaho's Clearwater National Forest."

Peter was intrigued by Dan Cohen's many varied interests. The breadth and scope of his knowledge, coupled with his enthusiasm, convinced him that Dan Cohen was indeed a unique individual.

"There's excellent fishing on the Kineret, about a two-hour ride from here. And the water is just about the bluest I've ever seen ... maybe we could go one day."

"I'd like that," said Peter sincerely.

Throughout the exchange, Rebbitzen Cohen and his daughter had brought to the table what seemed like a never-ending supply of food, beginning with a variety of salads.

These were followed by hot chicken soup with dumplings for the first course, and after one spoonful, Peter could not remember when he had tasted anything so delicious.

"Is there some sort of secret spice you use, Rebbitzen?" he wanted to know. "This soup is simply unbelievable." She smiled broadly at the compliment. "No, there's no secret spice. I think *Shabbos* food always has a special flavor, am I right, Danielle?"

"It's absolutely true," agreed Danielle as she put a large bowl of salad in the middle of the table. "It's something I noticed right away, Dad. All the food in Israel tastes great, especially the fresh produce, but on *Shabbos* everything tastes better."

After he'd drained the soup down to the last spoonful, roast chicken followed, with steaming hot potato *kugel* that Danielle had raved about in her phone calls to him over the past several months.

"You've got to try the *kugel*, Dad," she said, as if on cue. "It's out of this world."

He was more than happy to comply, and he wasn't at all disappointed. The luscious, crispy crust was golden brown, and the smooth potato puree melted in his mouth.

The roasted chicken also had a marvelous flavor, as did the salads.

But it was the special feeling of warmth with which the dishes were presented that made the meal truly memorable.

"Here, please try this," offered the Rebbitzen as she passed him another savory dish.

"Would you like some more couscous?" asked Dan.

Peter ate until he was pleasantly satiated, but he also experienced a contentment that was not just from the food.

He was beginning to feel that he was also a member of

this warm family, realizing it had been so long, he'd almost forgotten what it was like to … belong. It hadn't always been this way. When Beth had been alive, they'd entertained friends and acquaintances on occasion, and though the food had been store-bought or catered, a feeling of camaraderie had prevailed around the dining table. When Danielle was young, she and her friends would run off to play while the adults conversed. Sometimes the dinner parties would last late into the evenings, and Danielle would fall asleep, curled up on the small floral chaise in her bedroom.

That had been a lovely time, but it was fleeting at best. It all came to an end when Beth became ill and then passed away. He had never again entertained in the house. Afterwards, Danielle had often opted to eat dinner at friends' homes, and he'd stay late at the office, working. Suddenly, his lack of any family life aroused a sense of longing that was never so acute until that very moment.

It was easy to understand how Danielle had grown so attached to this young, caring family. They obviously filled a void for his daughter, and Peter felt incredibly grateful to them.

Dan sang several songs, showing Peter the proper places to follow in the prayer book, which was referred to as a *siddur*. He found it confusing that there were so many words to remember, but it appeared as if Danielle knew them all.

He followed along, but although he found the texts interesting, he was far more fascinated by Dan Cohen, himself. Peter had many questions that he wanted to ask, but he hesitated, fearing that they might be too personal.

Finally, over dessert, he had his chance. The small children had sauntered sleepily off to bed, and it was just the four of them at the table. The candles had burned down, the melted wax dripping onto the silver tray beneath.

He was so drowsy and sated that he was loath to move from the table.

And, so, over tea with iced chocolate cake, he asked Dan Cohen the question that had been nagging him the entire evening.

"Can I ask you a question, Rabbi?"

"Only if you call me Dan," he answered good-naturedly.

"Of course, Dan," he hastily corrected himself. "I hope it's not too personal. "

"I doubt that. People ask me questions all the time," he responded. "What would you like to know?"

"Well, I …" began Peter, not knowing quite how to proceed. "You mentioned growing up in Rochester. I'd like to know, were you always observant? I mean, were your parents? I hope you don't mind my asking."

Dan laughed.

"Is that all? Believe me, I've heard the gamut. As a matter of fact, when I was a child, my family wasn't all that religious, but before my *bar mitzvah*, my parents sent me to a sleep-away camp in the Catskills. In retrospect, it was the greatest gift they could have ever given me. I became friends with Orthodox kids, and that was it. I went to a yeshiva to learn as a teenager, and I've been learning Torah ever since."

"Were they upset?"

"They were thrilled, actually. In time, they became observant, as well, making their kitchen strictly kosher and keeping *Shabbos*. Just that knowledge gives me a tremendous amount of comfort because they both passed away in the last ten years."

He then added, "My daughter Rena is named after my mother, Renee, and Shmuel is named after my father, Samuel."

"They're lovely children."

"Thank you." He paused and beamed at his wife.

"Fifteen years ago this very week, the end of February, I was fortunate enough to meet my wife, and shortly after the wedding, we decided to pack up and move to Israel. And we've been here ever since."

"Fifteen years?" Peter could hardly believe it. "You must've married young."

"We were certainly young," agreed his wife. "I think it's better that way. We decided to grow old together."

"We weren't blessed with children for nearly the first ten years of our marriage," he continued in a more somber tone. "Esther taught full-time at the girls' seminary in Jerusalem, and I taught part-time. Now, with the children, *baruch Hashem*, we've reversed our roles; I teach there every day, and Esther teaches there part-time."

"Is that how you met Danielle? From the school?" he asked.

After an awkward silence, Danielle said quietly, "Dad ... I'll fill you in on all of that later."

Now *that* had piqued his curiosity, but he decided to switch gears a bit. "So, how did you and your wife meet? If you don't mind my asking, that is."

"Not at all. It's one of my favorite stories, actually," the Rebbitzen answered. "I was nineteen years old, from Brooklyn, and my brother learned in the same yeshiva as Dan. It was time for me to start the dating process, because in my family's circles it's customary to marry young. My brother kept pestering me to agree to a date with Dan Cohen."

"You mean, a blind date?"

"Well, it's actually referred to as a *shidduch* date, but it's essentially the same idea. Someone usually suggests that both parties meet, thinking they would have much in common. In my case, however, I said no."

"Why?"

Danielle leaned forward, "I've never heard this."

"I never told you this?" she continued. "Well, I did say no, based upon the mistaken assumption that we had very little in common. Coming from a small town in Rochester, Dan had a different background, and here I was, a girl from Flatbush. I was young and naive, and I flat out refused, assuming we would have nothing in common."

"Weren't you insulted, Dan?" asked Peter jokingly.

"Oh, I didn't know anything about it, actually," he replied cheerfully. "Thankfully, her brother didn't clue me in on any of this until later."

"What was it that made you change your mind?" Danielle asked.

"Well, it was a flat tire, actually," giggled his wife. "Remember your old, broken down Chevy?"

Dan laughed nostalgically, nodding his head. "That junk heap used to break down every two blocks."

"Yes, and one night he was driving my brother home from the yeshiva and the car's tire blew out, probably from some broken glass by the alley. Anyway, he had to come in to use our phone to call the tow-truck …"

Peter and Danielle were silent, waiting for her to continue.

"… and I must say, I will never forget how perfectly calm Dan remained. I remember thinking how agitated someone else would be, having to be delayed, towed, not to mention the expense involved. It would be understandable to be aggravated under such circumstances, but he was laughing and talking to my parents, as if nothing happened. I was impressed. Of course, we didn't speak to each other at the time, but soon after, I informed my brother that I'd changed my mind. I started thinking that perhaps growing up in a small town has its advantages. People might not get so rattled over small things. And the rest, as they say, is history."

Peter and Danielle sat in rapt attention, charmed by the heartwarming story.

Too soon, the meal had come to an end, and Dan distributed the Grace After Meals booklets, which were referred to as *bentchers*.

How would he ever be able to remember everything?

Wait a minute ... he didn't have to remember anything. In nine more days, he'd be on a plane back to Chicago, back to the familiarity of his normal routine ...

After he'd finished following along, Peter stretched and rose from his chair. Glancing at his watch, he was shocked to discover that it was after midnight, Israel time.

It had been a very lengthy meal; it had been so pleasant, though, that the time had passed quickly.

"Can I help clear the table?" Peter offered.

"No, of course not. You're our special guest," Rebbitzen Cohen insisted.

"It's late," Dan remarked. "Maybe Danielle should take you next door and help you get settled for the night."

Peter thanked the Rebbitzen profusely for the wonderful meal, and after shaking hands with Dan Cohen, he followed Danielle out of the apartment.

They wordlessly made their way through the dark corridor, and Danielle fumbled with the key that opened the door to the neighbor's apartment.

"Pumpkin, it's pitch black," said Peter. "Is there a light switch in this hallway?"

He began to feel his way, but she stopped him.

"No, Dad," she said. "You can't do that on *Shabbos*, and besides, I just opened the door."

She led the way into the mostly dark apartment, whose only source of light came from the kitchen where a single fluorescent bulb had been left on under the cabinets.

"Are you serious?" he asked incredulously. "If I can't turn on the light, how will I see what I'm doing?"

She smiled. "You'll be fine, Daddy. You know, there's no work on *Shabbos* of any kind. We take a rest from our daily routine. Think of it as total relaxation, like a mini vacation every week."

"Turning on a light doesn't seem like a lot of work to me," he said doubtfully.

"Nowadays, that's true. But years ago, that wasn't the case. They had to make fire for light, right? Well, the modern-day equivalent of fire is electricity, and that's definitely not allowed on *Shabbos*.

As an attorney, he could have thought of innumerable arguments to contradict her if he hadn't been so tired.

And if he hadn't been so content to be there with her.

"All right. Whatever you say, Pumpkin."

There were two wooden chairs adjacent to the small table in the kitchen, and they sat down. Peter had thus far enjoyed himself more than he could have possibly imagined and was reluctant to let the evening end. Additionally, he had so many questions he wanted to ask his daughter, he hardly knew where to begin.

To his surprise, Danielle led the way.

"So, Daddy, you're probably wondering how I got interested in all of this. It probably seems weird to you, right?"

He contemplated his words carefully before answering.

"To be perfectly honest, it did at first." He paused and rubbed his hands together. "I'll admit I was pretty worried about Rabbi Cohen, in particular, what sort of person he was … but now that I've met him and his wife, well, let's just say, I think I'm beginning to understand."

Danielle literally let out a breath, not even aware that she'd been holding it.

"That's what I was hoping you'd say. They're such wonderful people, Daddy, and the lives they lead are so beautiful, I just couldn't help but be inspired."

Peter asked softly, "What about your friends?"

She looked puzzled. "Which ones?"

"Which ones?" Peter asked. "Hello? I'm talking about Kim and Rebecca. You came here with them around nine months ago, and you never left, remember?"

"Oh, of course," she replied, a bit flustered. "Kim and Rebecca. I guess I owe them a debt of gratitude, since they were sort of responsible for this whole journey of mine …."

"They were?" Peter asked, astounded. "How is that possible?"

"Indirectly, I guess," Danielle clarified. "Remember tonight? When you asked if I'd met the Cohens through the school? Well, it didn't happen that way."

Peter waited expectantly.

"It's a little embarrassing, to be honest, the way the whole thing came about," she admitted sheepishly, playing with her hair. "It was kind of … well, it was a dare. Kim and Rebecca and I actually started to part ways almost immediately after we got here."

"What happened? You were like sisters for as long as I can remember," Peter remarked.

"It's true, but this trip just accentuated our differences, I guess. I wanted to experience the country, go touring, learn more about our heritage and the like. Kim wanted to eat out at all the best restaurants, and Rebecca wanted to go to clubs. Then we wound up at the *Kosel*, the Western Wall, you know, for the first time. It really hit me, Dad. The way all the Jews *daven*, I mean pray ... it just blew me away."

He was amazed to see his cherished daughter struggling to compose herself.

First her voice broke and then the tears followed, welling up in her large brown eyes and then spilling over her cheeks, as if they had been repressed and were now finally released.

"I felt so close to Mom," she sobbed. "I felt like she was watching over me. I know it sounds silly. I felt she had something to do with why I felt so close to G-d, like He was watching over me, hearing my prayers."

Her father reached into his pocket for a tissue, which he offered her.

She continued, "Kim and Rebecca thought that I'd flipped." She blew her nose.

"What was the dare?" he wanted to know.

"You know how there are observant people who walk over to secular Jews at the Wall and invite them to their homes for *Shabbos*?"

He wasn't aware of this, but he let her continue.

"Kim and Rebecca dared me to accept the first person who asked me, figuring no one would ask and I wouldn't really go through with it. Well, someone did ask me ... that person was Rebbitzen Cohen, and I accepted her offer to stay for *Shabbos*, and like you said, I never left."

It was a sobering thought, indeed, how his daughter had

so radically changed because of an adolescent dare. He was grateful that it had been the Cohens who'd welcomed her into their lives. He shuddered to think of the scenario that could've been, with people less scrupulous.

"Whatever happened to Kim and Rebecca?"

"They went back to America after calling me all sorts of names. They think I was brainwashed."

Peter was still, keenly aware of the color in his face rising.

"You didn't think so, too, Dad ... did you?"

He chuckled, knowing he couldn't hide the truth from his daughter.

"Maybe a little." He looked at Danielle. "Maybe more than a little."

She grinned. "The first Friday night, when Rabbi Cohen sang *Aishes Chayil*, the song about the woman of the home ... Dad, you won't believe this, but it was like ... like Mom was at the table. I could feel it."

She paused, waiting for his response, her eyes still filled with tears.

He cleared his throat and took her hand in his.

"Pumpkin, I believe you," he said quietly. "When I took a nap this afternoon, Mom came to me in a dream ... it's hard to recall the dream exactly, but she was definitely in it."

"Are you sure?" she leaned forward eagerly.

"Positive."

They were both quiet, lost in their own thoughts. Danielle blew her nose once more, wiped her eyes and took a breath.

Peter was savoring the time spent with his precious daughter. She seemed so poised and mature, not to mention all of her newfound knowledge of Judaism ... he couldn't help but look at her with a sense of tremendous pride. He was already dreading the separation that would occur when he'd leave in little more than a week.

Danielle was experiencing profound relief at the course of events that had miraculously unfolded. She'd been apprehensive about her father's visit for nothing. While he hadn't exactly embraced her new way of life, he certainly hadn't rejected it.

It was a start, and she was grateful beyond measure.

"It's getting late," she said, rising from her chair. "I think I'll go next door. Do you have everything you need?"

"I think so, thanks," he said, reaching across the table to hug her.

He stood and stretched.

She walked slowly toward the door, calling over her shoulder, "Good night, Daddy. You won't forget and turn on the lights or anything, will you?"

He nodded. "Don't worry, I'll be good."

She smiled at that, still wiping her eyes.

They said good night, and he closed the door behind him.

He sighed wearily and massaged his temples. As he mechanically prepared for bed, he couldn't help but feel a sense of irony. He'd traveled to this remote corner of the world to talk sense into his daughter ... but in actuality, it had been Danielle who'd done most of the talking. And now, here he was, parading about in the dark because he had promised his daughter that he wouldn't turn on the light; it was a sort of role reversal, just another aspect in this totally unexpected turn of events.

He suddenly remembered a snippet of conversation from several days prior, when he'd gone out to dinner with the young attorney from California.

What had he said? "You know what they say, if you can't beat 'em, join 'em .... I might just find religion myself."

It had been said in jest, of course, and the lovely Ms. Morgan had smiled politely.

He was jolted out of his thoughts by the sudden ringing of a phone. It was his cell phone, on the table in the other room. He quickly sprinted for it, but then stood still.

It was surely Ray, with more questions to ask him. He probably didn't realize the time difference, and it most probably was important.

He gave Danielle his word that he wouldn't turn on a light, but surely this was different. Ray Adams just needed a moment of his time, he was certain.

It wouldn't count, would it?

It was just a phone call, after all … who would know?

He wrestled with himself for several seconds, alternating between feeling utterly ridiculous and experiencing surprising bouts of stubborn resolve … to take a rest from the world and give the world a rest.

He let it ring.

CHAPTER 8

Sarah awoke from a dreamless sleep and looked around the room, disoriented. It was only after several seconds that she recalled where she was, and the familiar feelings of hot dread and panic resurfaced once more. She struggled to resist the feeling of helplessness, determined not to wallow in her own despair.

She swung her legs over the edge of the bed and was pleased to discover that, for the first time, she could do so without experiencing a sense of vertigo. Her head was not throbbing, and for that she was grateful. She stood up and felt stronger than she had the day before.

Surely, this was a good sign. She could recall where she was and even why she was there, so she forced herself to cling to the hope that today would be the day that she would remember, at last.

How badly she wanted to remember who she was, where she lived.

She was ready to reclaim her life.

She wanted to go home.

Only she didn't know where that home was.

She walked over to the table in the corner, restless and

unable to keep still. It too was white, much like everything else in the cold, sterile room. Curious about a small drawer she spied under the laminate table top, she opened it.

There wasn't much in the drawer except for several sheets of paper, some cotton swabs and a miniature mirror.

She cautiously held the mirror up to her face, eager to gaze at her likeness, and yet apprehensive at the same time. She wondered if her own reflection would be enough to jog her memory.

She gasped when she caught her image in the small mirror.

It was like staring into the eyes of a stranger.

Who was she?

Her amber-colored hair was plastered beneath swaths of bandages, her left eye looked bruised and her face was covered with little cuts and contusions ….

Who was she?

Did anyone care?

She could feel the tears beginning, but this time she quite literally forced herself not to give in to them. Crying would get her nowhere. She was steadfast in her resolve not to let another day go by mired in self-pity … there must be something she could do to hasten her recovery ….

But what?

She put the mirror, face side down, back in the drawer with a bang. And as she did so, something odd caught her eye.

To her astonishment, there appeared to be writing of some sort on her left hand.

Bringing her hand up to eye level, she was amazed to discover what must've been her own writing scrawled on the inside of her left wrist, written in ballpoint pen.

Go to police station across the street. File a missing person's report.

She smiled, buoyed by her own ingenuity. Although she couldn't recall writing herself the message, her spirits lifted. She walked to the window and gazed out into the street below.

It took her a short time to locate the building, but sure enough, she noticed the glass and brick edifice diagonally across the bustling intersection.

Hopefully, there'd be someone there who would help her.

Her plans were interrupted when a middle-aged, redheaded nurse bustled in with a tray.

Sarah discreetly placed her left arm behind her, not wanting to draw attention to the writing on it.

"Good morning, dear," she said cheerfully, with a patronizing manner that made Sarah wince. "Good to see you up and about! You look loads better, simply loads ... you probably don't remember me, but I was actually here when you were brought in."

That aroused Sarah's curiosity. "No," she replied. "I don't remember much of anything ... tell me, who brought me here? How did I get here?"

"To be perfectly honest, I'm not really sure," the nurse responded, speaking slowly and carefully as if she were speaking to a child. "The paramedics, I assume. You were in pretty bad shape, though, and I remember thinking what a shame it was, with you all gussied up in your designer clothes ... you looked so fancy ...."

Finally, that was a clue.

The nurse continued, "I'm so glad we're feeling better today, aren't we?"

We? Sarah thought. *Ugh. If she'd be any sweeter, I'd get a cavity.*

Amused by the thought, Sarah's lips turned up at the corners. It felt so good to smile again.

The nurse didn't seem to notice as she took her blood pressure, popped a thermometer in Sarah's mouth and set the tray down on the bedside table.

"It's a lovely day outside," she continued, in the same condescending manner. "Finally, a mild day for mid-February. I can't stand the bitter cold, and I just won't drive in the sleet and ice … you know, I'll bet that had a lot to do with your accident. When you were brought in, the weather was simply treacherous …."

A thought occurred to Sarah.

"Uh, where are my clothes?"

The nurse blinked. "Excuse me?"

"The clothes I arrived in, where would they be?" Sarah asked, looking down at her drab hospital gown.

"Oh, my goodness, that's a good question," the nurse said vaguely. "They have to be around here somewhere … they're usually put into a locker or closet."

She walked to the corner of the room and opened the door to a small cabinet.

"Ah, here we go," she sang out. "They're right here in this bag, safe and sound."

"Thank you," Sarah murmured, trying to downplay her piqued interest.

It was a relief when the nurse left the room, calling over her shoulder, "Rest up, dear. I'll check in on you later."

Sarah immediately went to the cabinet and held the bag of clothing with shaking fingers.

Would the clothing be the trigger that would help her to remember?

Opening the bag, she slowly took out her tattered, rumpled clothing, which were still damp and cold and smelled of snow.

She lifted a velvety cashmere scarf, smart jacket and long

woolen skirt from the bag. The nurse had been correct; from the texture of the fabric and the smart tailoring, the clothing appeared to be incredibly expensive. The buttery high-heeled boots were nestled on the bottom of the bag, and as she drew them out, she noticed that the heel on the right boot was dangling, literally hanging by a thread.

If her heel had come loose, that would easily explain how she'd have taken a nasty spill on the icy pavement.

The more she thought about it, the more certain she became ... how utterly preposterous it seemed to her now, to have lost her memory and be hospitalized over a silly boot.

Could that have been all it was? Or was there something else that had been the catalyst? Would she ever know?

She started to shove the boots back into the bag when she realized that if she was to take any sort of action, she'd be in need of them. Her mind racing, she figured that since the nurse had just been in, she must've been making her morning rounds at that very moment ... which left her with a narrow window of opportunity, at best.

She decided to seize the moment without considering the consequences. She was determined to act now, with alacrity, as her heart started beating furiously from the adrenaline coursing through her veins.

She hastily got dressed, as quietly as she could. She began to pry the other heel, which was also somewhat loose, from her boot, manipulating it back and forth till she was able to yank it off. Now she had two matching boots, which would make her far less noticeable than if she were limping on one heel. She retrieved the small handheld mirror from the drawer. Holding it up to her face, she couldn't help but wail softly when she saw her disheveled appearance.

The bandages ... she had forgotten about them. What was she to do?

She peered into the remainder of the bag, hoping to find something, anything that she could use to get rid of the gauze, but there was nothing.

She came to a swift decision. Holding the mirror with one hand, she gently peeled the bandages away from her head. It was not an easy task, as the bandage was long, but she unwound it quickly until it was completely removed. There was another, smaller bandage stuck to her head that she left in place. She then took the cashmere scarf and draped it over her head and around her shoulders. Holding up the mirror once more, she nodded at her reflection.

It was definitely more acceptable. Hopefully, no one would notice the bruises around her left eye.

Before she lost her resolve, she opened her door, furtively glancing in both directions of the white, tiled corridor. To her profound relief, it appeared deserted.

Taking a deep breath, she rapidly made her way down the stretch of corridor, having no idea where she was headed, glancing wildly about for an elevator.

She finally spied the elevators up ahead ... she was almost within reach, when she heard voices behind her. She immediately walked to her right, through a door that had been left ajar, until the people had passed.

Holding her ear to the door, she could hear their voices; they were doctors, discussing patients' therapies, medications and various procedures, while standing at the elevators for what seemed like an eternity.

Sarah, swathed in her cashmere shawl, began to perspire. Sweat beaded on her brow and began to trickle down the side of her head. Feeling flushed and a bit faint, she forced herself to breathe. She remembered the words from her chart ... fluids and rest ... but she was in no position for either ....

Just move, move ... please move ... she thought.

At that very moment, when she thought she couldn't hold out any longer, the elevator doors opened and the doctors vanished from sight.

Opening the door slightly, Sarah peered cautiously out, and finding the coast clear she took her chance. She made her way to the elevators and pressed the button, fearful all the while that someone would see her. Then she realized that her room was located in an ideal location, right near the elevators and away from the nurses' station. Had it been located differently, she doubted that her escape would have been that easy.

Essentially, that's what it was for her ... an escape. She felt like a prisoner within these walls, and she needed to get out. Most importantly, the key to her identity lay outside of these walls, of that she was sure, and she was determined to unlock the mystery of her life.

Mercifully, the doors opened, and she entered the elevator. *So far, so good*, she thought, breathing a sigh of relief.

What would happen if the nurse found her room empty?

Sarah quickly dismissed such a negative scenario.

"Just think positive thoughts," she said softly to herself, desperately trying to ignore the weakness in her knees.

She knew she had to get past the main desk, and her knees were literally knocking together from nerves.

The floors were descending down ... apparently, she had been on the sixth floor. Five ... four ... three ...

In a sudden panic, she glanced down at her wrist.

Her hospital identification bracelet ... she had forgotten to remove it.

She pulled with every ounce of her strength, and she felt it pop off her wrist just as the doors opened onto the main lobby. Squeezing it in the palm of her hand, she walked into the main lobby and proceeded toward the double doors.

"Miss? Excuse me?" Someone was calling after her.

Just be calm, she thought. She turned around.

The man at the admittance desk, dressed in a security guard uniform, was motioning her to come back.

Sarah took a deep breath and walked toward the desk.

"I think I'm lost," she said apologetically. "My friend had a baby early this morning and I'm here to visit her."

The elderly gentleman nodded. "You're lost, all right. Maternity is the next building over. You need to go outside and make a left. They're building an indoor walkway but it won't be finished for a while. Sorry for the inconvenience, Ma'am."

"That's okay," she replied. "Thank you."

As she walked toward the exit, her heart began to resume its normal staccato, but her insides were still knotted in fear.

Where had that come from?

She hadn't an inkling as to how that ingenious excuse had popped into her head, but she was incredibly grateful that she had been able to pull it off.

As she walked through the glass doors, a cold wind greeted her. It was downright frigid outside. Hadn't the nurse said something about the weather being mild?

If she'd lied about that, how could she be sure that she hadn't lied about other things, such as her very reason for being in that frightening place?

Sarah blinked in the sunlight, marveling that on such a cold day, the sun could shine so brightly. She walked to the corner crosswalk crowded with people, rehearsing the reason for her escape … *Chicago Police Department … file a missing person's report ….*

At last, the light turned green, and she crossed the busy intersection with the crowd. There was something awfully familiar about that … she had the strangest feeling that she'd done this before, and quite recently ….

Up ahead she saw the building she had spotted from her room. She felt inordinately pleased, triumphant even, with what she'd achieved.

She'd set out to accomplish a goal, and she had done just that.

Well, not exactly. Just how she'd broach the subject to the police was another matter, one that she hadn't thought through. Still, she was pleased with all she'd accomplished thus far.

She followed several people through the massive glass entry doors.

She stood for several moments in the lobby, unsure of her next plan of action.

"Can I help you?"

She turned to face a kindly-looking young officer who couldn't have been more than twenty-two years of age, with flaming red hair and masses of freckles.

She breathed a sigh of relief that he was so young and probably inexperienced; hopefully, he would fulfill her request without asking too many questions.

"Yes, thank you, Officer … ?"

"Smythe, Ma'am. Officer Smythe."

"Yes, Officer Smythe, I'd like to file a missing person's report."

At that, he straightened his shoulders and assumed an air of responsibility.

"Yes, Ma'am," he cleared his throat. "Will you come with me, please? I can help you with that."

He led her to a small, crowded cubicle and proceeded to offer her a chair. He then walked behind his chair and took a form from a desk drawer, looking eager.

"How long have you been on the police force?" she asked, in what she hoped was a pleasant tone of voice.

"Four months, tomorrow," he answered cheerfully. "All right, what is the name of the missing person?"

She swallowed. "I'm … not sure."

He raised his eyebrows a fraction of an inch.

She continued, "I don't think you understand … it's me. I'm the one that's missing. I've been in an accident, and I can't remember my name, or where I live. That's why I'm here …. I'd like to know if there's been anyone asking for me."

He looked at her, wide-eyed. Fidgeting in his chair, he cleared his throat several times, seemingly at a loss as to how to proceed.

"Well, Ma'am, I'm not sure …"

"Please help me," she implored. "I was in an accident, I tell you. A terrible accident."

She was clearly on the verge of tears. The young officer asked her, "What sort of accident was it?"

"I – I fell. My high-heeled boot skidded on the ice, I believe."

He stared at her stupidly, his mouth agape.

In a rush she continued, desperately, "Isn't there some sort of database you could check? Someone of my description who's been missing for a few days? I must have relatives who are worried about me …. I have to find out who I am."

Her voice was rising shrilly, and the young officer looked at her with pity. From his expression, it was evident that he thought she was mentally unstable, and he was unsure what to do in the bizarre predicament in which he found himself.

"I suppose I can ask my supervisor," he said slowly, scratching his head.

"Thank you," she responded shakily.

He got up from his desk slowly, looking behind him as he walked toward the office of his supervisor.

Sarah fought feelings of panic.

What if they all thought she was crazy? Would they send her back to the hospital? Maybe the supervisor would understand ... surely, he's had more experience ... he must've seen cases like this before.

She saw him speaking at the doorway with another police officer, and together they kept glancing in her direction as she squirmed uncomfortably in her chair.

Officer Smythe walked toward her with his supervisor, who was tall with a dirty blonde crew cut and steely gray eyes. She estimated him to be in his early forties.

Sarah disliked him instantly.

"This is Detective Robert Miller, Ma'am," the younger officer explained in his infuriatingly slow manner. "Why don't you follow him to his office down the hall, and you can discuss this further."

She was determined to explain her situation without losing her cool; it was the only way that she could expect some help. She absolutely had to appear like a reasonable person.

Getting up from her chair with all the dignity she could muster, she nodded to the redheaded officer and followed the other detective to his office.

He gestured to a chair and then seated himself behind his desk, an air of superiority and an odd, lopsided smirk on his face. For a split second, Sarah had the strangest sensation of having met him before ... his deep-set eyes, the jutting jaw ... were definitely familiar.

"Have we met?" she asked.

"Excuse me?" he asked her coldly.

"Nothing, it's just that … you looked a bit familiar. Never mind."

He leaned back, his broad frame encompassing much of the chair. She saw his name tag clearly above his shiny badge.

Detective Robert S. Miller.

"So what's all this nonsense about?" he began.

"There is no nonsense," she replied. "I was speaking with …"

"Yeah, I know … you said you're here to file a missing person's report, but then you indicated that you're the missing person. Lady, I gotta tell you, that's a first." He leaned back in his chair, chuckling, although he didn't appear amused.

"Well," she began defensively, swallowing several times.

He continued, "And I don't particularly have patience with folks who have some hidden agenda … it usually means someone's lying. So why don't you tell me the real reason you're here?"

She wasn't emotionally prepared for such a cynical assessment of her situation, and she stammered, "But it's true. I was in an accident."

"Sure, sure, you were," he said nastily. "You claim that your high heel got caught on a grate …. I heard all about it. Look, if you don't know where you live, where are you staying now?"

Her face flushed. She couldn't quite bring herself to inform him of the fact that her current residence was the psychiatric ward of the hospital across the street.

"That's what I thought," he said brusquely, shuffling papers on his desk. "I'm tired of people like you wasting our time. What's the matter, your husband's not giving you enough attention?"

Tears welled up in her eyes. "I told you, I don't know …"

"Well, then, let me make myself clear," he barked. "Show up here again, and I'll arrest you, okay? How's that?"

Frustration quickly turned to anger.

"Arrest me?" she fumed. "On what grounds?"

"On what grounds?" he laughed. "Listen to you … you sound like you know your way around, don't you? You probably have a rap sheet a mile long …. I know your type. Beat it, lady, I'm serious. We've got work to do."

"You haven't answered my question."

"Oh, yeah," he snarled. "I can arrest you on the grounds of harassing a police officer."

"You can't do that."

"Try me." His voice was suddenly so challenging, his sneer so ugly, that she became frightened.

He was vicious enough to do just that.

And whom would the judge believe?

She wouldn't stand a chance.

She got up from her chair and left his office without a backward glance, hoping her outer, confident veneer belied her quaking insides. She kept walking until she was safely out of the building.

The cold outside air felt welcoming, for she suddenly felt terribly weak. The physical and emotional exertion was too much, and leaning against the outer brick wall for support, she felt her legs sagging beneath her.

She chided herself for being so foolishly impulsive. Her teeth were chattering, as she was still in a weakened state. What had she been thinking? Her daring, little excursion had not only been fruitless, it had very nearly gotten her into trouble with the law, making her situation infinitely worse.

What was she to do now? Where could she go?

She spied a bench at the corner and made her way to it on rubbery legs. She reached the bench and sat down, taking shallow breaths.

That detective had some nerve speaking to her like that ... wasn't it his job to help people? He didn't believe a word that she'd said, not that he'd let her get so much as a word in edgewise. He'd mocked her accident, as if he hadn't believed that she'd actually slipped on the ice ....

Suddenly, Sarah felt her blood grow cold.

She tried to remember what his exact words had been.

She'd never said that she'd caught her heel on a grate.

Had the detective known more about her accident than he'd let on?

Fear became a taste in her mouth. She felt alone in a sea of strangers, unable to trust anyone. She felt unsafe where she sat, thinking anyone could harm her ... she looked wildly about, in a frenzy of alarming paranoia.

The old woman crossing the street ... did she gaze at Sarah in peculiar fashion, or had she only imagined it? The two men in business suits and tweed overcoats, did they glance at her, and then nod to each other, knowingly?

All at once, the sheer fright and uncertainty became too much for her to bear, and she knew she had to take flight, yet again. Miserably, she realized that her only recourse would be to return to the same hospital from where she'd escaped.

She had no choice; there was nowhere else to go.

She lifted herself from the bench, and when the traffic light turned green, she crossed the intersection with countless other pedestrians, her heart beating wildly in her throat, suspicious of everyone and feeling very vulnerable.

Once she reached the other side, farther away from the police station, she felt a bit safer.

Now that she was standing outside the hospital, she focused on her next plan of action; namely, reaching the safety of her sterile, white room, undetected. She felt overwhelmed by the task ahead of her, since she couldn't recall where that room was located, and someone was sure to see her.

She'd had much luck when she'd left, but she didn't expect it would go as smoothly upon her return.

To her right, she soon glimpsed a large family, two parents and several adolescent children, who were entering the glass doors of the hospital, and she impulsively decided to follow them as closely as possible. One of the members carried a plant, another a sign that read *Get Well Soon, Grandma*.

The children were speaking with each other so animatedly, they didn't observe Sarah crouching behind them.

The children followed their parents to the front desk.

"Beatrice McArthur's room, please," said the father.

"Make a left, take the elevators up to the fourth floor," the guard replied.

The family continued on, and Sarah did the same, staying in close proximity behind them until they'd reached the elevators. Undoubtedly, the person at the front desk had assumed she was with them, although nothing could have been further from the truth.

They were a family, and they all had each other.

She, on the other hand, had no one.

The intimacy they shared reinforced her feelings of being utterly, completely alone.

The elevator doors opened and she followed them in.

"Which floor?" the mother asked her.

For a second, she couldn't recall, but then she remembered. "Six, I think," she replied. "Thank you."

The family exited on the fourth floor, more people entered and the elevator continued its upward climb.

Five … six …

The doors opened and she walked out, fearful of any repercussions ahead of her. Hospital patients were not allowed to just don street clothing and go gallivanting around whenever they felt like it, of that she was certain.

She quickly made her way down the corridor, pleased that things looked a bit familiar, at the very least.

She couldn't remember her room number … did it even have a number?

She opened a door on her left, saw a woman asleep in her bed and closed the door quietly behind her. Further down, she opened another door … they all seemed alike. This time, there was a man sitting in a chair. He didn't seem to see her.

Fighting a rising feeling of panic, she walked a bit more. She'd have to find her room soon, for someone was sure to come this way. How would she explain herself?

She opened the next door, her pulse beating so furiously she thought she would faint.

Any moment now, a nurse was sure to come along and demand to know what she was doing … but at that very moment she realized that she was finally at the door of her room.

The bed was unmade, and the windows were as she'd remembered them.

Closing the door behind her, she walked to the small corner cabinet. She saw the discarded bag that had contained her clothing, and the rumpled hospital gown on the chair.

Everything appeared to be as she'd left it.

Incredulous that she'd had such good fortune, she quickly changed back into her drab gown, stuffing her clothing into the bag once more. She unwrapped the shawl from her head and added it to the bag.

She was just climbing back into her bed, when the door burst open.

It was the nurse, who looked wild-eyed with fright and anger.

"Just where have you been?" she demanded.

"Um, I just –" She swallowed. "I was just …"

"You can't just roam around … I was scared half to death when I came to check on you a few minutes ago and you weren't in your room. I even searched the ladies' room next door. I was just about to call security!"

No doubt, the nurse would've found herself in tremendous trouble had the hospital's security determined that her patient had truly gone missing, and Sarah astutely ascertained that that was the only reason she hadn't already made the call.

"I'm sorry … I just, I don't know. I guess I got confused," she finished, lamely.

"Confused?" the nurse looked at her suspiciously. "You can't meander around here, it's against hospital rules. You've had a head injury, and we wouldn't want you to harm yourself …."

"I'm feeling much better," she quickly replied. "I'll be fine."

"I'm glad to hear it," the nurse responded doubtfully. She took a quick look around the room, nodded to herself that all appeared to be in order, and went to the door.

To Sarah's utter horror, she heard the key being turned in the lock.

She was being locked in her room, and she was helpless to do anything about it.

It was just too much. Sarah's eyes filled with hot tears that rapidly spilled down her cheeks, but she felt too drained to wipe them away. It was so unfair, being locked in her room like a common criminal.

What had she done to deserve such unjust treatment?

Sarah's mind wandered.

Didn't she have any sort of patient rights? Was it illegal for her to be locked in her room? Could she sue the hospital for this harsh treatment, or were they within their legal rights?

Just as soon as the thoughts entered her mind, something else occurred to her.

I must know a lawyer, she thought. *Maybe I'm even married to one ... why else would I be thinking along those lines?*

She reached over the foot of the bed, retrieved the clipboard with its attached pen, and wrote on the inside of her wrist once more:

You know something about law. Try and find out more.

Meanwhile, in the police station, Detective Robert S. Miller left his desk. He went into the courtyard behind the offices, ostensibly for a smoking break.

No one needed to know that he'd quit smoking six months earlier.

He flipped open his private cell phone and made the call.

The call was brief, for he didn't speak much.

He listened mostly, nodded, and after several seconds, he tucked the cell phone into his pocket and made his way back to his desk.

CHAPTER 9

Sunlight streamed in the small, boxlike room, and Sarah blinked her eyes, willing them to open. Sleep had eluded her for much of the night, and she'd only finally drifted off toward daybreak. Nighttime was the worst. During the day, it took all of her energy to keep her feelings of hopelessness at bay; in the middle of the night, it was nearly impossible to keep the terror from overwhelming her.

She was so very much alone.

From the time that she'd been locked in her room, her whole existence had seemed unreal, the stuff of which nightmares are made. The dreadful nurse had checked on her sporadically throughout the day through the small window on her door, a distrustful look upon her face … when her shift had ended, she'd informed the evening nurse to keep her room continually locked.

The loneliness and fear, coupled with intense boredom, had almost driven Sarah to the breaking point. The only thing that helped calm her nerves were the colorful, albeit juvenile, cards that Anne Lewis had given her. All night long, she sat on her bed looking at them, memorizing every detail.

They were solid, living proof that Anne Lewis existed.

She would return in the morning. She would.

She instinctively knew that Anne could be trusted … and in a world that made no sense, having someone to trust meant everything to Sarah. She could not help but review in her mind the peculiar meeting that had taken place in the police station. It was obvious that the police officers had not believed her. She had been naïve and foolish to place her trust in utter strangers. When Sarah tried to determine what to do next, to chart her course of action, it became apparent that she had only one recourse.

Anne Lewis was her only hope. She got out of her bed and paced the room.

How she hated that room … but what she despised the most was the sheer, humiliating impotence she felt. At that very moment, a family member could be trying to determine her whereabouts, and she was powerless to aid in her own discovery.

The frustration of it all was beginning to gnaw at her.

It was just so totally, unequivocally unfair.

Ironically, the very same feelings of frustration indicated that she was healing, for in the beginning of her hospital stay, she was totally consumed with her physical ailments and pain.

The only pain she felt now was from deep within her, an emotional, searing ache that gnawed away at her. *She had to remember … who and where was her family … were they looking for her? At this very moment were they agonizing over her disappearance?*

There was no respite from her thoughts, and she paced the room continually in a circular motion, pausing to rest on the chair for several moments, only to resume her pacing once more.

Slowly, slowly, mercifully … the darkness outside her window began to wane, replaced by streaks of light in the sunrise.

Sarah watched it all from her window, and as the last remnants of darkness began to recede, she felt a bit stronger and more confident. Surely, with the new day and all its infinite possibilities, things wouldn't seem so bleak. And there was something comforting about watching the dawn break over the Chicago skyline, almost as if she'd done the same thing before, and not that long ago ….

She began to alternate between feelings of hope and despair, and when she thought she could no longer bear her own thoughts, she heard a key in the door and Dr. Anne Lewis entered.

Sarah exhaled, letting out breath that she didn't even know she'd been holding.

"Dr. Lewis!" she exclaimed, rushing toward her.

Anne Lewis smiled warmly.

"Wow, that's got to be the nicest reception I've had in a long time," she remarked brightly.

"I'm so happy to see you," began Sarah, suddenly on the verge of tears.

"I'm equally as happy," Anne replied with a puzzled look on her face. "You look so much better, it's remarkable … there's something you want to tell me, isn't there?"

Sarah nodded.

"What is it, dear?"

Sarah paused, looking at the doctor for what seemed like the very first time. She took in her brown hair, which she now realized was a wig, her large gray eyes, her kindly smile … surely, she was a woman who could be trusted.

She knew it with an intuition that couldn't quite be explained.

Sarah sat down on the bed, and Anne pulled over a chair.

She took a deep breath and began.

It all came out as a jumbled monologue, though she'd

rehearsed it half the night, but she spared no detail. At times speaking quickly, at times her voice muffled with sobs, she managed to relate her daring, undetected escape from her room to the police station, including the officer's cynical threats, and her hasty retreat ….

She ended with the most devastating and cruelest detail of all, that she found herself locked in her room like a criminal who could harm herself and others.

With the last detail, she could no longer restrain her tears. They flowed freely, not only from fear but also from unadulterated indignation.

"… and I fully intend to sue when I leave this place! What the nurse did was unconscionable, a basic violation of my civil rights!"

Anne Lewis sat mesmerized throughout Sarah's soliloquy, her mouth agape. It was only when Sarah had finished that she thought to ask the question.

"How did you know the police station was across the street?"

"You'd mentioned it to me, and I was afraid that I'd forget, so I wrote a note to myself on my wrist."

She held up her wrist, which was now scribbled with different words. Anne held up Sarah's slender wrist to better read it.

"Why do you believe you know about the legal field?" asked Anne.

"I guess because I fully intend to take legal action against that nurse. I mean, the situation hardly warrants locking me up, am I right? It's not like I'm a danger to myself or to others … I think it's a blatant violation of my rights as a human being, and as an American citizen!"

Her voice became so sure, so impassioned, that Anne Lewis burst out laughing.

"You know, dear, I think if you aren't already a lawyer, you should be!"

That brought a half-hearted smile to Sarah's lips, and she wiped the tears away with the back of her hand.

They were both silent for several moments. Anne spoke first.

"You know, you did leave the hospital, which is clearly against the rules. You could have suffered some sort of setback ... I'm sure the nurse was only thinking about your well-being, don't you?"

"She had no way of knowing that!" Sarah retorted.

"That's true," murmured Anne. "Still ..."

"Please," Sarah pleaded. "You're my only hope, Dr. Lewis. Anne. Please, please, discharge me from this place .... I hate it here. It's driving me crazy. I don't belong here, really, I don't."

Anne Lewis just looked at her for a long moment.

"You don't belong here," repeated Anne very slowly, her facial expression confirming Sarah's impassioned plea.

"What?"

"What you just said. You don't belong here ... you know, you just might be on to something."

"What do you mean?"

The kindly doctor got up from her chair, went to the corner table and lifted up the small, handheld mirror.

"What do you see?" she asked, holding up the mirror for Sarah to see.

She gingerly held up the mirror to her face. In truth, she'd been avoiding gazing at her reflection, for it was disconcerting, staring into the eyes of a stranger.

She saw her varied cuts and contusions, the bruises that were turning every color of the rainbow, her disheveled hair, the bandage ... *her tanned face, seemingly incongruous with Chicago's winter weather.*

"Do you see what I see?" persisted Anne. "Your coloring doesn't suggest that you're from around here, and being born and raised in Chicago, I can immediately detect a Midwestern accent."

"You can?"

"Yes, and sweetie, you don't have one. My guess is that what you said is correct. Perhaps the reason why things seem so unfamiliar is because you aren't from around here."

Sarah was quiet, slowly absorbing these words that made so much sense. "That could explain why my relatives haven't been asking for me around here, right?"

"That's possible, I suppose," agreed Anne. "Though with databases nationwide, it only takes a click of a button to find out what's going on, but you could be onto something ...."

"If I'm not from here, how did I get here?"

"Vacation, perhaps?" she offered. "Or maybe you've just relocated. Or maybe you have returned to the Chicagoland area after an extended period of time elsewhere ... the possibilities are endless."

Circles, circles ... it was a totally confusing maze that Sarah could not navigate, returning to the exact place from where she began. It was all so impossibly frustrating.

"Please, Anne, please," begged Sarah. "I'm so much better, really. Please discharge me. I can't bear to stay here another night; I mean it, I'll go crazy!"

Anne looked at her with compassion. From the time she noticed the Jewish star that Sarah's grandmother had given her, Anne Lewis had taken more than her usual interest in this young woman whose tragic circumstances touched her very deeply.

"Look, you're obviously feeling much better, and I don't blame you for wanting to leave. But, realistically speaking, where would you go?"

Curiously enough, she hadn't thought of that. A white hot feeling of dread crept up her throat as she realized that the doctor was indeed correct.

She had nowhere to go.

"Unless, of course ..." Anne Lewis began.

"Unless what?"

"Unless, well, I suppose you could stay at my house for a few days ...." Her voice trailed off. It was against her professional judgment, but still she felt compelled to make the offer.

The doctor then nodded, as if coming to a decision.

"You know, that might just be an idea," she continued. "Studies show that anxiety or stress of any kind can definitely impede the healing process ... perhaps being in a calm, stress-free environment will aid you in your recovery, will help you to remember."

Sarah looked at her gratefully, humbled by the woman's empathy and generosity. She could scarcely believe that she was offering to take her, a virtual stranger, into her home!

"Would you really do that for me?" she asked incredulously. "Would the hospital allow it?"

"True, there are ethical problems to consider. As your doctor, there is no way I'd be able to house you."

Sarah was quiet, her heart sinking.

"On the other hand, I can easily recommend a different psychologist, preferably someone who's more knowledgeable in the field of amnesia. If you weren't under my care, I see no reason why you can't stay at my place for a few days, do you?"

It sounded so perfectly logical, so reasonable, that for the first time in days, Sarah allowed herself the luxury of feeling hopeful.

Indeed, things were starting to look up.

Anne then looked at Sarah quite seriously.

"I want you to know that I wouldn't do this unless I thought you were much better. Physically, no doubt you're on the mend ... psychologically, however, it's a different story. The trauma you've experienced would be extremely stressful under any circumstances, but I do believe that your anxiety is compounded by just being in this hospital ... am I right?"

"Yes, that's true," answered Sarah, anxious to agree and thus confirm Anne's decision.

"All right, well, if your memory is to return, you need to feel safe. Calm. Away from here. Do you understand what I'm saying?"

Sarah nodded, so happy that their conclusions were perfectly in sync. Dr. Lewis had the capacity to understand that Sarah felt trapped and that these feelings were only exacerbating her anxiety ... every second that ticked by within these walls was almost too much for her to bear.

If a golden halo had floated down from the heavens at that very moment and hovered above Anne Lewis, she could have not appeared more angelic to Sarah. This angel, this absolute saint of a woman, understood her, and was helping her to escape.

It seemed almost too good to be true.

"Thank you," she whispered, suddenly at a loss for words.

"Don't thank me yet," cautioned Anne. "There's some red-tape that I need to take care of first, some channels I'll need to go through. Remember, I wouldn't be able to treat you, as that would raise a lot of ethical and moral issues and violate professional boundaries. However, if I am no longer your doctor, I am just opening my home to you as a friend, all right?"

"I understand."

She continued, "I'll speak with Dr. Cooper about getting you discharged. We're perpetually short of beds around here, so I don't think it'll be much of a problem. And I'll refer you to Dr. Karen Hayes, to help you through this. Don't worry, she's top-notch. Fair enough?"

"Yes. Thank you," she repeated.

Anne smiled. "I should warn you, my youngest son is getting married in a month, and if I said the house is in complete disarray, it would be the understatement of the century."

"I don't mind."

And she didn't. She did not know where Anne Lewis lived, nor did she care.

Anywhere was better than where she was.

Anne laughed as she added, "How are you at addressing wedding invitations?"

Sarah smiled, happy to know that there might be some way she could thank Anne for this incredible gesture of hospitality.

Anne smiled, squeezed her shoulder, promised she'd be back as soon as she could, and left the room.

Now there was nothing left to do but wait.

In retrospect, it wasn't all that long, but to Sarah it had seemed like an eternity. Much later that same day, a new nurse had come into the room to take her vital signs. As the nurse prepared the thermometer she commented, "So, I hear you'll be out of here soon." She then popped the thermometer into Sarah's mouth with a brisk, efficient air.

"Really? Whe–"

"Hold still."

After a minute, she withdrew the thermometer, saying,

"Yes, you're scheduled to be discharged tomorrow morning, I understand. How does that sound?"

It sounded wonderful. She felt humbled, grateful ... but also fearful.

Who knew what the future held in store?

Even after the nurse had left, Sarah had tossed and turned late into the night, unable to sleep. And when sleep finally came, her dreams were disturbing and very troubling ...

She was walking down a long corridor that seemed somehow familiar. Had she been there before? Was it the hospital in which she found herself? No, it didn't seem to be ... though it seemed like a hospital of some kind ... rooms with narrow doors flanked the hallway on both sides. Where was she?

She did not know, but she continued walking forward, propelled by some inexplicable, inner force.

She had to persist, she had to walk to the end of the hallway, and open the last door on the right side.

A little farther, a little farther ...

The doorway was almost within reach, and she was keenly aware that someone just beyond that door was waiting for her. It was a heady feeling, but she was nervous and at a loss for words.

She came to the door, which was slightly ajar.

She pushed it open and walked into the sparsely furnished room.

Unaware that she was standing there, a woman was sitting in a large wing chair facing the windows beyond with her back to Sarah.

She had to make her presence known, she had to make the person turn to face her ...

She opened her mouth to speak, but no sound came out.

She wanted to scream, "Turn around! Turn around! Here I am!"

But the figure in the chair continued to face the window, oblivious to her presence in the room.

And no matter how hard she repeatedly tried to catch the shadowy figure's attention, she could only manage a silent scream with no sound at all coming from her throat.

Sarah woke up, sweating, her heart pounding …

What did it mean?

She wanted to stay in the dream before it receded into nothingness and lucid thoughts crowded her consciousness. She groped around wildly for a pen, straining to see in the darkness.

She sat up abruptly, and to her dismay, her head throbbed with surprising intensity. Pressing her hand over the bandage, she waited until the stabbing pain subsided.

Her head had been feeling so much better, but now she was experiencing the same pain, and she was alarmed.

She'd have to remember to tell Anne Lewis about it.

On second thought, maybe she'd rethink discharging her.

She decided not to tell her.

Gingerly, Sarah got out of bed and felt her way to the table. The nurse had left a sheet of paper there along with a pen, as Sarah had requested. However, when she took pen in hand, she realized the dream was gone.

Tears of frustration burned her eyes as she made every effort to recapture the elusive dream, but it was useless. It had been important, she thought. A clue.

Perhaps it was only wishing thinking, but she was desperate to attach some significance to this dream; it couldn't possibly be meaningless … perhaps it could reveal some mysterious piece of the puzzle that was the sinister labyrinth in which she found herself.

There was no hope; the dream was irretrievably gone. As flimsy as a vapor, it had vanished.

However, sitting on the bed, as the sun was rising, she soon realized that for the first time she could feel justifiably excited.

Today was the day!

She hurriedly dressed in the rumpled clothing that was stuffed into the corner closet, noticing that the clothing still had a lingering, wintry scent. There was no hope for it; she'd have to wear her boots with the broken heels until she could buy new ones.

With what money? Her mind raced. She didn't remember her name, much less her bank account numbers. What had become of her wallet, her purse? Had it been lost in her accident, somehow? Had it been stolen?

Just as these new, disturbing thoughts began to crowd in on her, the door opened, and to her profound relief, it was Anne Lewis, herself.

"Good morning!" she said brightly.

"I'm all ready to go."

"Yes, I can see that," she replied. "However, I have to be here until three. You can wait a little while longer, can't you?"

Sarah couldn't hide the disappointment in her voice as she answered, "I guess so."

"The good news is that Dr. Cooper has given you the green light, and I've spoken with Dr. Hayes. She's agreed to take your case from here on, all right? There are ethical boundaries that I just can't cross, so as much as I'd like to treat you, I simply cannot."

"Right. I remember."

"Good. So just hang tight until three and I'll see you then."

She was walking to the door when Sarah said, "Thank you. Thank you so much."

Anne turned to her and smiled. "When you see that stack of wedding invitations, you aren't going to be thanking me, I can assure you!"

"I'm up for the task, don't worry."

Anne gave her the thumbs-up sign as she exited the room.

Leaning back on the bed, she suddenly thought of something. Reaching for her neck, she grasped the chain that held the faded Jewish star. She remembered telling Anne Lewis that her grandmother had given it to her as a gift. It was comforting beyond measure to know that she, indeed, had a grandmother … she did have family. Perhaps it wouldn't happen that day, and maybe not even the day following, but she felt hopeful that one day soon she'd be reunited with them, wherever they were.

The day was long but uneventful. In the later part of the morning, Dr. Cooper came by for a few minutes, to check her bandage, mostly.

"I think we can remove that," he said. She was so pleased to be rid of the bandage, she didn't even wince when it smarted as he rapidly removed it from her head.

"Try not to get the area wet for several days," he cautioned. "I wouldn't want the lacerations to become infected."

"Okay."

"All right, then, you're good to go."

"Dr. Cooper?"

"Yes?"

"How much longer before I start to remember?"

He scratched his jaw. "To tell you the truth, I'm a little surprised that you aren't already able to recall more ... the injury wasn't all that serious. Now, don't take this the wrong way, but ..."

He paused.

"What?"

He appeared to weigh his words carefully before he said in a low tone, "It just might be that you don't want to remember. I've seen it before."

She swallowed, digesting what he'd said.

It couldn't be true ... could it?

"Sometimes a problem starts out physically and winds up emotionally," he continued. "I could be wrong, of course. I'm sure Dr. Hayes will help you sort it all out."

He left, leaving Sarah with her never-ending, racing thoughts.

Could it be true? Could something have happened to her, something so frightening that she willed herself not to recall it? Or was it the accident itself?

As was becoming the norm for Sarah, she found herself with so many questions, and precious few answers.

Three o'clock finally arrived, and she was as ready as possible when Anne Lewis breezed through the doorway. All Sarah had with her was the clothing on her back and the cashmere shawl draped around her for warmth.

Sarah didn't give the room a backward glance as they left, walking toward the elevators that to Sarah looked guiltily familiar.

"How many days have I been here?" she asked softly.

"You were brought in Wednesday evening," Anne replied.

"Today is Monday, so you haven't even been here a full week, which is truly remarkable. You're very lucky."

They didn't speak much in the elevator ride downstairs.

"I parked in the garage," Anne explained when the doors had opened.

Sarah followed her out of the hospital lobby to the garage next door, and she once again felt the punishing shock of cold air as she walked outside.

"It's freezing," she chattered.

"Actually, for Chicago, in mid-February, it's a beautiful day. Chicago is known as the windy city, so we're grateful when at least it's sunny."

Sarah was almost numb with cold as she followed Anne into the darkened garage, and she shivered as they waited for the car to be brought around.

"You know, you're really not dressed warmly enough."

Why did she have the strangest suspicion that someone had uttered nearly the identical words to her, in the not-so-distant past?

Anne continued, "We're around the same size ... maybe I can find a warmer coat for you in the house. I must have one in some closet, somewhere."

A silver sedan arrived and Sarah gratefully slid into the interior, which was warm compared to the outside.

The thought crossed her mind that here she was, in a car with a woman she barely knew, and she didn't feel frightened. A bit anxious, perhaps, but the hospital had been infinitely more upsetting.

Anne drove with expert skill through the busy traffic, leaving the crowded streets of downtown Chicago behind them as she made her way toward the Outer Drive.

"This is Lake Shore Drive," she explained. "Look, there's

Lake Michigan to your right."

The lake was vast and wintry gray, and the expanse of it followed them nearly the entire route.

"Do you live near here?" Sarah asked.

"About twenty minutes away," she answered. "I live on the North side, in an area called Lincolnwood."

"Oh."

"Does any of this look familiar to you?"

"No, not at all."

Anne didn't look surprised by this, somehow, but she remained silent.

Sarah tried to absorb every detail of her surroundings, from the tall, graceful buildings that rose on her left to the lake view, flanked by a brick promenade on her right. There were many people on the promenade, many walking, some cycling and quite a few running. Every single one of them was cognizant of his or her own identity, and had people they belonged to and who belonged to them. Sarah felt a twinge of envy.

How wonderful it would be … just to be in possession of that basic birthright. Would she ever be able to take that for granted again?

She forced those negative thoughts from her mind, choosing instead to focus on her relative good fortune and what she had to be grateful for. Thanks to the woman seated on her left, she was at last a free woman, warm, safe and protected.

It wasn't long before Anne veered off Lake Shore Drive, heading west. Anne noticed the city blocks, with older brick buildings huddled closely together. They drove down several long city blocks that looked much the same before they came to an intersection where the neighborhood appeared a bit more upscale. Sure enough, the streets rapidly became less crowded, and as Anne drove down Lincoln Avenue, she remarked, "This is Lincolnwood. We're almost home."

Home.

How lovely the word sounded, and the positive images that it conjured were difficult to ignore. Still, Sarah was keenly aware that they were not traveling to her own home. They were heading to the home of Anne Lewis, where she would be a guest.

Would she ever see her own home again?

That was another piece of the ongoing puzzle of her life.

Anne turned down a lovely tree-lined street, with larger houses. Newer construction was interspersed with stately older homes, and the normalcy of the suburban scene was reassuring to Sarah. Though the houses were built close to one another, the quiet street held a peaceful atmosphere that was very appealing.

Anne entered her driveway, with the crunch of gravel beneath her tires, and Sarah looked at the older brick structure that was Anne's home and Sarah's present refuge. Although the house looked quite large, it didn't appear at all imposing; rather, it seemed warm and inviting.

"Here we are, Monticello Avenue." Anne exited the car, fumbling with her keys at the front door, and Sarah trailed after her.

Sarah noticed the graceful staircase in the foyer and the warm cozy kitchen beyond. To her left, a mantel over the living room fireplace was covered with framed family photographs, and Sarah couldn't help but feel a bit wistful. This truly was a real home, in which laughter and the members of this family had shared love in abundance.

Did she have such a home, somewhere? And if so, where was it?

When she'd unwrapped her shawl in the front foyer, she

looked to her right, spying the cluttered dining room. Every inch of the table was covered with what Sarah assumed were wedding invitations. There were piles of them stacked precariously in an attempt at order. It was at that moment that Sarah did something she hadn't done in quite a long while.

She turned to Anne, and they both burst out laughing.

CHAPTER 10

"*Come in.*"

Anne Lewis opened the door to the bedroom to find Sarah sitting at the tidy corner desk, pen in hand.

"Oh, good, I see you're working on your diary."

"Yes," Sarah replied proudly. "I'm almost finished for today. I think Dr. Hayes will be pleased."

"Oh, I'm sure she will be."

"When will we be leaving tomorrow?"

"Oh, probably around ten or so. Your appointment is not until eleven."

"I'll be ready."

Anne smiled, wished her good night and shut the door behind her.

Sarah resumed her writing, thinking yet again how very blessed she was to have met a person like Anne Lewis. Kind and patient, she had opened her home to her, a virtual stranger. She looked around the small room, which had been her home for the past week. While her room in the hospital had been cold and sterile, this room was warm and cheerful.

There was a large, maple sleigh bed in the corner, with a

matching dresser under the windows that faced the back yard. The room had an eastern exposure so it was sunny and bright, especially in the morning when Sarah first opened her eyes. She'd felt instantly at ease and safe within these walls from the very first moment she'd entered this room.

There was a definite warmth to the house in general; it enveloped Sarah and gave her hope. There was so very much to write, so many pent up emotions just waiting to be released, but her hand began to ache in earnest. She was beginning to feel the strain from all of the writing she'd done this past week. So Sarah reluctantly put down her pen to massage the cramp in her hand. There would be more than enough time later to catch up.

Time. It was the one commodity that she possessed in abundance. Time had become her friend as well as her greatest nemesis … if only she knew, somehow, when this period of uncertainty in her life would come to a close and her past would magically surface in her consciousness. Sometimes she fantasized that one morning she would wake up to an unending collection of images and memories. Often, though, when she remembered Dr. Cooper's words, she wondered whether she had willed herself into this deep forgetfulness because she wanted to totally distance herself from her past. Then, she'd give herself a mental shake, firmly resolving that no matter what the circumstances were, she still had to know about her past and claim her identity. The uncertainty weighed upon her, giving her no rest.

For now, she had no past and no future. She could only live in the present.

She decided to read through the pages that she'd laboriously and painstakingly already written. Dr. Karen Hayes, a prominent psychologist, was a believer in a diary system for her amnesia patients, and from what Sarah had gleaned, she'd achieved a modicum of success with this method. Sarah recalled her initial phone conversation with Dr. Cooper, just hours after she'd been released from the hospital.

"What percentage of her patients are cured?" she had asked hopefully.

"There's no way of knowing that," Dr. Cooper had brusquely replied. "Aside from the confidentiality issues, there's something much more obvious."

"What is that?" Sarah had asked, bewildered.

"True retrograde amnesia that lasts over twenty-four hours is pretty rare. There aren't that many cases that aren't compounded by some other specific issue."

"Such as?"

"Such as a host of mental illnesses, from bipolar disorder to schizophrenia ... but fortunately that doesn't seem to be the problem here. Dr. Hayes has achieved success in this field, so I'd like you to try her diary method. Write everything down for one week before your appointment. I'll be in touch with her to see how it goes."

His approach left her no room to argue, so she could have hardly refused. Truthfully, however, she felt somewhat hesitant to put all her thoughts and emotions down on paper.

To Sarah, it had seemed like a gross invasion of privacy. She'd never even yet met Dr. Karen Hayes, and to share her innermost feelings, to bare her soul, in effect, was embarrassing, and even seemed unnatural. She'd discussed the issue at length with Anne late Monday night, her very first night there. They'd shared steaming mugs of hot tea around the large kitchen table and weighed the pros and cons.

"What do you have to lose?" offered Anne.

"Besides my dignity?" answered Sarah. "I understand why it's important to write these things down ... maybe it'll help me remember faster."

"Exactly."

"But why can't it just stay private? Why does this doctor have to read it?"

"Well, if she's to help you recover, she needs to know more about you. And what better way to learn about you than directly from you?"

Sarah was quiet, pondering this logical conclusion.

"You don't have to worry about her showing this to anyone, of course," Anne reassured her.

Without thinking, Sarah added, "Oh, of course ... doctor-patient confidentiality, and all that. It would be illegal."

Anne's eyebrows rose a fraction of an inch, but she didn't comment. She just quietly slid a large notebook toward Sarah, with a gentle nudge. Sarah opened it, looking at its pristine, white pages, which would be privy to all her innermost thoughts and fears.

"Who knows what the trigger will be?" persisted Anne. "Like I said, you've got nothing to lose. Try it."

And so Sarah had begun to dutifully write down all of her thoughts, emotions and experiences. Before long, she had become thoroughly engrossed in the process, keenly aware of her feelings and her desire to express them. It was cathartic for her to pen her thoughts each night, and she actually began to look forward to that quiet time with her diary, eager for the words to come forth.

Although she noted that the first entry was the day she'd arrived at Anne's house, Sarah felt that the first day really began when she awoke in the hospital. Since she was unable to recall her life before that moment, everything started from that point onwards.

It was gratifying for Sarah to realize how very far she'd come in so little time.

She would have preferred writing on a laptop rather than writing by longhand into a notebook, but Dr. Hayes was adamant that she write the diary the old-fashioned way. Anne had explained that seeing her own handwriting would be beneficial to them both, in any case. She ascertained that Dr. Hayes would be able to analyze aspects of Sarah's personality through her handwriting, and for Sarah, perhaps it would be yet another link that could help her to remember something, anything ....

Even a tiniest fragment, the smallest shard of a fleeting memory, might be the trigger she'd been hoping for.

Additionally, the writing had kept her quite busy, and she was grateful for that. She didn't have that much to keep her occupied. She'd kept her word and studiously addressed all the wedding invitations, yet that had taken just two days. It had been pleasant enough addressing them at the dining room table. Anne had been at work and the house had been quiet. She'd addressed them in her neat, cursive penmanship, flourishing the letters with curlicues to add a touch of calligraphic elegance.

Anne's son was to be married in less than a month, at a hotel in downtown Chicago. Because of a printing error in the first batch, the wedding invitations had been sent out late, so it was essential to get them into the mail as soon as possible. Anne was very grateful and remarked that the job revealed that Sarah had organizational skills.

Sarah now opened the notebook to the very first page. Anne

had said she'd be ready to leave about ten o'clock the next morning for their appointment with Dr. Hayes. The house was quiet, as everyone had gone to bed. It was only Sarah and her diary, and in the serene, dark safety of her bedroom, Sarah opened the small notebook and began to read from the very first entry.

Monday, February 16

Dear Diary,

I hardly know where to begin. From the moment I awoke in the hospital until now, Anne Lewis has been there for me, every step of the way. She handed me this notebook last night, with instructions from Dr. Hayes.

"Write it all down," she said. "Dr. Hayes wants to read what you'll write, next week. This diary just might hold the key to a lot of answers."

She hasn't let me down yet, so I'll try to keep my end of the bargain. I will attempt to put pen to paper ... to express every emotion that I'm feeling. I apologize if this isn't in any sort of order. My thoughts continue to remain chaotic, darting back and forth like the small sparrows I see outside my window. I find that I get distracted easily, partly because there are so many lapses in my memory ... there are just giant, black holes that I can't help but wonder about ... and I worry whether they will be there forever. There's a level of anxiety that's perpetually there, an ever constant presence, and it gnaws at me.

On a more positive note, there is a slight sense of peace that I'm now experiencing. Just being here, in Anne's lovely home ... it makes me feel safe. The world is a vast, frightening place. I have no idea who I am and where I belong, and so naturally the thought of leaving the confines of this home is terrifying to me. I know that I'll have to leave next week, because I have an appointment with Dr. Hayes. Anne promised that she would drive me to the appointment.

I've noticed that I scare easily. I don't know if this was always the case or if it's a direct result of everything that I've been through. It's the oddest sensation not knowing oneself ... it's like I'm living with a stranger. And that stranger is myself. I have to think long and hard about my basic likes and dislikes.

Certain things are easy. I know I like coffee. Other things are infinitely more difficult. For instance, as I was sitting today addressing the invitations for Anne's son's wedding, I was wondering if I have a favorite color. Oh, by the way, his name is David. Anne's youngest son.

See what I mean? My thoughts are scattered. I was thinking of going back and correcting what I wrote, to put it in some sort of logical order. I decided against it. If Dr. Hayes reads this, I want it to be accurate. I tend to like everything in perfect order. Again, I'm not certain if that's just the way I've always been or if it's a direct result of the accident. I'm not a psychologist or anything, but it would make sense for me to want to have some sort of control over my life, wouldn't it?

In any case, I have no idea what my favorite color is, or if I have one. Favorite song? No idea. Favorite book? Not a clue. I cannot express how frustrating it is not to know myself. I see myself in the mirror and it's like I'm looking into the eyes of someone I used to know a very long time ago. It's the oddest sensation. This situation consumes me. It is the very last thing I think of before I go to sleep at night, and it's the first thing that greets me each morning.

Who am I? Will I ever know?

Tuesday, February 17

Dear Diary,

I finished addressing the rest of the invitations today, and I'm feeling quite proud of this relatively small achievement. I'm also thrilled to help out Anne, albeit in such small measure. How will I ever repay her for what she's done for me?

I met Anne's son, David, briefly today. He drove Anne home, since her car is in the shop. What a nice young man. He doesn't live at home during the week because he dorms at the Yeshiva, I was told. A yeshiva is a school where Jewish boys learn the Torah, which is the Bible, Anne explained to me. David wants to be a rabbi, like his older brother, and he is studying for the Rabbinate. I'm finding the whole thing fascinating, truth be told. Anne is a very religious woman. She says prayers every morning, I noticed. I also observed that she mouths a small prayer before she eats food, and a prayer when she's finished with her meal.

Anne is a wonderful cook. Last night, she made a delicious lasagna for dinner, which was truly incredible. I don't know much about myself, but I'm fairly certain that I don't know how to cook. I don't think I have many domestic talents, in general. For example, Anne gave me a lot of clothing she found in the back of her closet for me to wear. Some were in need of mending, and the like. She gave me a spool of thread and a needle to move buttons around. I'm embarrassed to admit this, but I simply have no idea what to do. I didn't want to appear even more pathetic than I already must appear, so I thanked her and took the clothes to my room, where they are stacked neatly on the dresser. I truly believe that I have never done sewing of any sort, though I'm not quite sure how I know that. I'll try and tackle that tomorrow, though the task seems daunting, indeed. Perhaps I'd enjoy the challenge.

On a different note, I found out a piece of disturbing information last night.

Anne's husband passed away five years ago.

They had a very close and wonderful marriage, Anne confided to me with a forlorn expression on her lovely face. My heart ached for her.

"Was he sick?" I asked.

"No, it was very quick," she replied. "He didn't suffer." She didn't elaborate, and I didn't want to pry. There are pictures of them everywhere … on the mantel, on the walls … constant reminders of what she had, and lost. He was a nice-looking man, a black skullcap on his head, a broad smile on his face. He was a doctor, Anne mentioned, and they had had much in common.

"He was my very best friend," Anne told me softly.

Poor Anne … how she must've suffered these past five years … and soon she'll walk her son down the aisle, alone.

Maybe not remembering is not the worst thing ….

Wednesday, February 18

Dear Diary,

Anne has two sons. The oldest lives in Israel and his name is Aaron. His wife, Rachel, is also originally from Chicago. They have a young son, whose cards I dutifully returned to Anne. It seems funny to me now that Anne gave me those cards to study. It seems like a long time has passed between then and now, and I'm a different person than I was at the time. In any case, Anne's grandson's name is Eli, and he is quite adorable. I often find myself looking at their pictures that are displayed prominently over the mantle. There are masses of pictures everywhere in the house. Obviously, Anne misses them greatly; it must be terribly hard to have children living so far away. Still, they are due to arrive before the wedding, and I'm sure that Anne is counting the days until her family is reunited with each other. As for my own situation, I have yet to be reunited with anyone or anything ….

I am eagerly anticipating meeting Aaron and Rachel, and little Eli. Small details, like names, have become very important to me. I repeat them in my mind, terrified of forgetting even the most inane of minutiae. I cannot begin to fathom why it has become so important to me to retain every trivial fact that I come across, but that's just how it is. Maybe it's because I don't know what my own name is, and so I hunger for knowledge of any sort. Actually, that brings me to another topic … a topic that is quite personal in nature.

Anne said that I have to write everything down, and so I shall, but it's difficult knowing quite how to proceed ….

The fact is, I've become very interested in learning more about my Jewish heritage. Truth be told, I've had a lot of time on my hands, and much of that time has been spent in quiet solitude. Since I cannot recall anything from my own past, all I've been reflecting upon is Anne.

Anne's family. Anne's practices. Anne's beliefs.

I've come to the stunning realization that Anne does not merely live her life the way most others do. Every aspect of her life is fraught with meaning. Pardon the pun, but I've "observed" so much about observant Jews, and the details are endless ....

For instance, Orthodox Jews do not eat meat and milk at the same time. I never knew that; at least, I don't believe I ever did. There must be six hours that elapse after a meat meal before one is allowed to eat a dairy meal. After a dairy meal, however, one only has to wait fifteen or twenty minutes, and it's best to rinse out one's mouth.

Staying at Anne's home is definitely turning into quite a learning experience ... obviously, I don't know all that much about religion, but each day I discover more. I've been adhering to the rules of the house to the very best of my ability. When I'm in the kitchen, clearing up the breakfast dishes, I keep the dairy plates away from the meat area, just as Anne instructed. Anne said that she can't get over how quickly I've picked things up. I've actually become a giant sponge, eager to soak up all that I can. Whenever I learn a new fact about religion, it gives me a sense of satisfaction, which I find calming. Additionally, it keeps my brain occupied, and for several moments I can actually breathe, eager to escape my own, inner turmoil and focus on something other than myself. What sweet relief!

Anne has been so very kind to me ... any time she's able to say something complimentary, she makes sure to. What a magnificent person. And the rituals she follows, such as never eating meat and dairy together, or the prayers she recites ... it doesn't seem all that strange to me.

Truthfully, in my innermost heart, I do believe that there is a G-d. Somehow, the more I witness Anne's customs, the more my belief in Him seems to deepen. It's rather comforting to me, to realize that I'm not really alone in this vast, precarious world.

Oh, don't get me wrong; I'm not saying that observant life is for me, or anything like that. I just have developed an ... appreciation of sorts, a fascination, one could say ... and to Anne's credit, she has never pushed me in any way to adhere to her rituals. Still, I often find myself watching her, eager to learn something new.

On another note, I saw a picture of David's bride, Aliza, and she seems lovely. She looks demure and sweet, and I'm sure that they'll make a wonderful couple. Secretly, I can't help but worry about their ages; they're just so young. David is only twenty-four, and his bride is only twenty-one years of age.

I find myself wondering how old I am. It's a peculiar sensation, indeed, not to know how old one is. When is my birthday? I grow despondent whenever I think of such things, so I continue to try and focus my energies elsewhere.

Anne gave me two books to peruse at my leisure, and I've been reading these books voraciously. I try to convince myself that it's just to escape the monotony, but who am I fooling? These books contain so much knowledge … I simply can't put them down. The first one is a book of names, since Anne doesn't know what to call me, and I refuse to be called "Jane" – as in Jane Doe. No, that would be too humiliating.

I still haven't chosen a name that I like, but I've learned a lot about names, their meanings and origins. I discovered that the name Aliza means "joy." How fitting … Anne deserves to have joy in her life, and no doubt this blessed union will make Anne proud and happy.

The other book is simply brilliant, as it explains a lot of laws and customs that Orthodox people follow. It is called *The Book of Why, When, and How* and I must say it contains a staggering amount of information. It's written in such a clear, concise manner that makes it quite easy to follow. For example, I know that I'm a Jew, but I know so very little about being one. This book actually explains at length how a person is automatically a Jew if the mother is a Jew. I was never aware of that … it must mean that my mother was Jewish, which brings me to more, never-ending riddles ….

Where is my mother? Is she alive? I yearn for

answers, but there are only more questions. Right now, Anne has been filling the role of surrogate mother with grace and aplomb, but each day that passes by I wonder if my real mother is out there, somewhere, worried about my safety. I'd like to allay her fears, since I am very well cared for, but of course, it's futile to think along those lines ....

I'm truly fascinated by this book, and aside from reading it each chance I get, I've also taken notes on it, hoping I'll remember small details. There are so many things I'm certain I never knew. It all makes perfectly logical sense, and I feel like each day I'm making remarkable, new discoveries. I may not know who I am or where I fit in, but I'm learning much about the world, nonetheless. There is also a lot of Jewish history crammed into the book, which is intriguing, as well. For a nation that's been persecuted all through the ages, it's truly remarkable how far the Jewish people have come.

I feel proud to be a Jew.

Thursday, February 19

Dear Diary,

One would think that the President of the United States was arriving tomorrow. The entire household is preparing for tomorrow evening. It is the Sabbath, the day of rest. Even I have heard of that, I'm quite sure. It definitely sounds familiar, anyway. Anne calls it *Shabbos*. Before she left for work this morning, she compiled a list of things for me to do. It was a very detailed list, and so it wasn't difficult to follow. I defrosted the chicken and meat that had been in the freezer, and I even baked a cake all by myself.

I followed a recipe that had been left on the kitchen counter, and to my delight, it wasn't all that complicated. It rose in the oven perfectly, and it smelled fabulous.

I was inordinately pleased with this small accomplishment. I tidied up the dining room and put the white tablecloth on it, as per Anne's instructions. On *Shabbos*, Anne uses her fine crystal and china. Anne said that it's in honor of the Sabbath Queen, who "visits" the home each week. Additionally, David and Aliza will be eating the meals here, and the excitement is almost palpable. I am looking forward to it more than I ever could've dreamed possible, but again, there isn't a moment that goes by that I don't wonder if I have family who are interested in my whereabouts. Will the Sabbath Queen whisper all the elusive answers to me when she visits?

How I wish that it could be so easy.

Each day when Anne comes home from work, I ask if there's been any news on that front. And each day she shakes her head. She's been to the police countless times on my behalf, asking if there's anyone missing who matches my description. The databases are filled with drawings of missing women, but the artists' renderings don't match my profile, and the women listed have been missing for far longer than I have. I even saw a copy of a police form that she filled out on my behalf. It was signed by Officer Robert S. Miller.

I remember him as the malicious police officer who mocked and threatened me. I never told this to Anne, thinking that in my weakened state, I may not recall events exactly the way they occurred.

I do remember the forceful thrust of his jaw, his cold, menacing eyes, and feeling frightened and overwhelmed. He didn't believe me at the time, but surely he must feel differently now, since Anne explained to him my unusual situation. It truly does not matter, however, since he informed her that there have been no inquiries on my behalf.

So far, nothing. And so I continue to wait, plagued by uncertainty.

Where is my family? Why aren't they looking for me?

Perhaps I have no family. Maybe Anne is the closest thing to family that I've got.

Sunday, February 22

Dear Diary,

How can I possibly begin to describe the wondrous course of events that has transpired this weekend? I will attempt to put into words what my tumultuous feelings are, but it will be most difficult. I have so much to write; my emotions threaten to overwhelm me. I suppose I'll begin with Friday. The preparations for *Shabbos* lasted all afternoon. The heavenly smells coming from the kitchen were indescribable. Anne is an outstanding chef. David was home, dressed in a black suit and a matching black fedora hat. He left for synagogue at the start of the *Shabbos*, the house became quiet and expectant, and then ... and then ...

Anne did something I wasn't expecting her to do.

She lit candles.

And when the candles were lit, she covered her face with her hands, mouthing silent prayers. An aura of calm pervaded the home, and a blessed sense of peace permeated my very being. When I saw her serene face reflected in the glowing flames, I began to cry.

I could not stop. The cries were primal, seemingly coming from a place within me that had lain dormant for ages. Whatever it was, it had awakened within me a powerful yearning that even I cannot fully comprehend.

Anne put her arm around me, explaining that these emotions were coming from my very soul. I believe it to be so. At first, I thought I was crying for myself. Here I was, a guest in someone's home, unsure of myself or my future

... at times it seems like too much to bear. But I quickly realized that I was crying because I was recalling someone else lighting candles on Friday night ... someone dear to me. I could almost make out the fragmented memory, but it's an elusive shadow ... a tantalizing glimpse that is just beyond my grasp.

I'm not certain who it was, or whether she's still alive today, but I'm quite certain that I did at one point have someone close to me who lit the Sabbath candles.

If only I could remember her name ....

In any case, Friday night was a pivotal night for me. The holiness of the night somehow awakened my spirit, that's the only way I can begin to describe it. The wonderful meal, the lively discussions, being part of a family ... I can't ever remember feeling so hopeful and yet so wistful, at the very same time. I must've cried for two hours straight, but my sense of purpose has been renewed.

If I came away from the meal with anything at all, it was with the knowledge that there is most definitely a Higher Power. If I ever had doubts before, they are extinguished for good. Just seeing the light emanating from everyone's faces was all the proof I could ever need. I am quite sure of this. For reasons even I cannot begin to fathom, this is my current situation, and I am determined to make the most of this time that I possibly can.

There are books on all sorts of Jewish themes in Anne's home. I fully intend to utilize this time to learn more about Jewish practices. I am eager to begin, in fact.

Shabbos was magnificent, and I genuinely felt melancholy when David made the blessing at the close of the Sabbath. Aliza was here, as well, holding a large candle high above her head.

"I always held the *Havdala* candle high," she murmured to me. "My mother said my husband would be tall. I guess she was right."

We laughed, but at that moment an interesting thought occurred to me. Every single practice that religious Jews observe seems to have some sort of purpose, some sort of meaning. Events are not random, and customs are not haphazard. There seems to be a rhyme and a reason for most everything, and all one needs to do is ask.

And I have been asking. Questions keep pouring forth in an endless stream, and to Anne's credit, she responds to each of my queries with patience and insight.

I feel changed, somehow. *Shabbos* has changed me in ways I cannot fully recognize, but nonetheless, I sense a difference within myself. I am a bit less fearful, and there is the renewed sense of there being a light at the end of this dark, foreboding tunnel ....

Sarah closed the notebook sleepily and turned off the light. There was such truth to what she'd written, but she felt as if she'd only scratched the surface. There was so much more in her heart and in her soul, and so much beyond words.

She couldn't shake the feeling that, somehow, everything that had happened to her had been for a reason. True, she couldn't possibly begin to guess what that was, but all the same, a sense of peace had replaced her tortured thoughts.

Instead of questioning her fate, she had begun to accept it.

It was a step. And the very next day, she was to take another step in her recovery; namely, meeting Dr. Hayes for the first time, who would read her diary.

Her stomach fluttered anxiously at the thought of being out in public, for she'd been sequestered in the safety of Anne's home for the last week.

It was a long time before she finally fell asleep.

CHAPTER 11

SUNDAY, FEBRUARY 22
7:54 P.M.
AMERICAN AIRLINES,
EN ROUTE TO O'HARE
INTERNATIONAL AIRPORT

Peter awoke from a fitful doze, his neck aching him something fierce. He never had been the type to sleep much on flights, but the exhausting flight from Tel Aviv had thoroughly drained him. Kennedy Airport had been a nightmare of delayed flights, lost luggage and angry travelers, and he was grateful to finally be en route to Chicago. He just hoped that his bags had followed him, as well.

He took out his wallet and found the small, red parking stub, exactly where he'd left it ten days earlier.

Ten days.

Could it have been a mere ten days ago when he'd parked his car in the O'Hare lot? How strange … it seemed like eons ago. How could so much have happened?

He was fully awake now, the pain in his neck receding. And as he fingered the small parking ticket in his hands he began to think back, eager to review in his mind the incredible events that had transpired in such a short time span.

He had gone to Israel with only one objective, and that was to talk some sense into his daughter, to explain that her interest in Judaism was the result of being young and easily impressed. He had taken this journey for the sole purpose of helping his daughter to see the light.

Instead, quite inexplicably, the reverse had occurred. Instead of doing the talking and being the one in control, he had spent his time there mostly listening and learning. He had experienced in that environment such a profound sense of serenity that, for the first time in his life, he'd felt a totally welcome feeling of inner peace. Some inexplicable void within him, of which he'd been completely unaware on a conscious level, had been miraculously filled, and in a way he could never have imagined. In the past, he had dismissed all religions, believing they were confining, primitive and irrelevant in a modern society. Now he was beginning to believe that just the opposite was true. Now, he felt happily free to explore with an open mind beliefs he had previously dismissed. He was excited about the prospect of embarking into previously unexplored areas of thought, and the feeling was heady and intoxicating. And all of this had occurred in the process of learning more about his daughter in the past ten days than he had ever before.

If anyone had seen the light, it was he.

He settled back in his seat and let his mind travel back to the first *Shabbos* at the Cohens. It had been magical; there was no other word to describe it. The feelings he'd experienced had been nothing less than amazing. How could he have ever imagined a world so far away where modern day Jews and the stereotypical Jews of yesteryear were adhering to the same beliefs and performing the same rituals so harmoniously?

He was never even aware that such a world existed. There had been so much that he'd been unaware of, it was simply staggering. He'd often thought of himself as an educated man, quite accomplished, successful and educated, not only in his chosen field, but across a wide range of subjects that he could discuss with some degree of sophistication. This trip to Israel had changed his perception of himself, and he wondered if he'd ever look at things the same way again.

Thinking back, he realized when that very special moment had occurred. It had been a moment like no other … a lightning bolt, an electric shock wave that had pummeled him with such force, he had to literally hold on tight so as not to fall. It hadn't happened throughout that first *Shabbos* at the Cohens', marvelous as it was. No, the moment had happened on the next day, Sunday, only a week earlier, when he had traveled to Jerusalem with Danielle.

He remembered the experience perfectly, every detail etched in his mind with total clarity. He doubted that he would ever forget it.

They had taken a taxi, and Danielle was eagerly pointing out to him various sights along the way. The ride had been smooth, and as they climbed steadily upward toward Jerusalem, Danielle had directed his attention to several objects nestled in the hills, on either side of the stretch of highway.

"See those, Dad?" she asked. "They're tanks, reminders of the '67 war, when the Jews recaptured Jerusalem."

He knew precious little about the history of the Jewish state, but as he gazed at the burned out tanks, which were nothing more than twisted pieces of metal, he felt a lump rise in his throat. He wondered how many young lives had ended in that war, and he couldn't help but think of Eden, the young man he'd befriended on the plane. Once again, he offered up a silent prayer for his safety.

Before long, they were rising higher, about to enter the hallowed city of Jerusalem. It stirred something within him, a marvelous excitement. Here he was with his daughter, about to enter the city that Beth had spoken about numerous times, and for which so many generations of Jews had an abiding loyalty.

Wouldn't it be amazing to travel to Jerusalem? Beth had said. *To explore all the archeological ruins of the old temples? Wouldn't it be exciting?*

I'm here, Beth! he wanted to shout. *I'm here with Danielle, and we're on our way to Jerusalem!*

He verbalized nothing aloud, of course, but he had the strangest notion, the oddest idea that somehow Beth was aware of it, anyway, wherever she was.

"Look, Daddy, over there," she'd pointed.

To his right, he had seen a small hill covered with flowering shrubs and greenery. Hebrew lettering was etched in the carefully planned landscaping.

"It says 'Welcome to Jerusalem,'" said Danielle.

It was truly remarkable to him how knowledgeable she'd become. It seemed as if there was nothing of which she was unaware.

Soon they were in the bustling city center, and Peter had been astounded at how modernized it all seemed. While Bnei Brak had seemed old world, the center of downtown Jerusalem was totally contemporary with tall modern buildings, new cars, throngs of fashionably dressed pedestrians and traffic crawling at a snail's pace.

He remarked, "Wow, Jerusalem is certainly more bustling, am I right? Look at this traffic!"

Danielle answered, "It's a bigger city, Dad. Remember, you

were in Bnei Brak for *Shabbos*, when there's no traffic. Believe me, during the week, it's pretty chaotic there, as well."

He recalled the odd sense of melancholy that he'd felt the evening before, when *Shabbos* had come to a close. Outside, the traffic lights in the city of Bnei Brak had begun to work once more, and inside the Cohen apartment, yet another ritual was taking place.

What had it been called? He couldn't remember.

Danielle had held a candle high in her hand, and Dan Cohen had made the blessings over the wine, signaling the end of *Shabbos*. Peter had been instructed to lift his fingers upwards toward the flame, and to smell the pungent cloves.

"On *Shabbos*," Dan explained, "we're blessed with a *'neshama yesaira,'* an extra, special soul. After *Shabbos* is over, that soul goes away, and so we smell the cloves to give us strength for the week ahead."

It had piqued his interest ... an extra soul ... he'd never before stopped to think of the soul he already possessed, not to mention yet another.

"Dad? What do you think?"

His thoughts had been interrupted by his daughter, who was gazing at him strangely.

"Sorry, Pumpkin, I didn't hear you. What did you say?"

"I asked if you'd like to go first to your hotel and get settled before we go to the *Kosel*, the Western Wall."

"Yes, that's a good idea. I'll get settled first," he murmured.

He'd been in an agreeable mood. If Danielle had suggested that they both fly off to the moon together, he'd have probably acquiesced in a heartbeat. He smiled at the thought of the two of them on a rocket ship, off to explore other galaxies ....

And isn't that what they were in actuality doing? Looking

through the cab windows, he ascertained that the surroundings may have as well been on another planet, that's how far removed he felt from reality.

Or was it the other way around? Perhaps the true reality was right there, at that very moment, and it was his life in Chicago that had been unreal, a dream.

It was all so confusing. He looked at Danielle, but his daughter just stared demurely ahead, unaware of her father's chaotic thoughts. Seeing her so serene, so comfortable in her identity, calmed him, and he was able to relax once more.

Before long, the taxi pulled into the circular driveway of the hotel. Peter had exited the car to pay the driver and had followed Danielle into the large marble lobby of the hotel.

To his pleasant surprise, the hotel was lovely, with a chic décor and modern amenities. Danielle had settled herself on a couch in the corner lobby to wait for him. His bags were whisked upstairs, his room key and packet of information was efficiently handed to him, and overall it seemed like any other upscale hotel.

Only the view, he noted, was unlike any other he'd ever witnessed. He had opened the door to his room on the fourth floor and immediately saw that the large windows faced the gates of the Old City of Jerusalem. Drawn to the windows, he'd stood there for several minutes, gazing at the sun-drenched Jerusalem hills extending toward the horizon.

It was a majestic sight.

He tore himself away from the windows, and quickly changed into walking shoes. Danielle had said that he'd need them, for they would walk together to the Western Wall. He then grabbed his room key and wallet and hurriedly made his way downstairs to where Danielle was patiently waiting.

He'd found her curled up on a small corner chair, book in hand, writing copious notes.

"Ready, Pumpkin?"

"All set." She tucked her papers into her bag and they started off.

"School work?" he asked.

"Yes. We're having a test in a week and I haven't started studying yet. It's really hard."

"What subject?"

"The laws of *Shabbos*," she'd answered. "You wouldn't believe how much there is to know, Daddy."

The thought had occurred to him that just a few days before, he'd have been alarmed by this bit of news, but now all he could feel was satisfaction. He felt surprisingly proud of what his daughter was doing, and of the path she had chosen.

As they had set out down the long driveway, he'd lagged behind Danielle, calling out, "Hey, slow down! Your old man isn't used to walking so fast."

She'd happily obliged as they walked in sync. For several minutes, neither had spoken, each content to walk in silence. After they'd passed through the Jaffa Gate, Peter thought about how many invading armies throughout the centuries had passed through these ancient portals. Then Peter had broken the silence.

"Pumpkin, can I ask you something?"

"Sure, Dad." She'd looked up at him expectantly.

"Did you ever hear of Robert Frost?"

"Huh?"

"Robert Frost. Did you ever hear of him?"

"You mean, the poet?"

"Yeah, the poet."

"Sure, I guess so. We learned about him in high school, I think."

"That's the one." He'd paused. "He wrote one particular poem that I've always liked."

"Really? I never knew you liked poems."

"I like this one. Your mother did, too. He called it 'The Road Not Traveled.' It's the last part, the last few sentences, that I've been thinking about lately. Want to hear it?"

"Okay."

He recited softly as they continued walking:

"Two roads diverged in the wood, and I –
I took the one less traveled by,
And that has made all the difference."

They were both quiet for a moment, walking in amiable silence through the famed Jaffa Gate, each lost in their own thoughts.

"You see what I mean, don't you?" Peter had finally said. "You could've taken the same road as everyone else. Your old classmates, your old friends ... but you chose not to. You chose a different road for yourself, and even though I was more than a little skeptical at first, I have to say that I feel differently than I thought I would. I'm really proud of you, Pumpkin. I think the road that you're traveling is the right road for you, I really do."

Danielle had stopped in her tracks when he'd uttered these words.

"Really, Daddy? You have no idea how happy this makes me. I've been needing to hear it, I guess."

"Really, truly," he'd reiterated. "It's probably too late for your old man, but I definitely think you're on the right track."

They were a few simple words, but they had been enough. They didn't speak of it again for the rest of the walk. Peter had been content to absorb the tumultuous activities of the Jewish Quarter, this fascinating world that was such a contrast of old and new in which he'd found himself.

And it had truly been a world in itself. Danielle had pointed out to him the old stone dwellings that the Jewish people lived in in the Jewish quarter, a stone's throw from the Western Wall.

"See that gate, Dad? A Jewish family must live there."

He could scarcely imagine an entire family living behind these ancient stones, but Danielle had remarked how she'd stayed for a *Shabbos* here once, and inside it had been lovely. Peter had seen young children, the very pictures of blissful innocence, burdened with backpacks, running home from school happily. It had been almost noon, and he had wondered if these children came home for lunch, or if it was the end of the school day.

It was a world unlike any other he'd previously encountered, veritably untouched by time. It was almost as if the current world of which he was so much a part had ceased to exist. Children laughed and played in the narrow courtyards, and mothers hurried by, clutching their infants tightly in their arms.

There was something blissful about the scene, something … something …

Holy.

And before he knew it, he was walking down the stairs with his daughter and could already see the hallowed Western Wall.

"Do you know what the *Kosel* is, Dad? Why it's so precious to us?"

"Not exactly," he'd replied sheepishly.

"I didn't either," she'd whispered. "It's actually a piece of the outer wall that enclosed the Temple. The temple that was destroyed two thousand years ago."

"Wow."

"As a matter of fact, since it's your first time here, the normal custom is to cut your garment a little, as a sign of mourning."

"Cut? Like, with a scissors?" he'd asked incredulously.

She saw his alarmed expression and laughed. "Don't worry. Today is *Rosh Chodesh*, the first day of the new Hebrew month, so you don't have to."

"Oh." He had been given a reprieve, much to his relief, but he wasn't sure why.

How did his daughter know so much?

They continued walking in the direction of the Western Wall where he heard a cacophony of sound like he'd never previously heard.

"What in the world is that noise?"

"Birds. I think they all come here to sing."

It was true. He could see the birds and hear their joyous, riotous sound.

"Do you know that Rabbi Cohen once told us that before the Jewish people recaptured Jerusalem, the birds had gone? Simply vanished. And soon after we'd reclaimed the *Kosel*, the birds returned."

He hadn't known this, of course.

The Wall was soon in plain sight before them.

The thought that this was the actual place that the Jewish people had traveled to for so long, and with such hardships, was a sobering thought. He found himself wondering how many people had come here to pray over the ages, beseeching a Higher Power to help with all sorts of problems. He figured the number was astronomical.

After being checked by soldiers at a checkpoint, Danielle had motioned for him to go to the separate men's side, and she quietly slipped over to the women's side. As Peter walked, carefully checking that his *yarmulka* was still on his head, his sense of awe had heightened. Here were Jews from all walks of life, joined together for one purpose only … to pray at the holiest site. His pace had quickened along with his heartbeat.

He was soon facing the Wall. Coming closer, he saw many crumpled slips of paper stuffed into every nook and cranny of the ancient stones. He saw a young boy to his right writing something on a small scrap of paper, rolling it up, and trying to insert it into a miniscule crack.

They were notes to heaven, and miraculously, they all seemed to fit.

Everywhere that he looked he saw rolled scraps of paper and could only imagine the variety of scribbled secrets, dreams and desperate requests that people from all over the world had deposited there.

Peter had gazed at the people around him. There were men in Chassidic garb, men with knitted *yarmulkas* and even a few teenaged boys who appeared secular and unaffiliated with any sect. There were also soldiers, their rifles slung over their shoulders, who were touching the Wall, deep in prayer. One group surrounding a young boy was celebrating a *bar mitzvah*.

As he'd stepped closer to the Wall, the noise seemed to cease, replaced by a hushed lull, as if sound had become muted.

Tentatively, he had lifted his hand and touched the smooth, ancient stone.

It was as if a bolt of electricity had shot through the stone and penetrated into his very soul.

Long buried, wave upon wave of emotion took him by

surprise, rising to the surface in a fraction of a second.

G-d Himself was here, he knew.

And He was listening.

Peter Strauss found himself shaking uncontrollably, and he leaned his head against the Wall, whispering.

Help me, G-d. Please help me. My parents are no longer alive. I lost my wife. My daughter is all I have left. She's trying to do what's right. Please help her. I think it's too late for me ... I don't know where to begin.

The stone felt wet next to his cheek, and he tasted his tears.

Please. Please. I don't know how to pray, but I know that You're listening. Please help my daughter on this journey. Keep her safe and healthy. Please watch over her and protect her. Please ...

He was shuddering, quaking with sobs.

Time had ceased to exist.

He'd stayed there, transfixed, for quite a long time. He had been loath to move from his hunched position, afraid to shatter the power of the moment. His concentration was absolute, and his motives had never been so completely sincere.

Finally, he composed himself, at least outwardly, wiping his tears with his wrist, and reluctantly walked away from the Wall.

It had been an experience like no other. Potent and humbling at the same time, he'd been made quite aware of his own insignificance. In the vast configuration of the world, he'd never felt smaller, like a mere speck in the infinite cosmos. And yet, he'd never felt more important.

G-d Himself had heard his prayers, he knew.

He was accustomed to being in a courtroom and pleading his case before a judge and jury, but this had been entirely different.

His most successful jury trial hadn't even come close

to bringing him as much satisfaction as being heard by the Heavenly Judge.

Deep in thought, he hadn't noticed Danielle walking toward him, a look of concern on her face.

"Dad? Are you okay?"

He looked up. There was Danielle, in her coat with her pink scarf, looking at him expectantly.

"Oh, yes, I'm fine, fine ..." he'd murmured.

She'd looked at him sympathetically.

"It can be intense, I know," she'd said.

They had walked together, and Danielle had suggested lunch.

"There's a bagel place not too far from here, in the Jewish quarter," she'd said.

"Oh, fine, fine," Peter had answered.

He seemed capable of giving only one word answers at the time. It was as if he'd had the wind knocked out of him. Time and space had been suspended, and even sound seemed a bit altered ... he kept hearing a distant, buzzing noise.

"Dad, is your cell phone ringing?" Danielle had asked.

"What? Oh."

The buzzing had indeed been coming from his cell phone, which he'd turned to vibrate.

Checking the number, he realized it was Ray.

It was only six o'clock in the morning, Chicago time, but Ray Adams liked to get an early start. He looked at the phone.

"Aren't you going to answer it?"

He shook his head. He felt too emotionally drained to deal with Ray at that particular moment.

Danielle had looked like she wanted to say something, but she didn't.

They soon had found the bagel store, a charming little

eatery with outdoor tables and chairs. Drained, Peter had sat down on one of the chairs, and Danielle went to order.

How well he remembered the feeling of bewilderment as he'd sat on that chair, waiting for Danielle. He had hardly known what to do himself ... he knew he'd had a life-altering experience, but his elation had been mixed with a wistfulness. What now, he'd thought. What now?

Just what was he going to do about it?

"*Ladies and gentlemen,* please return your trays and seatbacks to their proper position. We're now approaching the Chicagoland area."

Peter gave a start. He'd been reliving his trip in such detail, he'd all but forgotten that he was on a plane back to Chicago. He was so exhausted, his normal sleep-wake schedule so distorted, he was having a hard time differentiating reality and fantasy.

But the question remained. He'd discovered a newfound sense of clarity, of purpose, on his trip to Israel. But what could he possibly do about it? How would he incorporate this reality into his life?

He had lingered at the curb, saying good-bye to his daughter. He had felt as if his heart would crack in two. The bond that they'd forged in the past ten days had been deeper than he could've possibly imagined. He'd felt closer to her than ever before, and all too soon, it had been time to say good-bye.

He knew she'd be fine, that she was in the very best of hands.

He was more worried about himself. How would he be able to get on that plane? Would he be able to resume his previous life, pretending that nothing had changed?

Something *had*, in fact, changed. Something wondrous and

miraculous, something spiritual that couldn't be put into words.

The idea of just blending seamlessly into the old routine, trying and settling cases, closing deals with ease, just one of the millions of nameless, faceless people in the higher echelons of corporate America ... the thought depressed him.

The plane touched down.

Weary travelers, grabbing their bags, waited for the doors to open. And when they did, the passengers filed out of the aircraft like well-behaved, sleepy children.

O'Hare. The busiest airport in America, a virtual maelstrom of motion, teeming with thousands of people ...

Peter had never felt more alone.

After he'd retrieved his luggage, he made his way via the underground walkway that connected to the parking garage. The air at once felt chilly and brisk, as if reality was slapping him in the face.

Had he been in a dream the last ten days? What was existent, and what was not?

His car, quite real, was there, exactly where he'd left it. Throwing in his valises, he slid behind the wheel and followed the signs out of the garage. After paying the attendant, he drove toward the highway that would take him home.

The traffic was awfully congested, the cars moving at a snail's pace.

No matter, he thought.

He was in no hurry.

He opened the massive oak doors that led into his entry foyer, his voice ringing out, "Gilda? Gilda, I'm home."

There was no answer.

Frowning, he walked over to the round mahogany table that sat in the center of the foyer. There, perched against a riotous display of silk flowers in a marble vase, was a note. He picked it up.

Mr. Strauss,

My mother's companion is out of town this weekend, so I'm staying with her. She has, unfortunately, declined in recent weeks and cannot manage alone. I'll see you Monday evening. All the mail is on the desk in your study. I hope you had a nice trip.

Gilda

He dropped his suitcases in the foyer and slowly walked up the circular staircase to his bedroom. He was conscious of the noise of his footsteps on the granite floors, of the stillness of the house. It was a large, grand house, decorated in the most elegant fashion.

But it was empty.

That reality was true on many levels, he realized. He also sensed his inner void with each step as he climbed the graceful staircase, his footsteps muted on the rich plush carpeting. He wearily sat down on a bedside chair in his room and buried his head in his hands.

Closing his eyes, he could easily conjure the many experiences that he'd shared during the past week with his daughter. Every detail was still so vivid, he wanted to keep replaying them in his mind, lest he forget.

He recalled a conversation that he'd had with Dan Cohen and Danielle when they'd traveled up to the Northern regions of Israel on Wednesday and visited the beautiful sites there.

Dan had taken his fishing gear, and true to his word, they'd fished in the waters of the breathtaking Lake Kineret, adjacent to the charming coastal town of Tiberias.

The water had been blue and placid, and the three of them had been content to just relax, the fishing lines stretched into the water. Peter couldn't ever recall such a feeling of inner peace. He had not planned on asking the question, and reflecting back on it now, it was surprising how effortless, how natural it had seemed at the time. The question had been utterly spontaneous, and he hadn't felt at all self-conscious when he'd asked it.

"So, Dan," he'd ventured. "If there was one thing I could take on, just one ... what would it be? What do you think?"

Dan had been quiet, mulling it over.

"You mean, one *mitzvah*? One commandment?"

"Yes. Just one."

He nodded, as if coming to a decision. "I'd have to say *Shabbos*. It's not easy, especially at first, but keeping the *Shabbos* transforms the entire week. The whole week becomes suffused in spirituality, and it changes one's whole perspective."

"I see."

"*Shabbos* is a gift," he continued. "It's a treat. Every week you get to stop the daily grind, unwind, enjoy your family, learn more ... and then, when it's over, you feel ready to take on the challenges of the following week. I don't know what I'd do without *Shabbos*."

Danielle was nodding. "It's true, Daddy. When I think of my old life, my old friends, when Saturday was just another day ... I could never go back to that."

"I understand that," he'd agreed. "Really, I do. But for me, it's just too hard. Impossible, even. I have work, clients, business ... it all just can't stop."

"Do you always go to work on Saturday?" Dan had asked.

"Usually not," he'd admitted. "But I almost always bring home work. And if a crisis is imminent, I'll just work right through it. The phone is always ringing on Saturdays … I guess I'm a bit of a workaholic."

"What about if you're away? Who is handling the workload now?" Dan had asked.

"There are two partners in the firm who are on top of things, Ray Adams and Lee Ross," he had explained.

Strangely, it hadn't been difficult unburdening himself to the young rabbi, although by nature he was quite guarded about his private life. In actuality, it had been a relief to talk about his work, something he didn't often get a chance to do. And Dan Cohen had listened to him patiently, and most importantly, non-judgmentally.

Danielle had asked an interesting question.

"What if you had a nasty cold?"

"Excuse me?"

"What if you were in bed with a nasty cold, Daddy? Would you answer the phone then?"

"I guess not."

"So, you'd be willing to let the phone ring in case of a cold, but not for the *Shabbos* Queen?" she'd persisted.

"I honestly couldn't say, honey. I've never been sick a day in my life!"

They had laughed.

The weather had been idyllic, the sun shimmering on the placid surface of the lake. Later, when they were hungry, Peter had treated his daughter and Dan to an early dinner at a lovely restaurant perched right on the water.

The food had been delicious.

"I can't believe this is a kosher restaurant!" Peter had enthused. "This rivals some of the best restaurants in Chicago."

"Glad to hear it," Dan had said warmly. He'd passed the bread basket. "Here, take some more."

They'd stayed until the sun had dipped lower in the sky, and Dan Cohen had taken him to a small synagogue several blocks away, where men had gathered for evening prayers. He couldn't quite get over how natural it had seemed for all of the assembled men to simply stop whatever it was they were doing and pray.

Dan had already explained the significance of praying with a group.

A "*minyan*," he'd called it.

"Ten men is the minimum," he'd clarified.

Once again, Peter had not prayed. He'd stayed toward the back of the group, who'd gathered outside a small stone building. He'd found it a bit odd that they hadn't gone inside; rather, they'd prayed where they were, in a courtyard of sorts. None of the passersby or casual onlookers noticed, as if this were just a common routine.

Standing in the back, Peter had wondered whether he was considered one of the ten men or not. It hadn't mattered in the end, for there were at least twenty men gathered there.

And before he knew it, it had been over, and the small crowd had dispersed, returning to whatever they'd been previously engaged in doing.

The whole event had seemed quite natural to the men assembled.

But to him, it had been quite a moving spectacle ....

Everything that had happened during the course of his stay had seemed to hold some deeper significance for him. On his trip, everything had occurred in bright, vivid technicolor … he clearly remembered thinking how his life, as he knew it, had been a study in pale, drab grays beforehand ….

Peter rubbed his eyes, trying to pull himself together.

How long had he been sitting in that chair, reminiscing about his trip?

He glanced at his watch, astounded to realize that over an hour had passed. It was nearly midnight and he had to be at work the next morning.

His stomach rumbled with hunger, but he ignored it as he slowly trudged around the room, preparing himself for bed.

He was rummaging through his suitcase to find his toothbrush when he saw it.

The black velvet *yarmulka* Danielle had given him.

He held it in his hands for several moments. Then, feeling a bit foolish, he put it on his head, adjusted the bobby pin and looked at his reflection in the mirror above the console table.

Who am I kidding? he thought.

I'm not a part of that world.

Still, it felt oddly … comforting. He missed his daughter fiercely, and wearing her gift made him feel a little closer to her. He decided to leave it on. After all, who would know?

Rifling through his things, his fingers closed around a book. Now that was odd … he didn't recall packing a book into his luggage. Lifting it out of the bag, he read the title.

"*The Book of Why, When, and How — Explaining Hidden Meanings Behind Many Jewish Laws and Customs,* by Rabbi Reuven Bergenstein."

Smiling to himself, he opened the jacket cover and read the inscription:

Dear Daddy,

Thank you so much for understanding what this "voyage to teshuva *(return)" means to me. Having your support in this quest means more to me than words can say. Here's a little something to read on the plane. I hope that this book will answer a lot of your questions ... and who knows? Maybe it will start you on your own wonderful journey. Hope to see you soon!*

Love,
Your little girl,
Danielle

He felt as if his heart would burst.

He knew that quite a few of his colleagues and acquaintances had children around the same age as his Danielle. Yet, he was hard-pressed to think of any who were as thoughtful, as determined ... as mature as she was. Somehow, she had turned into a lofty, and at the same time, wonderfully grounded adult.

He knew Beth would have been proud.

He placed the book gently on the nightstand beside his bed. He most definitely wanted to read it, but it was so late at night, he was simply too exhausted to think clearly.

It was only after he'd gotten into bed that a new thought entered his mind.

Maybe I don't quite fit in the world I'm in, either.
Where do I belong?

There were no easy answers as he tossed and turned, before finally falling into an exhausted sleep.

CHAPTER 12

Sarah sat on the edge of her bed and opened her diary. She paused several seconds, and then began to write.

Monday, February 23

Dear Diary,

I am a little nervous. Today, I will go downtown with Anne, as I have an appointment with Dr. Hayes. As strange as it may seem, I haven't been among people in such a long time. I still find the idea of venturing out into the unknown a bit terrifying, but I suppose that cannot be helped.

Dr. Hayes doesn't exactly make house calls, I gather.

Besides, the outing will do me good, in all probability. Anne told me that her office is in a large office building on Michigan Avenue, and though that sounds frightening to me, I'm sure that the best thing for me to do is face my fears head on.

Anne will be with me, after all. What could happen?

I keep checking myself in the mirror, and I honestly have to admit that I look much better, at least outwardly. My bruises have faded, my cuts have healed, and no one could guess the ordeal I've been through.

I am wearing a nice sweater and skirt that Anne gave to me, quite modest, and I appear very presentable. This saint of a woman quite literally gave me the clothes off her back. I don't know how I will ever be able to repay her.

Sarah closed the diary. There was a lot more to write, always more, but for now it would have to suffice. The appointment was for eleven, and Anne probably wanted to be on her way. She quickly picked up the diary, tucked it under her arm and gave one last look around the cozy room. She pulled on the cashmere shawl over her clothing and left the room, shutting the door behind her.

Downstairs, in the entry foyer, Anne was putting on her gloves.

"Ready, dear?"

"Yes, I guess so."

Anne saw her worried expression and said, "Don't worry. She won't bite, I promise."

Anne grabbed her car keys from the console table, and as she did that, Sarah glanced out the window. A black Mercedes with dark windows drove ever so slowly down the street.

Did it pause in front of Anne's house, or did she only imagine it? Hadn't she seen the car the very day before do the very same thing? Was this at all significant?

Anne must've caught her alarmed expression, for she said,

"What's wrong? You look like you've seen a ghost."

Sarah swallowed. "Did you see the car that just drove by?"

"No."

"A black Mercedes just drove down the street very slowly. I'm almost sure that I saw that car before …. I think even yesterday, the same car cruised down this street. I think it even stopped in front of the house."

"Maybe it was looking for an address," replied Anne, doubtfully. 'I mean, who do you think it could be?"

"I don't know. I just get the strange feeling that I've seen the car before." Sarah paused, thinking. "You know, now that I think about it, I think that car has passed by the house nearly every day I've been here … what could it mean?"

Anne burst out laughing. "It doesn't have to mean anything nefarious, dear. The people who own it could live on the next block!"

Feeling foolish and overly fanciful, Sarah followed Anne outside, greeted by the brisk, chilly Chicago air.

The black Mercedes was nowhere in sight.

Had she imagined the entire episode? Was her mind playing tricks on her?

They got into Anne's comfortable car, and Anne expertly backed out of the driveway, heading back toward downtown. Sarah felt quite anxious, but sitting next to Anne, she tried to convince herself that all would be fine.

It just had to.

The monotony of traffic irritated him. In fact, everything that morning seemed to exacerbate his restlessness. Peter was running late, a characteristic that was quite unlike him. He hadn't had time to shower or eat a bite of breakfast, since he'd overslept. He threw on his clothing haphazardly as he ran down the staircase, taking the steps two at a time. Gathering his briefcase, he slammed out of the house, sprinting to the car.

He was usually punctual and efficient, his routine neat and clearly defined. For years, he'd headed to work with nary a glitch. Even when Beth had been ill, he'd managed to be at work by nine sharp. But this morning, everything had gone wrong. His alarm clock had failed to go off at the scheduled time, and he couldn't recall if he'd even remembered to set it.

Gilda hadn't yet returned from her mother, so his coffee urn hadn't been turned on, not that he'd had time to drink it. He'd tried calling Danielle, but she was only able to talk several seconds. She'd expressed relief that he'd gotten home safely, but she'd had to catch a bus to take her back to Bnei Brak from Jerusalem. Or had it been the other way around? It had been an awful connection.

He'd hung up recalling the blue sky of Jerusalem, and feeling a sadness that he couldn't quite understand, and didn't have the time to explore. The abysmal traffic had Peter grinding his teeth and clenching and unclenching his fists on the steering wheel.

The final straw had been the large sign over his parking garage.

Closed for repairs. Use garage on Wacker Drive.

He had been parking in the same garage for at least ten years and it had never been closed before, to the best of his knowledge.

Muttering under his breath, he tried to maneuver his car around the small alleyways, which were all one-way. This was more than a mere nuisance, for it would sure add an extra twenty minutes to his already tardy arrival at the office.

After what seemed an eternity, he finally found a parking space in a different garage and hurriedly made his way toward his building. Even the weather matched his thunderous mood, for it was chilly and overcast.

He briskly entered the marble lobby of his building almost at a run, calling to the two women in the elevator, "Hold the elevator, please!"

To his chagrin, they didn't seem to hear him, and so he ran toward the elevator, hoping to catch their attention. He was too late, and the doors closed just as soon as he approached.

He stood there for several seconds, his mind racing furiously.

Wait a minute … wasn't that … ?

No, it couldn't be …

Strangely enough, he could have sworn that one of the women in the elevator resembled the attorney he'd met from Los Angeles. What had her name been?

Sarah Morgan.

But that was impossible, after all. The conference had been over weeks earlier. No doubt she was back in California, and this other woman had merely resembled her.

Another elevator opened, and when he was whisked up to

the twelfth floor, where the Law Offices of Heller and Strauss had conducted business for over a decade, he promptly forgot all about the woman in the elevator.

As he strode down the corridor toward his office, an elderly custodian pushing a trolley cart filled with cleaning supplies stopped in his tracks and grinned at him broadly.

"Shalom!" he exclaimed.

"Shalom," Peter mumbled, wondering how in the world Ray Adams had managed to inform the entire building of his trip. Subtlety had never been one of Ray's finer attributes.

"Welcome back!"

"Welcome back, sir!"

"Hey, buddy, how are ... you?" Ray looked at him questioningly.

Peter walked around the office, shaking hands, thanking everyone for their good wishes.

But when he dutifully said, "It's great to be back!" the words sounded hollow and insincere.

Was it great to be back? He certainly didn't feel celebratory as he made his way to his private corner office, greeted by stacks of work on his desk ... and was it his imagination, or did his entire staff seem to be staring at him?

He wearily shut the door to his office and sat down with a thump behind his desk. Everything looked familiar, from the broad mahogany desk in the center of the room to the gleaming artwork on the walls. His gaze took in the many certificates on the wall, his diplomas from institutions of higher learning and the many awards and plaques he'd received for his firm's philanthropic and communal work.

He was already forty-five years old, and his forty-sixth birthday loomed ahead. He knew that he'd accomplished much in his life, but for some inexplicable reason, it didn't seem to fill a newly discovered void within him.

A void that he'd never been aware even existed. His trip to Israel had been an awakening, and waves of self-doubt had begun a ripple effect.

For the first time in his life, he resented the pile of work on his desktop, and it confused him. Work used to feel fulfilling and productive, and now it just seemed annoying and burdensome.

His thoughts were interrupted when Ray Adams knocked on his door, and then bounded in before Peter could even muster the words, "Come in."

Ray was never big on social pleasantries, but it had never bothered Peter in the past.

"Okay, Peety-boy, we've got a problem in the Monagrane case," Ray began, sitting his small, wiry frame in one of Peter's oversized chairs.

"Which case?"

"Monagrane Industries, you know, the shareholders, remember?"

"Oh, sure, sure," Peter muttered.

"Anyway, would you believe that Judge Karakas wants to prohibit two key witnesses from testifying? I have a corporate securities expert and an accountant. I tried every argument I could think of, and it all fell on deaf ears."

"What was his reason?"

Ray paused. "He said that Lee Ross was dilatory in providing witness identification to Monagrane's attorneys."

"Well, was she?"

"She's been going through a nasty divorce, man, I don't

know … maybe she missed a deadline. Still, Judge Karakas has it in for us! This is huge! What do you think I should do?"

Peter was quiet for a minute, pretending to mull it over. Truth be told, he could hardly bring himself to care about the outcome of the case.

"I guess just go ahead with whatever you've got. When is the trial?"

Ray stared at him disbelievingly.

"You're not serious, are you? The Monagrane case … hello? The trial is next month!"

"Sorry, I guess I'm a little jetlagged … anyway, just go ahead. In any case, you don't have much choice, do you?"

"I guess not," responded Ray slowly. His ever-sharp eyes fixed on Peter, missing nothing.

"Okay," he began. "This is Ray you're talking to, buddy. Spill it. There is something going on and I want to know what it is."

"What do you mean?"

"What do I mean? I'll tell you what I mean." He took a deep breath, as if unsure how to proceed. "The Peter I used to know would have had the Judge's clerk on the phone this minute, trying to see what could be done. The big Peet-O I used to know would be trying to file a last-minute motion, anything, to desperately try and salvage the situation. And here we are, you're as calm and cool as a cucumber, telling me to go ahead with what I've got … and I've got nothing!"

Peter wearily massaged his sudden aching temples.

"Ray, what do you want me to say?"

Ray just looked at him, waiting.

"All right, I'll admit, I'm a little … out of sorts this morning. It's my first day back, it was a twelve-hour flight … my daughter is still there …"

"Is that the problem? She's still in that cult, isn't she?"

"IT'S NOT A CULT."

"Whoa, whoa … sorry." Ray narrowed his eyes. "Wait a minute, wait just one little minute … that's it. Oh, man! They got to you, too. They got you, didn't they?"

Peter chuckled, but the faint flush that crept into his cheeks belied his mirth.

"You didn't answer the question," Ray said accusingly, watching Peter closely.

"Come on, Ray, give it a rest … we're here to run a law firm, not to discuss religion, remember? Do you want me to call Judge Karakas' chambers? Would that make you feel better?"

Ray got up from his chair and reached into his wallet. He pulled out a business card from the billfold and handed it to Peter.

"I'll call Karakas if you call this number."

Peter looked at the card. "Karen Hayes? Who is that?"

"Some sort of shrink. My ex has been hounding me to go for years. Dude, it might help to talk to somebody …."

"Why in the world would I need to see a psychiatrist? I'm exhausted from a long trip, but I'm not crazy. What's with you?"

Ray held up his hand. "Don't take it the wrong way, buddy. It just might help to talk this over, that's all. I'm being your friend. I think you … just might … need to talk … to a professional."

It was at that moment that Peter's eyes followed Ray's, and understanding was beginning to dawn on him. Ray had been staring at the top of his head.

Peter felt his face flame with embarrassment as he reached up to the top of his head, mortified to discover *that he was still wearing the* yarmulka *that Danielle had given him.*

No wonder everyone had been gaping at him … and the custodian …

"Ray, I can explain …" he began.

Again, Ray held up his hand. "No need, buddy. This is America, and you can do what you want."

"You don't understand …."

"Whatever. Live and let live, right? It doesn't change anything between us."

"It's just that Danielle …"

"Just call the number. Talk to the lady, really, my ex swears by her. Of course, my ex has always been deranged, but who knows? Maybe she's right about this shrink. Better yet, you can go down and make an appointment. She's in our building, fourth floor. It's all about convenience, buddy."

"But …"

"Don't mention it, any good friend would do the same …."

"But I just … Danielle gave it to me as a gift, I was just trying it on …." Peter sputtered, to no avail.

Ray had already left his office.

Peter sat down in his chair with a thump, the embarrassment he'd earlier felt swiftly replaced by indignation.

Of all the nerve … a psychiatrist, for goodness sake … it's a free country, after all … people are entitled to wear whatever they deem appropriate ….

Another thought occurred to him. He was the senior partner, and he could wear whatever he felt like wearing, and no one could tell him otherwise. Why in the world did he feel the need to apologize? What purpose did it serve?

He leaned back in his chair, grinning to himself.

He left it on.

CHAPTER 13

Sarah breathed deeply in the crisp Chicago air as she walked. Huddled in Anne's old down jacket, she nestled into its warmth as she continued her walk around the quiet streets. The weather was much nicer than it had been on that first Monday when she'd traveled downtown to meet Dr. Hayes for the first time. Her fears had been unfounded, she'd been pleased to discover. They'd had two sessions since then, each Monday, and the meetings had gone quite well. They'd discussed many diverse topics, and to her extreme relief, Dr. Hayes had turned out to be a very thoughtful, calming influence. There had been one particular point, however, that Sarah had found intriguing, and it was this point that she kept returning to in her mind. She was pleased to realize that she could recall their last conversation, word for word.

"When will my memory return?" she'd asked.

"I like to think of the mind as a vast ocean," Dr. Hayes had answered. "Memories are like tiny ripples, floating along. One day soon, I predict, something will trigger those dormant ripples, and before long, waves of memories will flood you. I've seen it happen, trust me."

"But what will trigger it?"

"It's difficult to say because it differs from person to person." Dr. Hayes had gazed at her over the rims of her small glasses, which were perched on the end of her nose. "There is almost always a trigger, though. Something that acts as a conduit to transport you back to the life you once knew."

"What if the life I once knew wasn't as good as the life I have now?" Sarah burst forth.

Briefly, no one spoke. Shocked by her own admission, Sarah's mind raced.

Could Dr. Cooper have been right? Is it that she just didn't want to remember? Surely, it was impossible ... it just couldn't be.

Sensing Sarah's confusion as if she were able to discern every word of her inner dialogue, Dr. Hayes just smiled and nodded, knowingly, waiting for her to continue.

"I just feel so ... conflicted," admitted Sarah slowly. "At the beginning of all of this, all I wanted was to remember my name, who I am, where I live, my family ...."

"Don't you still want that?" asked the doctor, gently.

"Of course I do," Sarah stated unequivocally. "It's just that ... that ..."

"Why do you feel conflicted? What's changed?"

"I – I've changed," stammered Sarah. It was so hard to put her tumultuous feelings into words, to verbalize aloud how the tremendous influence of staying at Anne's house these past two weeks had impacted her very soul.

"Anne is a religious woman, Orthodox ... and being at her home these past two weeks has really ... I mean, I don't know all that much about being observant, of course ... still, I just know that I never ... I mean, before ... it's hard to explain ...."

Dr. Hayes gazed at her thoughtfully.

"Anne's Orthodox way of life appeals to you, then?"

"Yes, yes, very much," agreed Sarah.

"Now, let me see ... since you weren't observant before, this leaves you at a crossroads. Once you begin to recall your past, you'll leave Anne's home and return to your former life. I'm sensing that this is causing you some anxiety, leaving this newfound knowledge behind. Is that correct?"

"I ... I guess so, yes."

"How can you be certain that you weren't observant before the accident, if you truly can remember nothing from your past?"

"I just know that I was completely secular ... organized religion of any kind is so foreign to me. Anne has had to explain literally everything ... believe me, I just know."

How could she possibly explain the profound joy she'd experienced when Anne had lit the Shabbos *candles, a joy that was so deep, she had wept from the sheer beauty of it ....*

How could she explain the sense of heightened awe she'd become accustomed to when Anne's son would recite the blessings at the Shabbos *table ...?*

It was inexplicable, to be sure, how of late her thirst for details of the past had become tempered with a thirst of a different kind.

"Fair enough." Dr. Hayes paused. "Why couldn't you continue learning about your religion, then, say, after you've healed? Why do you need to live in Anne's house to pursue this?"

That idea hadn't occurred to her. Somehow, in her mind, religion seemed intertwined with Anne Lewis, but all at once she realized how naïve and simplistic that was. Discovering more about Judaism wasn't something that couldn't be achieved on her own one day, if she was so inclined.

"You know, many patients take up yoga or needlepoint when

they're going through a particularly trying time," she continued. "And after that time has passed, many of them keep up with their newfound interests … what's the harm in that?"

"That's true," she said, although she knew in her heart that an interesting hobby wasn't the same as taking on a life-altering religious commitment. "I just wish I knew when …"

"Like I said before," continued Dr. Hayes, "it's impossible to predict when it'll happen. I truly believe, though, that in the days and weeks to come, more memories will return to you. Look how far you've come in this short amount of time. Let things unfold naturally … try not to be overly concerned about it, and it'll come on its own."

Sarah mustered a laugh. "I'm sorry, but that sounds impossible. I'm always on edge, Dr. Hayes. Everything is so up in the air, I just wish I could plan what will happen next."

"Okay. I'd like you to repeat what you've just said."

"Everything is so up in the air, I just wish I could plan what will happen next," she repeated.

"Classic type-A," murmured the doctor. "It's a common malady, this propensity for scheduling one's life. You'd be a lot less apprehensive if you realized the futility of planning. I know I could get into a whole lot of trouble for saying this, but an excess of prearranging is usually a waste of time."

"How can that be? People have to plan ahead," insisted Sarah. "How would things ever get accomplished?"

The doctor smiled knowingly. Sarah couldn't help but wonder if she was steering the conversation in such a way to uncover some deep, hidden truths about her, or if she truly meant what she said.

"Okay. Let's say … oh, I don't know … we're planning a picnic, the two of us. And we plan. We plan everything, who brings the food, who brings the drinks, everything. And then, when all of our best-laid plans are complete, and it's twenty minutes before I'm supposed to drive over to pick you up, I get an important call. A patient of mine is having a crisis and I can't go, after all. See what I mean?"

"But the picnic can be postponed," offered Sarah. "All the plans weren't for naught, were they?"

"They weren't for naught exactly, but they weren't helpful in the end, either. There are so many variables ... planning ahead doesn't always guarantee that things will work out. The point I'm trying to make is to try and relax, and let the natural course of events take over. The point is, stop fighting so hard to be in control."

"Lately, I've been tied up in knots," confessed Sarah.

"I don't doubt it, and who is it helping?" Dr. Hayes wanted to know. "I can prescribe some medication to help with your anxiety, but really, I think some good old-fashioned time is all you need."

"I'd rather not take anything."

"All right, then, let's just see how it goes. Since our time together is nearly up, I have two assignments for you for next week. First, keep writing in your diary every day, no exceptions. And second, take a walk every day. It will calm your mind and relax your spirit."

"A walk? You mean, outside?"

"Of course I mean outside. Why? Does the idea of being outdoors still frighten you?"

Sarah thought of the black Mercedes that had appeared to stop in front of the house on more than a few occasions. Anne had said that its owners probably lived in the neighborhood, and Sarah assumed she had been correct. Surely, there was nothing sinister awaiting her. Perhaps walking in the neighborhood would prove that.

"Not really, I guess not."

"Good. A brisk thirty-minute walk a day would do wonders for you. I'll see you next Monday."

The conversation had been played and replayed in her mind so many times that week, Sarah was able to recall each word verbatim. And, true to her word, each day she had ventured out and toured the lovely Lincolnwood neighborhood, just like she was doing at that very moment. To her utter surprise, these outings had become rather pleasant. Sarah had been pleased to discover that although Chicago's winters were brutally cold, the sun still shone most days, and the sky had remained clear for most of the week.

No strangers had bothered her on these walks. In fact, there were scarcely any people about the quiet neighborhood. It had given her time to think, to reflect. She knew she couldn't stay at Anne's home forever, as comforting as it was. Anne's son was to be married in ten days' time, and after the wedding, Sarah knew that she'd have to make some very concrete decisions regarding her future.

She was just strolling back on Monticello Avenue toward Anne's house when she saw it.

A black Mercedes with dark tinted windows, driving ever so slowly down the street, pausing in front of Anne's house.

Was it her imagination, or could she make out the driver leaning forward, trying to look into the large picture window in the front of the house?

Suddenly, she experienced a wave of anger. She was so *tired* of feeling afraid. Boldly, without thinking, she broke into a run, sprinting toward the car. She wanted to ask the driver what about Anne's house had him so curious, and why he was looking through the windows.

But then the driver, whose face was obscured under a large hat, saw her coming and quickly sped down the street and out of view.

Sarah paused by the curb, her heart racing, but otherwise feeling invigorated. Instead of being frightened, she had wanted to confront her fears and face them, head-on. The cowardly driver didn't stand a chance against her.

For the first time in weeks, she felt stronger, more confident.

She was healing, she knew, and it felt wonderful.

When she entered the house, she was greeted with the unmistakable smells of *Shabbos'* impending arrival, which buoyed her spirits even more.

She hurriedly went to tell Anne about what had happened.

FRIDAY, THE SAME DAY
3:45 P.M.
HELLER AND STRAUSS, LLC

Peter Strauss was feeling miserable. Every bone in his body seemed to be on fire. His neck and shoulders ached, his throat felt dry, his eyes burned and he couldn't stop sneezing. Everything seemed to be moving in slow motion. Peter sat at his desk, staring at the same stack of papers for hours on end.

Answers to interrogatories were tedious and dull but needed to be completed, all the same. He leaned back in his chair and closed his eyes. A second later, he quickly opened them when Ray came bursting in the door.

"Oh, man, you look awful!" he exclaimed.

"Thanks."

"I think you're coming down with something."

"I never get sick," mumbled Peter.

"Everyone is entitled to break a rule now and again," grinned Ray. "Go home. The day is almost over, anyway."

"No. No home." Peter muttered.

"Look, buddy, you're out of it. Now, go home before we all catch it. Really, I insist."

"Yes, Mother," replied Peter.

"Maybe you picked something up in Israel. I'm telling you, man, you've got to go home and sleep it off. It's Friday afternoon, you can take it easy the whole weekend."

"No sleep," murmured Peter, a hand over his stinging eyes. "Work to do."

"Look at you. You can hardly form a coherent sentence. Go home."

Peter opened his eyes. "First you want me to see a psychologist. Now you want me to leave."

Ray laughed. "I just think you're falling apart at the seams, dude. You need to take better care of yourself."

Peter was feeling so poorly that he didn't have the strength to argue.

"Fine, I'm going," he grumbled. He gathered his papers, stuffed them into his briefcase and unsteadily rose from his chair.

"Whoa, careful, there," Ray said. "You look like you might be running a fever."

"I've never had a fever in my life," insisted Peter.

He made his way out of the office, calling over his shoulder, "I'll see you on Monday."

Ray just looked after him, shaking his head.

The ride home was interminably long. His head throbbed, and it felt as if there was a fiery dragon behind his burning eyes. He drove slowly in the right-hand lane, allowing impatient drivers to pass him by.

What's wrong with me? he wondered. He hadn't felt quite like himself since he'd returned from his trip, but nothing like this … he was really feeling quite ill.

Finally, after what seemed an eternity, his car turned into the graceful curve of his paved driveway, and he lurched unsteadily from the car, loosening his tie as he stumbled toward the house.

Mercifully, Gilda was at the house, and she quickly opened the door when she saw Peter's car.

"Mr. Strauss, are you all right? What's happened?" exclaimed the alarmed housekeeper. "Is it Danielle?"

"No, no, Danielle's fine," Peter managed. "Just feeling sick … going to bed …"

"Let me help you," offered Gilda.

"No, no … I'll be okay … just need to lay down for a while."

It was a supreme effort for Peter to walk up the winding staircase, but at last he found his room and stretched out on top of his bed without even pausing to kick off his shoes.

Now that felt a bit better … putting his hand over his blazing eyes, he would've been able to relax a bit if it had not been for the furious pounding in his head. He felt shivery and cold, all at once. He was loath to move from his position, but he wanted to get under the covers, to nestle into their warmth. He suddenly realized that he was freezing … his teeth actually started chattering.

"Gilda?" he called out, chagrined to realize that his voice was barely above a whisper.

He couldn't ever recall feeling so ill.

Gilda peeked into Peter's room, never having done so before, knowing how her employer cherished his privacy. Still, the situation warranted it, and Gilda, years earlier, had gone to nursing school, though she'd never quite finished.

"Yes, Mr. Strauss? Can I get anything for you?"

"A blanket," he responded, his teeth chattering uncontrollably. "I'm cold."

"You're running a fever, I'm afraid," she replied. "I'll bring you some Tylenol, as well."

She quickly left the room, and before long returned with blankets, fresh towels, several bottles of water and a container of fever-reducing medication, which she left on his nightstand.

He suddenly felt so helpless. What would he have done if his loyal, trusted housekeeper hadn't been there?

He realized in a rush just how indebted to her he was.

The last thought he had before falling asleep was that she deserved a raise ....

He awoke, disoriented, wondering why the room seemed so hot. He then realized that in all probability it was his own fever that was the cause of the uncomfortable heat.

What time was it?

He leaned over and looked at the small clock on the night-stand, shocked to discover that it was nearly eleven o'clock at night.

He'd slept for nearly six hours straight.

Although he realized that he was still making up the lost sleep from his trip, the dull pounding in his head told him that he was, in fact, sick with some sort of miserable cold or the flu.

He ached all over and his throat felt dry. He felt so congested, it was hard to breathe. He blew his nose and wiped his streaming eyes. It even hurt to lean over and open the bottle of pills that Gilda had left for him. Swinging his legs over the side of the bed, he made a supreme effort to open the small jar. He swallowed two of the pills, followed by a long swig of cool water from a bottle on his bedside.

He could barely recall the last time he'd been ill, it had been so long ago.

He got up from bed slowly, annoyed that he'd slept in his good suit. It was crumpled beyond recognition. The phone rang. He slowly reached over to grab the receiver, when a thought occurred to him.

His hand paused in mid-air.

Wait a minute. Wait just a minute.

What had Danielle said?

They'd been fishing … they'd been talking … Dan Cohen had talked about *Shabbos* … he'd said that he'd often brought home work to do over the weekend … work just couldn't stop … and Danielle had said …

What if you had a nasty cold?

Would you answer the phone then?

So, you'd be willing to let the phone ring in case of a cold, but not for the Shabbos *Queen?*

And what had he answered?

I honestly couldn't say, honey. I've never been sick a day in my life!

In the darkness, he smiled to himself.

It was *Shabbos.* He, in fact, was sick in bed with a nasty cold.

And the phone would have to wait.

He slowly got up from the bed and made his way to the walk-in closet on the other side of the room. It was a bit hard to navigate around in the dark, but he didn't dare turn on a light.

Was this was some sort of a test? If so, he fully intended to pass it.

Somehow, the timing of his illness didn't seem coincidental, especially after the conversation they'd had. According to Dan Cohen, nothing in this life was ever coincidence anyway … it was all part of a Divine plan.

He could almost picture Ray Adams, howling with laughter.

What would he say?

Divine plan? Dude, you're an easy mark! You caught a bug! There were hundreds of passengers on the plane, and you picked up something nasty! You can't possibly believe that stuff, can you?

It didn't make any sense, he knew.

There had to be some logical, reasonable explanation behind all the fanciful thinking.

But what if … ?

A stubborn, niggling voice inside his head told him otherwise. And once again, he could hear Ray Adams' mocking voice.

You can't possibly believe that stuff, can you?

But he did.

Inexplicably, he believed it. All of it.

He opened the door to his room, allowing the light from the hallway to illuminate his darkened closet. He chose an old pair of pajamas and hurriedly got back into bed. He'd gone from being overheated to feeling freezing once more. He got under the covers, trying not to let his teeth chatter, and waited for the medicine to take effect.

It was going to be a long night.

He awoke hours later, drenched with sweat. Shaking off the heavy quilts, he was glad to discover that he felt remarkably better. The dull throbbing in his head had receded, and he felt less achy and chilled. He leaned over once again to check the clock. This time, the clock read nearly five o'clock in the morning, and he felt rested and awake. He hadn't slept so much in … well, years.

The room was still blanketed in darkness, and he was alone with his thoughts.

He'd already made up his mind that he wouldn't answer the phone the entire day. He fully intended to take the day off.

He was sick, after all. He had an excuse.

Work would just have to wait … the world at large would just have to wait ….

He closed his eyes once more.

And that's how it, indeed, turned out. Peter sat for hours that day propped against the enormous pillows, taking occasional sips from his water bottle, all the while leisurely reading *The Book of Why, When, and How.*

He was completely immersed in the book and could not recall reading something that so captivated his attention.

It was as if someone had just handed him a golden key to a new world that he'd never known existed … there was just so much to know … so much to learn ….

It was disconcerting to discover how totally unaware he'd been of his roots, his history, his people. It was stunning to realize that his daughter, Danielle, at such a young age, had grasped onto something so vastly different from anything that she'd known as a child.

It was further interesting to him that he'd previously viewed religious people as being alienated and out of touch with reality.

The irony was not lost on him that now it was he who felt alienated and out of touch. Although he considered himself to be an educated man, he couldn't help but feel woefully ignorant in these matters.

It wasn't a reassuring feeling in the least, and he was unaccustomed to feeling vulnerable. Still, he knew that in the current age of instant information, it couldn't be all that difficult to learn more, if he so chose.

He took several cat naps, and late in the day, he got up, stretched and walked around, relieved to be feeling stronger, more like himself.

As the sun dipped lower and lower in the sky, he felt better and better. And as the first stars emerged in the night sky, another thought occurred to him.

It was the first time that he'd kept *Shabbos.*
And it felt wonderful.

SATURDAY NIGHT, MARCH 7
11:45 P.M.

Maria Ramirez was a tortured woman. Ever since taking the diamond ring out of an abandoned pilot's case nearly a month prior, she had been plagued by guilt. And, even worse, as of late she'd had a few scares. Her two-year-old son had been having recurring nightmares. "Night-terrors," the pediatrician at the clinic had told her, but Maria was convinced that it was a bad omen. A chilling sign from above that her deed had not gone unnoticed.

Additionally, her elderly mother who lived with her had been having recurring stomach pains, and she would often moan in her sleep. Maria had not slept a full night in what seemed to be ages. Carrying her secret burden had become too much, and she knew she would find no rest until she made things right.

Walking along the deserted corridor in the bowels of the hotel, she kept glancing around her to make absolute sure that she wasn't being followed or watched.

There was no one in sight as she stealthily made her way toward the Fairmont's Lost and Found Room.

She opened the door with her key and turned on the light.

It was exactly where she'd last seen it, a beautiful Louis Vuitton leather pilot's case, pushed into a corner of the dusty room. It was truly amazing how many items had accumulated there over the years.

Maria wondered if any of the belongings were ever reunited with their owners.

No matter. She came on a mission and the deed had to be done.

She slowly withdrew the glittering diamond ring from the starched pocket of her apron, opened the side pocket of the luggage and replaced it back exactly where it belonged.

She zippered the pocket once more, murmuring under her breath, "I have learned my lesson, and I have now returned the evil thing. I will never again take what is not mine ... please make my mother better, and please take away the awful nightmares from my little boy ...."

She closed the light and walked into the dimly lit corridor of the hotel. A heady feeling of sweet relief flooded her as she walked down the hallway, her stride more confident with each passing step.

She was certain that her error in judgment had been forgiven and all would soon be well once more.

CHAPTER 14

As soon as Sarah awoke, she was aware of a feeling of anticipation that somehow pervaded the air. At first, she couldn't pinpoint what the excitement was about, since she was still shaking off a murky sleep. After several seconds, however, she knew.

It was David and Aliza's wedding day.

She was attending, of course, as Anne's special guest. There would be crowds of people there, but to her extreme relief, she wasn't experiencing much trepidation about venturing out into such a public venue. Weeks earlier, the very thought would've been enough to cripple her with extreme anxiety.

She knew she had come very far in her recovery, and for that she was profoundly grateful. True, she had declined attending the synagogue on *Shabbos* for David's "*aufruf*," when he would be called to the Torah in honor of his upcoming wedding, but that had been more out of compassion for Anne than from her own fears. Anne's oldest son, Aaron, his wife, Rachel, and their child were to be in attendance, having flown in from Israel late Thursday evening. Sarah secretly wanted Anne to enjoy her children's precious reunion, unencumbered with having to think about anything or anyone else. And so she'd stayed home, happily. Anne had been gone for hours, and it had warmed Sarah to see the delight that was plainly evident on Anne's face when she returned home late in the day, carrying Eli in her arms.

"Goodness, you're getting too heavy for your old grand-mother," she'd laughed as she set him down in the foyer.

He had stared at her, all big brown eyes and fair hair.

"Who dat?" he asked.

"This is my friend, Eli," she'd explained.

"Hi, there," Sarah had said with a smile.

He had returned the smile and then ran to the toy box that Anne had kept in the corner of the room, awaiting his visit. His parents had joined them later in the day, and she'd been thoroughly impressed with each of them, as well. They had been interested without being inquisitive, besides being genuinely friendly and non-judgmental.

It was not the first time that the thought crossed her mind that Anne had done a remarkable job raising her children, and she had found herself wistfully wondering if she would ever get that chance, one day ....

Shabbos had been beautiful, once again, and afterwards she'd felt twinges of melancholy that were soon replaced with the knowledge that at the end of the coming week, *Shabbos* would visit them once more.

She found herself humming as she got dressed, eager to attend her first Orthodox wedding. Of course, she couldn't be absolutely certain that she'd never before attended an Orthodox ceremony, but she highly doubted it.

In any case, she was well-prepared. The stacks of books on her nightstand, which she had devoured, had discussed many aspects of the Jewish wedding, from the ceremony to the many customs afterwards. It was still astounding to her that there was so much ... and every small ritual was suffused with so much meaning.

She had read with wide-eyed wonder all about the wedding

canopy, the *chuppah*, and how it symbolized the Jewish home ... how the breaking of the glass symbolized the destruction of the Holy Temple ... how even at times of joy, it is incumbent on the Jewish people to remember that they are still in exile.

To Sarah, every aspect of Orthodox life was infused with beauty, and reverence.

She could hardly wait to witness it all and share in Anne's joy.

She went down the stairs at a brisk pace to find Anne at the kitchen table, eating her breakfast.

"Good morning," Anne said. "Did you sleep well?"

She'd asked the same question for the last several weeks, and it never failed to lift Sarah's spirits.

She knew that there was someone who genuinely cared about her well-being.

"Yes, thanks. How about you, Anne? Were you too excited to sleep?"

"Are you kidding? I slept like a baby!" she paused, grinning. "I woke up every two hours."

Sarah poured the cereal in her bowl, careful to say the blessing, in English, before she ate from it.

Blessed are you, Hashem, our G-d, King of the Universe, who creates species of nourishment.

They ate in companionable silence while Anne read the morning newspaper and Sarah read her well-worn copy of *Judaism: Reasons Behind the Rituals.*

"How many times have you read that book?"

Sarah looked up to see Anne peering at her above her small reading glasses that were perched on the tip of her nose.

"I've probably read it five or six times," she admitted. "I can't help it. Each time I read it, I find it fascinating."

"I'll have to get you some more books," murmured Anne.

"Oh, by the way, we're supposed to be at the hotel at one o'clock. The photographer wants to take some family pictures early, since it saves time later on."

Sarah nodded.

Aaron, Rachel and Eli were staying at the home of Rachel's parents, and they would meet at the hotel later on.

"Is Eli going to walk down the aisle?" asked Sarah.

Anne beamed with pride.

"I believe he is. Won't he look adorable?"

Sarah agreed, knowing how difficult it was for Anne to have her only grandchild live so far away.

"Do you think that maybe Aaron and Rachel would ever consider moving back here?" Sarah asked.

Anne sighed. "No, they wouldn't. Aaron teaches full-time in the Yeshiva, and Rachel just started teaching in a women's seminary in Jerusalem. They're so happy there, and they have such a meaningful life there … no, I wouldn't even dream of asking them. That's the place where they belong."

Anne's face took on a wistful look as she added, "It's the place where we all belong, after all."

Sarah hesitated, but then asked, "Would you ever consider moving there?"

"Of course. I think about it all the time, actually. If I would take an early retirement, that would be the ideal place for me. Other than David and Aliza, there is nothing keeping me in Chicago, as much as I love the city. And when David becomes a full-fledged Rabbi, chances are they won't remain in Chicago."

Sarah was incredulous. "But, but what about this house? It's your home …."

"It's just a pile of bricks," answered Anne, as she sipped her coffee.

"But what about your friends?"

Anne smiled at her. "I'll take them with me, in here ..." she pointed to her head, "and in here." And she pointed to her heart.

"And what about all your memories ...?"

"Exactly the same. I'll take them with me. And I'll make new ones, and that's the best part."

The phone rang just then, and while Anne took her call, a thoughtful Sarah walked into the den to begin her morning routine. It was surprising to learn that Anne had dreams of relocating to Israel, and that leaving everything behind didn't quite seem to bother her. In a way, it was yet another reminder to Sarah that she wouldn't be able to stay at Anne's house indefinitely, and the day was rapidly approaching when she'd have to make a decision regarding her future.

She picked up the prayer book and began her routine. She'd started it about a week prior, and each day she added to it. They were short morning prayers, and she recited them in English, but each time she held the book in her hands and uttered the words, she felt a connection to the One Above. That feeling gave her tremendous comfort, for she knew that her prayers were not a mere soliloquy ... but more like a dialogue.

Inexplicably, she felt that she was being heard, even ... even ... Answered.

THE SAME DAY
12:20 P.M.

"*It's time to* go!" Anne bellowed up the stairs as she rushed around, trying to remember last-minute items to take with them to the hotel.

Sarah came down the stairs, already dressed in the beautiful finery that Anne had given her. It was an older gown of Anne's, still quite fashionable with its brown long skirt foaming around her ankles. She had pulled her hair back with bobby pins, letting the rest cascade to her shoulders, and applied makeup with a deft touch.

"Oh, my goodness," breathed Anne. "You look absolutely gorgeous!"

"Thank you, Anne."

"Didn't you want to change at the hotel?"

"No, that's all right. I figured this way, if your daughter-in-law needs the dressing room, it'll be easier."

"That was very thoughtful of you," Anne remarked appreciatively.

Anne bustled around, gathering several items off the console table in the entry hall.

They took one final look around and quickly exited the house, their arms laden with Anne's gown, a wig box and a small suit bag.

It was all so exciting, really. Sarah felt more vibrant and hopeful than she'd had in a long time. The weather, as well, was mild and clear, with a sparkling blue sky and fluffy white clouds.

Anne got behind the wheel and backed out of the driveway, and they were off.

They didn't speak much on the ride downtown, for traffic was terribly congested and Anne kept glancing at the small clock on the dashboard. They still had plenty of time, for they had left the house earlier than necessary. Sarah was content to look at Lake Michigan on her left and the graceful curve of tall buildings to her right, overlooking the water.

"Chicago is a beautiful city," she observed.

"It certainly is," agreed Anne. "Of course, I've never lived anywhere else. I was born and raised here, and raised my children here."

Sarah looked down at her own bare fingers, knowing in her heart that she'd never had children.

She simply couldn't have. She refused to believe that she would've forgotten them if she'd had ….

At last they exited Lake Shore Drive, bearing right onto the glittering Michigan Avenue, and continued for several blocks until Anne turned the car into the wide driveway of the hotel.

"Here we are," she said brightly. "Welcome to the Fairmont Hotel."

There was something about the way she said those words that gave Sarah a startling notion of déjà vu. Had someone once said something similar to her, or was it her imagination?

Her eyes were drawn to the graceful columns of the hotel, the intricate carvings on the pillars, the wide arc of the driveway and the royal blue livery of the doorman who opened the car door for her.

As she exited the car, the strangest sensation came over her … it all just seemed so familiar ….

Her breath came in small gasps as she peered around her, wide-eyed.

She had been here before.

She knew.

"Dear, are you all right?"

She looked up and saw Anne observing her closely.

"I think I've been here before," she whispered.

Understanding dawned on Anne's face.

"All right, easy now … that's wonderful news," she reassured her, taking her by the arm and walking toward the lobby. "Little ripples, right? Isn't that what Dr. Hayes said?"

They walked into the lobby and Sarah stood glued to the floor, absolutely mesmerized.

A mural, painted in riotous colors, wove its way around columns, and even snaked its way on the high ceilings ... the galaxies, the Milky Way ... the sun, moon and stars ... the green grass, flowering shrubs, breathtaking birds and species of every kind of animal, from the smallest insect to the largest, a most magnificent elephant with gleaming white tusks ...

It was a breathtaking scene, to be sure, but Sarah knew that her heart's furious beating wasn't from the beauty of the painting. It was from the fact that she believed with absolute certainty that she'd stood in that same exact spot before, gazing at the mural from the identical vantage point ... but not quite identical. Now, it was not just visually beautiful but much more meaningful ... her own perceptions toward it had changed, that much was certain.

As if in a dream, she turned to her left, listening to voices that echoed within her ... voices that resonated with sounds so clear, she could practically hear them aloud.

Beautiful, isn't it?

It is, indeed. The six days of Creation, if I'm not mistaken.

Exactly. As a matter of fact, I've heard that there was quite a scandal when it was first unveiled.

Really? How so?

Well, you know how it is nowadays with religion. It's a touchy subject all around ....

There was more ... but the sounds faded away as she felt someone tapping her on the arm, and she looked to her right, where Anne was staring at her with concern.

"You look white as a sheet, dear. Let me help you ... let's sit down over there."

Sarah followed Anne to the elegant brocade chairs in the corner of the lobby where she sank down, her knees wobbly and weak.

"You remember, don't you?"

It was more of a statement than a question.

Sarah managed to nod.

"Do you recall your name?"

Sarah shook her head, swallowing, "No."

Anne looked at her, debated with herself and then said, "Look, I can't believe the timing .... I wanted so badly to be here for you, but they're taking pictures ...."

This time, Sarah found her voice. "Go, Anne, go. Your son needs you. I'll be fine, really."

"Are you sure?" she asked, doubtfully.

"Yes, I'll be fine. I'm a big girl." She smiled, hoping to belie her innermost feelings of anxiety.

Anne paused once more, then gave her a thumbs-up sign, patted her on the arm and walked toward the family members who had begun to gather in one of the hallways leading to the ballroom.

The ceremony wasn't for several more hours, but getting dressed, makeup and pictures would all take time ... Sarah knew that Anne would be occupied for most of the afternoon.

She was alone, once more, with her thoughts.

She was fearful of what she would recall next. Like Dr. Hayes had said, the memories had come in waves, growing more forceful each time. Suddenly, she recalled a childhood memory of standing in the ocean and feeling the force of the undertow.

Sarah was terrified of drowning if the waves washed over her too quickly ....

Now, she could easily picture the distinguished gentleman who had commented on the mural. She could readily see his dark hair flecked with tinges of silver at the temples, the expensive cut of his suit, the sincerity in his smile ....

What had his name been?

She couldn't remember.

After several minutes, when she felt a bit stronger, she got up once more and walked over to the mural, eager to admire its vivid details.

She stood there for quite a while.

There had been someone else, she realized, who had come to retrieve her from that very spot. A man had walked toward them, with wire-rimmed glasses and reddish hair.

I'm Rob McCann, the event coordinator. Would you come with me, please?

Sarah instinctively knew where to go, and following her imaginary lead, she walked toward the right part of the lobby and down a long corridor to the very end, to the massive doors on the left. She knew that the doors opened into a colossal ballroom, and so when she opened them, she was not surprised.

The room looked different than when she'd last seen it. Instead of a raised platform, there was a dance floor that had been placed in the center of the cavernous room, and round tables were being set in preparation for the wedding that would be taking place in a few hours. People rushed around, seemingly oblivious to her presence, each busy with tasks that needed to be completed.

She walked inside the room, propelled by some invisible

energy that was forcing her to confront her fears and simply ...
remember.

She stood in the middle of the room, waiting for the moment
when it would come rushing back, feeling ready at last. As
if she could hear them rushing toward her and building to a
crescendo, *let the waves come*, she thought.

It was the not knowing that was the worst ... she had to
remember ....

Standing still as stone, she allowed the waves to engulf her.

*There had been people, an audience, listening to her in rapt,
silent attention.*

She had been a keynote speaker at a conference.

She'd spoken about mergers and acquisitions.

She was an attorney.

*She had been at her best, speaking with an ease, an inner
confidence, that had since eluded her. She could well remember her
feeling of triumph ....*

As the memories started to recede, Sarah's cheeks turned
pink with shame.

Had she truly been so terribly smug, so incredibly ...
arrogant?

Sarah put her hands over her eyes, wanting to somehow
hold the turbulent memories at bay, at least for several
moments more.

"Excuse me, Ma'am, can I help you?"

Sarah opened her eyes. A dark-haired young woman was
looking at her inquiringly.

She found her voice, saying, "No, no ... thank you."

"Are you part of the wedding party?"

For a split second, Sarah didn't understand, for she'd
been so wrapped up in her own tumultuous thoughts, she'd

all but forgotten the wedding that was to take place in that very room.

"Yes, yes, I am."

"Well, I'm afraid we have to clear this room now. We need to set it for later, I'm sorry."

"That's all right, thank you," Sarah murmured, and turned to leave.

Just then a novel thought occurred to her.

Turning back to the young woman, Sarah asked, "Pardon me, but is there a Rob McCann who works for the hotel?"

The woman shrugged her shoulders.

"I just started working here last week, so I couldn't say. Maybe the front desk could help you."

"Thank you."

Sarah walked out of the room, her legs still a bit shaky. It was very frightening to her, knowing that she was on the verge of discovering the truth, and not knowing if she'd welcome the reality.

She'd have to face it, regardless.

She walked through the lobby once more. There was no sign of Anne, and Sarah knew that the family was taking pictures, getting ready for the big event.

Sarah had her own life to contend with … she could feel it. She felt as if she was dangling on the precipice of a very large rocky cliff, and she required the very last bit of rope to pull her to safety. She feared looking below her.

One wrong move would catapult her into the stormy waves crashing below.

She thought furiously about how to proceed. Taking a deep breath, she forced herself to walk to the front desk, trying desperately to appear calm, at least outwardly. She placed one foot before the other until she was at last there, facing the woman behind the granite counter. The desk manager was speaking on the phone, and she motioned for her to wait.

Sarah gazed at the opulent interior of the hotel. From the gleaming granite counter to the magnificent chandelier that hung above her head, she took it all in. It all seemed wonderfully recognizable, and she reveled in the familiarity, having missed the sensation for so very long.

After several seconds, the manager hung up, apologizing profusely.

"I'm so sorry to make you wait. The wedding party is taking pictures in the Grand Suite, located just past those doors on the left."

Looking down at her shimmering gown, Sarah realized that it was most obvious that she was here to attend the wedding.

"Oh, thank you," she mustered. "But, actually, I had a question ... is there a Rob McCann who works here?"

"The event coordinator? He should be attending the wedding party. Just a second, I can page him for you."

Before Sarah could think, the manager paged him to the front desk.

Sarah's heart began to pound. *What now?*

What could she possibly say?

Excuse me, Mr. McCann, but I have a dilemma. I can recall your name but not my own. Do you know who I am?

It was so ludicrous, it was almost laughable, she thought miserably.

Several minutes passed and there was no sign of him. She was about to breathe a sigh of relief, thinking that perhaps she'd been mistaken, or maybe it was his day off, when she heard footsteps tapping behind her.

She turned around and recognized the man walking toward her. He stopped when he saw her, thinking hard.

"Wait – don't tell me," he remarked. "I pride myself on being good with names …."

He thought for several moments before he snapped his fingers.

"Of course, Ms. Morgan, isn't it? Welcome back to the Fairmont."

She stared, transfixed, unable to move.

Ms. Morgan.

Her name was Sarah Morgan.

Only it had really been Morgenstern. Her father had changed it when he'd remarried ….

A shadow of concern crossed over his face.

"Ms. Morgan? Are you all right?"

She mumbled, "Yes, I'm fine, thanks." And she walked quickly away, completely unaware that her gait was still uneven and wobbly and that Rob McCann stood gaping after her, finding her behavior odd in the extreme, as if she'd had one too many drinks.

There had been a ladies' lounge down the left corridor, she knew, and she practically ran to it, closing the heavy wooden door behind her. She didn't notice the elegant room around her, she could barely realize where she was … for wave upon wave of long-forgotten memories were crowding her consciousness, and though she put her hands over her face, she could hold them back no longer ….

Her father was dead.

Her mother had abandoned her when she'd been a young child.

No wonder there hadn't been any family inquiring after her.

She had no family.

She thought of her elderly grandmother, who had been

living in an old-age home the last time she'd spoken to her, and wondered if she was still alive.

When had she spoken to her last?

The element of time was a fragment that was still missing. Sarah was still a bit confused as to how much time had elapsed since the start of her ordeal. Additionally, there were other details that she still found elusive … such as where she had worked … it was on the tip of her tongue, but she couldn't place it quite yet ….

She sank on the brocade settee in the corner of the lounge area and waited for her hands to stop their violent shaking. There was a gilded mirror opposite her, and Sarah caught her reflection. Her skin had taken on a greenish tinge, and she felt ill in earnest. Her whole being was shaking now, the room was spinning ….

Breathe. Just breathe, she told herself. *Don't panic … there is nothing to panic about … Anne is here … perfectly safe … just breathe ….*

She looked again in the mirror.

For once, it was not a stranger who peered back at her.

Never forget who you are, Sarala, dear.

Her grandmother's words reverberated in her mind.

She had forgotten, truly forgotten, for years.

The irony was not lost on Sarah that it had taken a complete loss of memory for her to finally awaken, and remember …

Remember who she really was.

Remember that she, Sarah Morgan, carried a Jewish spark within her that had lain dormant for ages, waiting to be reignited.

Would her life ever be the way it was before the accident? Did she even want it to be?

There was one thought that gave her tremendous solace … she couldn't change her past history, but she would be able to chart a different course in the years ahead.

She sat there for quite some time, reflecting mostly on the happy years she had spent at her grandmother's cozy apartment, recalling small, random events, when her trail of thoughts led her to the first time she had seen her grandmother lighting two candles on Friday night.

She had just been there two or three days after her parents had separated, and she was feeling lost and forlorn. She had walked into the small dining room, and saw her grandmother bent over two candlesticks, her eyes closed in concentration. It was a stirring sight, and it had given her a feeling of peace.

"What are you doing, Bubbie?" she'd asked.

"Lighting the Sabbath candles, my darling child. Every Jewish woman does on Friday night."

"Really? I never knew that."

Her grandmother had come over to her and put her arm around her.

"You'll see, Sarala, dear. One day, you'll have a home of your own, with children of your own, and you'll light Sabbath candles, too."

"How do you know, Bubbie? How can you be sure?"

She had smiled warmly.

"Bubbies have a way of knowing these things, and, yes, I am absolutely sure."

Sarah blinked. The memory had been so real, and now that it was starting to fade, she wanted to hold onto it for a while longer. Her grandmother had been so utterly certain, so perfectly sure ….

Sarah's eyes filled with tears. Her life had not turned out the way her Bubbie had so confidently predicted. She had no children, she had no home ….

Or did she?

Thinking furiously, she was able to picture a diminutive apartment with high ceilings and exposed brick … a sunny window over the small kitchen island, a tiny bedroom off the living area. She was the owner of a tiny loft in Santa Monica, and it had cost a small fortune.

How had she been able to afford it?

She must've been quite successful in her field, but she still couldn't recall where she had worked. It was hovering close, so very close, but she just could not quite grasp it.

Sarah stayed where she was for a lengthy stretch of time, grateful to discover that her breathing had finally returned to normal and her trembling had subsided.

She stood up, feeling calmer than before. She knew what she had to do.

She opened the door and walked into the lobby once more, relieved that Rob McCann was nowhere in sight. She walked over to the front desk, surprised to find that the woman who'd been there earlier had been replaced by an older man with a shock of gray hair, thick glasses and a genial smile.

"Can I help you, Ma'am?"

"Yes, I believe so," she began. "My name is Sarah Morgan, and I've stayed here before, for a conference. I was just wondering if you could perhaps look up the date of my last stay here. I can't seem to recall the exact date."

His eyebrows lifted a bit, but if he thought the request unusual, he gave no indication.

"Morgan, is it? Let's see …." He typed into a keyboard that was partially obscured by the large vase of flowers on the lustrous counter.

"Hmm … that's strange," he murmured after several minutes.

"Really?" Sarah leaned forward. "What's strange?"

"Well, it says here that you checked in on February 8th, and your checkout was scheduled for the 11th. But according to this, there's no record of your checking out. It must be a mistake. I'll take care of it straight away, Ms. Morgan."

He typed again into the computer, and as he did so, Sarah's mind raced.

It all made perfectly logical sense … of course she hadn't checked out, for she'd awakened in the hospital. She was startled, however, to hear that she'd checked into the hotel on the 8th of February. Today was March the 8th … could it be exactly one month to the very day of her trip to Chicago?

She'd truly believed that much more time had elapsed. It was positively staggering that so much had happened to her in a few short weeks.

The elderly man looked up, peering at her through his thick lenses.

"You're all set, Ms. Morgan. Your credit card has been charged accordingly."

"Thank you," she responded politely. "I have one more question, though. Is it possible that I may have left something here?"

"Excuse me?"

"Sorry, it's just that … I think I may have left something here that belongs to me. A piece of luggage, something like that, I believe. Where would I be able to find it?"

She was well aware that her query hardly made any sense; it sounded highly suspicious, in fact, and yet she hoped the elderly gentleman would be able to help her, nonetheless.

"Well, let's see," he said, scratching his head in confusion. "There's a Lost and Found room for that purpose, but guests of the hotel aren't allowed down there."

"Oh, I see," said Sarah, wondering what her next step would be.

The man continued, "I suppose if you'd describe the valise to me, I'd be able to send someone down to retrieve it."

What had her luggage looked like?

She found herself answering, "It's a Louis Vuitton pilot's case, and it should have my name on the tag."

The words had come out of her mouth so effortlessly, almost without thought, that it had surprised her. Little details were rapidly returning, she realized, as she sat down on an elegant chair to wait for her luggage to be brought to her. She could now easily picture her car, a blue Jaguar, which had been her pride and joy. She could well remember how important acquiring it had been to her at the time, and how ecstatic she'd felt the day she had driven it home from the showroom.

She had equated material assets with happiness; she had drawn parallels between prestigious possessions and true success. She had felt so powerful, so completely in control of her own destiny ....

Until she'd learned the hard way that she wasn't the one in the proverbial driver's seat. No, she'd learned that there was most definitely a Higher Power who had been doing the steering all along. Thankfully.

It was almost unimaginable that she had been so self-absorbed, so shallow ... had her thought processes really changed so drastically in one month's time? Had she changed so very much?

Miraculously, she had. And she didn't intend to lose sight of the lessons she'd learned. No, not this time around.

She looked up to see a young bellhop wheeling her pilot's case toward her.

"Ms. Morgan? Is this your bag?"

She stood up to retrieve it, thanked him and then thanked the elderly man at the front desk, who nodded amiably, glad to be of service.

She wheeled the pilot's case back to the ladies' lounge, eager to open its contents, yet filled with unease at the same time. She couldn't help but wonder if she'd find some elusive clues; namely, where she had been employed when she had come to the conference. To the best of her knowledge, it was the only information that was still missing.

The ladies' lounge was once again deserted, and she was glad to be afforded a bit of privacy. She knew that Anne must have been wondering as to her whereabouts all this time, but she had to discover the truth. She simply could wait no longer.

She unzipped the pilot's case and removed its contents. Although the case was deceptively small on the outside, the contents were considerable. She sifted through her sleepwear, a wrinkled outfit, a cashmere sweater, a pair of high-heeled shoes, a makeup case ... everything appeared to be here. Nothing seemed out of order.

She hastily stuffed it all back and zipped it shut. She then opened the small pocket on the side of the bag, reached her hand in and slowly drew out a brilliant, round diamond ring that glittered in her palm.

She stared at the ring, feeling waves of panic rising

uncontrollably within her. Beads of sweat broke out on her brow and the taste of bile rose in her throat. She leaned her head back against the cool marble tile, until the room stopped its nauseating spinning.

Of course. Of course. The final piece of the puzzle …

After years of toiling laboriously at a large law firm, and not advancing in the manner she'd wished, she had forged out on her own and started her own firm of Morgan-Sloane.

She had become engaged to Michael Sloane, a man who had treated her miserably.

A man who had mocked and belittled her. Repeatedly.

And, baffling though it was, she had all but convinced herself that he had been worth the ups and downs. After all, he was driven and ambitious, much like her. He'd proven himself to be a hard worker. Together, they would make Morgan-Sloane one of the premier law firms in southern California.

Or so she'd told herself. And it had almost worked.

Until … until …

Until his animosity had become too much to bear. She remembered hurrying down the slushy pavement, skidding in her high-heeled boots, tapping out the word O-ver, O-ver, O-ver ….

She had been crying. Again.

Michael had called her all sorts of names, slamming the phone down in disgust. They'd quarreled about work, about money … it no longer mattered, since they were always fighting; she'd been used to it, but that particular time had been different ….

He hadn't wanted her to be in charge, but the reality was that she, and she alone, owned the firm. He had threatened to quit, and then he did.

She had known that their stormy, volatile relationship was over, at last.

It seemed inconceivable that she had allowed herself to be subjected to such shabby treatment for so long. Why hadn't she ended it years earlier?

Sarah opened her eyes. She knew the answer, though it was difficult to acknowledge, even within the deep recesses of her mind. To her shame, she had been willing to sacrifice everything, even her own sense of self, at the altar of success.

Or what she had considered success at the time.

How wrong she'd been ... how ridiculously foolish ...

Michael Sloane was a non-Jew, she thought miserably. That fact alone should have stopped her in her tracks. Temperaments aside, they were worlds apart. How could that not have disturbed her at the time? Had she no pride in herself, in her heritage?

She knew that on some level, it must have bothered her ... she had hesitated in bringing him to meet her grandmother, offering one lame excuse after another.

Her cheeks burned with indignation as she suddenly realized that, in all probability, he hadn't cared a whit about meeting her grandmother in the first place.

He had just enjoyed tormenting her.

She placed the ring back into the folds of the side pocket, and this time drew out a cell phone in a small case.

She held it in her hands, thinking hard.

She couldn't hide out in the ladies' lounge much longer, or in Anne's comfortable home, for that matter.

She had to go back.

Besides the myriad business matters needing her attention, there was the matter of returning the ring, ending things for good. She wanted no part of her previous existence. In fact, she could hardly bear to think of the person she'd been, for it was still too raw, too painful.

However, she needed to face reality. In all probability, her office was in a shambles; she had been gone for a month. She knew that in all likelihood, her secretary, Sharon Pierce, hadn't been able to cope with very much.

She didn't relish the prospect of facing stacks of work, and yet she anticipated tackling it unencumbered, for once.

If Michael had followed through on his threat, he was long gone, having quit weeks ago, and it was a relief to know that she'd be able to handle things her own way.

Free at last ... free to keep growing, to keep learning ...

She'd made mistakes, so many mistakes, but she knew that at last she'd found the right path, and she was on her way ....

She placed the cell phone back, its battery long expired. After closing her case once more, she remained where she was for a lengthy amount of time, pulling herself together and mentally preparing herself for how she would tell Anne.

Anne ...

She had completely forgotten about the wedding. Glancing at her watch, she was shocked to find that it was after four o'clock ... hours had passed since she'd seen Anne leave to take pictures. It was unbelievable to her that only hours earlier, she'd had no recollection of who she was ... what was it that Dr. Hayes had told her ... ?

There is almost always a trigger ... something that acts as a conduit to transport you back to the life that you once knew.

As she left the room and walked through the lobby once more, she spied the mural, knowing that it had been the exact trigger she'd needed.

What would have happened if the wedding had been at a different hotel? Would she have remembered on her own one day, perhaps under different circumstances? Or would she have remained as she was, a guest in Anne's home, unaware of even her own name?

She couldn't help but feel humbled at the incredible turn of events. The One Above was watching over her, guiding her, prodding her to remember. She couldn't help but feel that all of the recent chaotic events had occurred for reasons that still remained to be seen.

Gazing at the beauty of the painting, she felt it was a symbol of sorts. The mural depicted the artist's beautiful and very inspired rendition of the beginning of time, and wasn't she embarking on her very own beginning?

She knew that her life of old was over. She'd been given a second chance, and she fully intended to embrace it.

"Would it be possible for me to leave my bag here? I'm a wedding guest," she explained to the same pleasant man at the counter.

He surely must've thought her peculiar, and her requests unusual, but he good-naturedly accepted the bag and placed it behind the counter, until after the festivities.

Sarah walked toward the ballroom that was adjacent to the lobby, following the strains of music.

People were already gathered, some clustered around small tables, eating hors d'oeuvres, while throngs were gathered in front of the lovely bride, who was seated on a white chair, looking radiant. Anne was sitting to her left, Sarah noticed, and another woman, ostensibly the bride's mother, was seated to her right.

Extremely relieved, Sarah realized that the crowd of people didn't frighten her. She realized that what had frightened her all this time was the dread of her unknown past. When she had finally confronted it, her other fears had simply vanished, and were of no consequence.

Making her way through the crowd, she sought out Anne, who had caught her eye and motioned for her to join them.

She stopped in front of Aliza, whose white gown glistened so brightly, she looked positively ethereal.

"*Mazel tov*, Aliza," she exclaimed. "You look so beautiful."

"Thank you," the young bride replied with a warm smile, and went back to receiving well-wishers.

Anne patted a chair next to her that seemed to materialize out of thin air.

"Sit next to me, dear," she shouted over the music, which seemed to be getting louder in volume. "They're coming any minute!"

"Who is?"

"David, to cover Aliza's face with the veil … I hear they're getting closer!"

"You mean, the *badeken*?" Sarah asked.

Anne was about to ask her how she knew the word, when they both laughed. Sarah had read up on the Jewish wedding ceremony at length; Anne found herself wondering if Sarah knew more than she did herself.

The men were getting closer, sure enough. The energy in the room was intensifying and was so exciting, it was palpable as Sarah leaned forward, eager to witness the dramatic moment.

David was soon in view, being led to his *kallah* by his many friends, who were singing and dancing joyously. He came forward and shyly draped the snowy white veil over the bride's face.

Then came the blessings ….

Aliza's father, a tall man with a white beard, came forward, and placing his hand over her head, he repeated the famous line said to the Matriarch Rivka.

Our sister, grow into thousands of myriads. May your children inherit the gates of their enemies.

He then proceeded to give her more blessings. Sarah was inordinately pleased that she recognized the *brachos* from the books that she'd read.

The Angel who has saved me from all evil, he should bless the children, and they should be called by my name, and by the names of my fathers, Abraham and Isaac; and they should become numerous in the midst of the land.

Sarah blinked back tears. She found the whole scene to be so spiritual, so moving, that she couldn't help but choke up. She'd never been to a wedding prior that had moved her to tears, but then again, this wasn't the sort of wedding she'd have attended in the past.

The men didn't linger after that; the band started up once more, and the singing from David's friends rose to a crescendo as they led the way before him, dancing him toward the other room, where the *chuppah* would take place.

In the midst of everything that was happening, Anne turned to her and whispered, "I can't take it anymore. You've got to tell me. Do you remember?"

"Yes."

"Everything?"

She replied simply, "Yes."

Anne exhaled, taking it in. "What is your name?"

She swallowed.

"My name is Sarah. Sarah Morgenstern."

Anne squeezed her hand.

Nothing more was needed, and as the crowd began to disperse, winding its way toward the *chuppah*, they stayed behind. Anne handed her a book of Psalms to say, wanting her to utilize that special time to beseech the One Above to bless her children with a long, healthy and wonderful life together.

Sarah opened her book and began to recite Psalms in English, with praise and humble thanks of her own, grateful tears now dropping freely from her eyes.

CHAPTER 15

She gazed around the lovely little room once more. It had been a large measure of comfort to her these past weeks, and she would miss it. The cheerful curtains on the windows that overlooked the yard gave her a feeling of security, of warmth. She checked around one last time, making sure that she hadn't forgotten anything behind. Anne had insisted on giving her several outfits, and she'd agreed, for they'd been modest, and Sarah knew that they would have to suffice until she could go shopping. She intended to buy a new wardrobe, for her clothing of old had become distasteful to her. Anne had found it interesting that the idea of long skirts and sleeves that fit past the elbow did not seem archaic or restrictive to Sarah. As a matter of fact, the idea appealed to her very much, for she knew that the signal she would send to the world was that she was modest and G-d-fearing.

No longer would she be a slave to society's views on fashion, and the thought was profoundly satisfying, even … even …

Liberating. Yes, she was free to serve her Creator in the manner of dress that was unpretentious and comfortable, and she could shake off the heavy albatross of societal norms for good. The irony was not lost on Sarah that she had previously equated the term *modest* with being meek, and she'd previously considered people who were unassuming to be downright submissive. She knew now that nothing could be further from the truth. Dressing modestly was her choice to make, and she knew that, if anything, it heightened her sense of self, her sense of purpose.

She silently said good-bye to the room, wondering if she'd ever see it again, knowing in all likelihood that she would not. Anne would one day sell the house and move to Israel to be near her children, and the house would have new inhabitants. She closed the door behind her and made her way down the flight of stairs, dragging her suitcase behind her.

Anne was seated at the kitchen table drinking a mug of hot chocolate.

"Good morning, Sarah," she began. "Did you sleep well?"

"Yes, thanks," replied Sarah, knowing how much she'd miss these morning chats with Anne. Anne had been like a mother to her, although in actuality their age difference made that impossible. Anne was only fifty years old, and Sarah had ascertained from her driver's license that she was thirty-six. Still, Anne had been so nurturing, so protective, that for the first time in her life, Sarah had felt as if she'd had a mother, and it had been wonderful.

Anne had helped her heal, body and spirit. Her confidence had returned, although it was tinged with a measure of humility, knowing how close she'd come to disaster.

She doubted that she'd ever have that smug feeling of superiority again, and she was thankful.

After completing her morning prayers, which were getting longer each day, she checked her bag once more and sat on the sofa in the living room to wait. Anne soon joined her and sat opposite her. Neither said much at first, and simply waited for the cab that was due to arrive any moment to take Sarah to O'Hare airport. Anne had offered to drive her, of course, but she had adamantly refused. The week of *Sheva Brachos* had been magnificent, but exhausting, and Sarah knew that Anne was simply drained. Anne had given her so very much; she just couldn't accept anything more.

Sarah looked around the familiar, cozy room. From the mantel covered with Anne's family pictures to the piano in the corner ... it had been her home for over a month, and it was wrenching to have to say good-bye.

As if sensing her inner dialogue, Anne asked, "Do you have your ticket?"

"Yes, it's an electronic ticket," she replied. "It's in my bag."

"Did you pack some food for the flight?"

"I ordered a kosher meal."

Anne smiled. "You know, Sarah, don't take this the wrong way, you know how proud I am of you, but ..." Her voice trailed off.

"I know what you're going to say, but it's just not like that."

"I don't want you to feel pressured into anything ...."

"You've never pressured me."

"I don't want you to feel obligated because you were in my home."

"Look, Anne," began Sarah. "I understand what you're saying, but it's not about feeling obligated. I want to do these things, really, I do. I want ... I need ... to find out more. I need to learn more about Judaism, so I can do proper *teshuva*, and become the person I was born to be."

Anne couldn't help but smile. "I'm so proud of you. Look how far you've come already."

"It's all thanks to you," said Sarah, simply.

"Not at all, Sarah. If I had anything to do with this, it was purely accidental." She pointed heavenward as she said this.

"*Hashem* put you there, at the right place, and at the right time," agreed Sarah.

"You've learned so much ... it's all happening so fast. I'm actually concerned that it might be too fast."

"What do you mean?"

"It's a life change, is all I'm saying," Anne reiterated. "It's not surprising that you feel this way here, but what about when you return home? You might discover that you feel differently than you originally thought, and I don't want you to ..."

"Don't worry," Sarah insisted. "I know that this is the right path for me. I just know it."

Anne looked thoughtful and nodded.

Sarah knew herself to be determined by nature, and when she put her mind to something, she was unwavering. She knew with every fiber of her being that this was not merely a lark, a quest she'd embark on without utter sincerity. No, she felt as if this journey toward *teshuva* was something that had been waiting for her, her absolute destiny.

She felt as if she'd been an understudy her entire life, waiting in the wings for the curtains to rise, only they never had ....

She felt that her previous life had been mere playacting; but she was now ready for her true lines, quite eager for her life to finally begin ....

This was extremely difficult to verbalize to others, even Anne, but she sensed that Anne understood her emotions, regardless. She'd been so stoic, so helpful to her the entire week, even with all of the *Sheva Brachos* preparations, even with Aaron and Rachel's departure, which was the hardest of all.

Sarah had been on the phone much of the week, making arrangements.

She'd called her credit card company, as well as her bank, to inquire about her finances. To her relief, everything appeared to be in order. She'd called Sharon Pierce, her secretary, but she hadn't answered, and the line had just rung repeatedly.

Sarah realized in all probability that Sharon had become too overwhelmed, having a self-esteem issue in the first place. She knew that when she returned, she'd have to hire new, more efficient staff. Poor Sharon.

The cab's horn jolted Sarah out of her thoughts. Anne had gone to the front door, remarking, "I think the taxi is here."

Sarah turned to Anne, suddenly at a loss for words. She'd been through so much, and Anne had been there every step of the way. She'd been a mentor, mother and friend to her, and it was difficult, if not impossible, to convey her appreciation. How would she ever be able to truly thank her for the many kindnesses that she had bestowed upon her? Sarah felt as if Anne had truly saved her life, spiritually as well as physically.

As if understanding all that was unspoken, Anne murmured, "First Aaron, Rachel and Eli had to leave, and now you, as well. The house will be so quiet, what will I do?"

There was nothing to say to that, and Sarah remained silent.

The cab honked once more.

"You really have to go, Sarah, the taxi is waiting."

"I don't know how I can ever –"

Anne held up her hand. "Don't say good-bye. We'll see each other again, I have no doubt."

"But I want to thank –"

"No need. I haven't done anything. It's I who should thank you."

"Oh, for goodness sake … for what?"

"For keeping me company. For keeping me occupied so I didn't have to dwell on the fact that my baby just got married … for addressing all those invitations … if not for you, none of the guests would have shown up!"

By that point, they were both laughing, mostly to cover the sadness they each felt at the thought that they would continue on their separate ways.

The cozy time that Sarah had spent at Anne's home had finally, inevitably, come to a close.

There were no words as Sarah hugged Anne with all of her might, unaware of the tears forming in the corners of her eyes.

The cab honked once more, impatiently, and Sarah walked down the steps, her pilot's case in tow. The driver placed her luggage in the massive trunk, and she opened the door, waving to Anne through the windows.

They waved to one another even as the cab drove away from Anne's house, and down the street.

Good-bye, Monticello Avenue … good-bye, Lincolnwood … good-bye my old self, she thought.

She had come to Chicago career-minded, but also materialistic and self-absorbed, and she was leaving the city quite the opposite. She had undergone the very beginnings of a life transformation, and she knew that in the days and weeks and years ahead, her growth would only continue. She knew that she'd always view Chicago as the place where it had all begun, and that this city would occupy a special place in her heart.

The cab sped down the expressway toward O'Hare, and Sarah's heart began to race in anticipation.

That feeling only intensified as they arrived, and after paying the driver, she exited the vehicle.

The airport was a colossal hub of activity, with people scurrying in all directions.

She waited patiently in line through security and then headed to the gate, wheeling her case behind her.

She easily found the gate and took a seat, already having printed out a boarding pass, eager to open her new copy of the book, *Finding Yourself: On the Path to Teshuva*, which had been a gift from Anne.

She opened it and read the inscription once more.

> *Dearest Sarah,*
>
> *Remember, one can never change the past … only look to the future. I wish you loads of* mazel *on your journey of* teshuva, *and remember that you are never alone. Hashem is always there as your ever-present, silent protector. I am here for you, as well. You know my number … please keep in touch.*
>
> *With love … Anne*

She closed the book, wanting to save it for the long flight ahead. Though it was a four-hour flight, she'd be gaining hours due to the time difference. She was due to arrive at eleven-thirty in the morning, California time.

Before long, they were boarding, and Sarah waited her turn with the other passengers. She had flown first-class on the way to Chicago and she'd had a limo service waiting for her at the airport, but she couldn't fathom the reason why. Did she consider herself royalty, a celebrity of sorts? Had she paid for such extravagances so she wouldn't have to associate herself with the lower class, with mere mortals?

This attitude now seemed not only foreign to Sarah, but even ludicrous.

She walked across the tarmac to the plane and found her seat. She held the precious book in her hands, itching to open to the first page and immerse herself in it. She held off, however, until after the take-off. While the plane taxied on the runway, she took out her copy of The Traveler's Prayer, and recited it in English.

Only after the plane had touched off the ground, climbing higher and higher, and Sarah had seen the tall buildings of the Chicago skyline fade in the distance, did she open the book and start to read.

An hour later, a flight attendant made her way down the aisle and leaned over. She apologized, "I'm sorry, Ma'am, but there has been a mix-up with your kosher meal."

Sarah looked up. "I beg your pardon?"

"I'm afraid that we can't offer the kosher meal to you, but you're welcome to have the first-class meal instead. It's our mistake. I do apologize."

Sarah didn't hesitate. "That's all right, thanks."

"Would you like the other meal? It's very tasty, I'm told."

"No, thank you. I'm fine, really."

"Can I get you a drink, then?"

"Ginger-ale would be great, thank you."

The smell of food all around her made her stomach rumble with hunger, but Sarah resolutely drank her soda, content to read her book the entire flight.

It was a marvelous read, and it had seemed to Sarah that the author was actually describing her. The author had managed to understand all of her deepest emotions, and connect with her on a personal level. She knew that she was not alone in her feelings, that many Jews from every walk of life would have similar experiences in their return to *teshuva*, though each person's circumstance would be different.

There was no timetable, for life was not a race. Naturally, the *teshuva* process took longer for some, while for others, the transformation was swift and absolute. There was so much to learn from the book that Sarah devoured it line by line, only stopping to dutifully write notes in the margins. She even left tabs on certain pages for future reference.

She hardly noticed when the plane began its descent into the Los Angeles area, but when the flight attendant spoke into the loudspeaker, Sarah returned her seat to its former position, reluctantly put down her book and stretched.

Glancing out the window, she recognized the thick brownish smog that enveloped the city like a tattered blanket, and wondered how she'd ever thought that the city was beautiful.

The plane touched down, and Sarah reset her watch to the current time. It was nearly eleven-thirty; they had arrived earlier than anticipated.

She followed the throngs of passengers off the plane, down the escalators and into the baggage claim area. There was no one there to greet her, not that she'd expected anyone.

The thought occurred to her that she had very few friends, having shunned close relationships of any kind in her all-encompassing pursuit of her career.

There was no one who had missed her absence, no one who had even noticed. It was a sobering thought, actually. Even if she'd achieved a modicum of success, with whom would she share it? Had the thought previously ever entered her mind? Had she ever thought of anyone besides herself?

She knew that there was one person for whom she'd cared a great deal. She thought of her grandmother in the nursing home, wanting desperately to see her.

After retrieving her luggage, she glanced at her watch, noting that it was still before noon.

She crossed the street to the airport's parking garage, and after getting a bit lost several times, finally spied her car, exactly where she'd left it.

Curiously enough, the sight of her car didn't hold any appeal to her. If anything, it brought back memories she longed to forget.

Although she was impatient to visit her grandmother, the urgency to see her mounting with each passing moment, she knew that there was one stop she had to make beforehand.

The time had come.

CHAPTER 16

Although Sarah felt a measure of relief that the vicinity looked familiar, and her car seamlessly navigated the streets almost effortlessly, she acutely realized that she was experiencing little joy at having returned home. She'd been away for over a month, not to mention going through a challenging ordeal; ordinarily under such circumstances, most individuals would be giddy with joy at having returned home. It seemed unnatural to Sarah that her surroundings held so little appeal to her. Had she ever really considered this to be her home, or was it merely the place where she lived? She was realizing the infinite difference between the two.

She headed east on Century Boulevard toward Santa Monica and turned left onto Wilshire Boulevard. After driving several blocks, she slowed down and turned the car into the lot adjacent to her office building.

She wondered what awaited her in her office. She envisioned stacks of paperwork piled high on her desktop, and Sharon Pierce knee-deep in files scattered over the floor, the phone ringing incessantly with clients who were demanding to speak with her. It was a disturbing scenario, and her pace quickened as she walked into the building toward the elevators.

She paced several minutes in front of the elevators, recalling that they were notoriously slow. Her office was on the third floor, and impulsively, she decided to walk up the stairs.

The stairwell was deserted, and Sarah quickly climbed the stairs and opened the door to her corridor on the third floor. She walked several steps toward her office, and then stopped dead in her tracks.

Her heart began to pound so violently she thought she would faint.

For there on the wooden door to her office, in gold lettering, was a sign.

Law Offices of Michael Sloane.

She dumbly stared at the sign, not quite comprehending, unable to grasp the ramifications of what she was seeing. She sagged against the wall for support, her breath rapid and shallow, furiously trying to think it all through.

It was a shock to her system, one of many that she'd endured in recent weeks. While it was blatantly obvious what had transpired in her absence, she still found it unfathomable, unthinkable. Never in her wildest nightmares had she ever thought she'd return to this.

Why had he done it? She knew the reasons ... all four million of them. That had been the firm's fee in the MeadowLane case, and there were countless other cases, just waiting to be settled.

Morgan-Sloane had been a gold mine. Michael Sloane had been greedy.

How could she have been so blind?

When she hadn't returned, he must have been beside himself with joy. Had that clouded his judgment? He couldn't simply have taken over her firm, for that would be tantamount to stealing her cases ... the very idea was so utterly unthinkable and unethical, even illegal. He could lose his license to practice law, should the proper authorities be notified.

On the other hand, he had practically gotten away with it. She'd been stowed away in Chicago, suffering from memory loss. Who in the world would have ever realized? Sharon Pierce? It was highly doubtful.

She quickly came to the realization that there was something missing. It seemed as if he'd taken an awful gamble, for how could he have taken the chance that she'd never return? It didn't make any sense.

There was only one person who knew the answers, and he was just beyond that door. The door itself had never before appeared so menacing to her, its stark wooden frame foreboding, as if daring her to enter. In fact, the entire corridor seemed frightening. The dimly illuminated passageway, which had at one time appeared so elegant to her, now seemed strangely ominous. Why had she never noticed it before?

Although she wanted nothing more than to turn and run, after waiting several minutes, she forced herself to open the door.

It hardly came as a surprise to her that the furniture in the waiting area had been rearranged. The leather couches that she'd painstakingly chosen for the space were now turned to the right side, with the reception area moved toward the left. Sharon Pierce was nowhere to be seen. As a matter of fact, at first there didn't seem to be anyone behind the reception desk, at all. However, as she walked closer, she spied a young woman on her hands and knees on the floor, sifting through stacks of papers that had ostensibly fallen, muttering under her breath how she was underpaid and underappreciated.

The woman quickly stood up when she realized that she was being watched.

"Can I help you? Do you have an appointment?" she asked warily.

She was petite with blonde hair, and had a definite air of indifference.

"No, I'm afraid I don't," stated Sarah, never before imagining she'd need an appointment to visit her own office.

The entire scene was surreal. She was in her office, yet it was no longer hers; she was speaking to a secretary that she'd never met. The furniture was familiar, but rearranged; she was in some sort of alternate universe. This just simply couldn't be happening ….

But it was. And she was determined to get to the bottom of it all.

"Is Mr. Sloane in?" she inquired, in as calm a voice as she could muster.

"I'm sorry, he's not. What's your name, please?"

Sarah evaded the question. "Do you know when he'll be back?"

The woman shrugged. "He went out for his lunch break, but he should return soon. As a matter of fact, that's where I'm headed, too."

She unceremoniously dumped the stack of papers on the desk, all the while muttering under her breath, and proceeded to the front door.

"Would I be able to wait here?" Sarah asked.

"Sure," she answered, carelessly. "Mr. Sloane should be back within the hour."

She left the room with a bang.

Sarah did not hesitate. She walked toward the back of the waiting area to the door that led to the suite of offices, praying it was not locked. Mercifully, it wasn't, and the doorknob turned easily in her hands.

She quickly walked to the back, where the file room waited. Turning on the overhead light, she hurriedly scanned the boxes that held the records of her many cases, knowing that they were stacked alphabetically, finding at last what she was looking for.

MeadowLane v. Henderson.

She opened the box with trembling fingers, taking out the numerous files. She didn't have to look very far, however, as the very document she'd been searching for had been nearly at the top of the pile. It was a legal release, pages long, confirming her suspicions. She skipped over the legal jargon, which simply stated that officers, designees, stock holders, subsidiaries and agents would no longer be held liable once the final settlement had been reached. There was a confidentiality clause, she noted, and she turned page after page, until the very end ... and there it was.

Michael Sloane's signature had been scrawled on the bottom of the page, and his signature alone. The Hendersons had settled the lawsuit weeks ago, and Michael Sloane had already pocketed the entire fee. She didn't know how he'd gotten around the fact that she was missing, but she had little doubt that it had been creatively convincing. She suspected that the Hendersons had wanted to put this painful chapter of their lives behind them, and so they'd agreed.

It had worked, plain and simple.

She put all the pages back into the box and shoved it back to where it belonged.

The box was strangely tilted ... would anyone realize that she had been snooping? This was essentially her office ... did it even matter?

She felt numb. All of her life, she had worked so hard, just to have it snatched away from her in the blink of an eye. She should've been consumed with fury, she should have been burning with justifiable righteous indignation, but, oddly enough, she seemed to be beyond feeling. If anything, her inner rage was directed mostly at herself. She'd put her trust into the almighty dollar, placing it above all else, so that her views had become distorted. Her whole outlook on life had been terribly skewed, so much that she'd been unable to discern unscrupulous characters from upright ones. If it wouldn't have happened with this particular case, it most likely would have occurred other times, with different cases.

She turned off the overhead light, exited the room and headed to her own private office. She was not surprised to find that the large mahogany desk was now turned on an angle, and her pictures were nowhere in sight. Furthermore, her diplomas and awards of achievements that had been prominently displayed on the walls had been removed, replaced by Michael Sloane's various diplomas and plaques.

Someone had been busy, indeed.

There were several smaller pictures on the mahogany credenza. As if being silently propelled in their direction, guided by some inexplicable force, Sarah walked over to look at them more closely. They were family snapshots, no doubt, but they weren't of her family.

As if in slow motion, she reached over and lifted up a framed picture, and blanched. She held one hand over her mouth to stifle a scream.

It was a picture that had obviously been taken several years earlier. Two brothers stood side by side posing for the camera, looking remarkably alike. They had the same eyes, and their jaws jutted out in similar sneers.

One of them was Michael Sloane. The other one was wearing

a policeman's uniform. It was none other than Detective Robert S. Miller.

Robert Sloane Miller.

Michael's half-brother.

No wonder he had appeared so familiar. She must have seen this picture beforehand, and she'd recognized him. Had he known who she was? How could he have known?

And then her blood ran cold.

Whimpering, she looked closer at the picture, her hand shaking so violently that it took a supreme effort just to hold it. The brothers were standing outside, in a driveway of sorts, and they were leaning back against a car ... a black Mercedes. Robert was extending his arm, proudly showcasing what must have been his brand-new car at the time.

Of course he'd known. He'd known all along ... which meant that Michael Sloane had been apprised of her whereabouts, as well. They'd practically kept her under surveillance, in fact. They'd kept a watchful eye on her, biding their time ... no doubt, they'd hoped her memory would never return.

But it had.

In sudden, stunning clarity, she remembered crossing the street in the frigid weather, trying to hurry to the other side. She began to relive the scene so vividly that she could practically feel the icy sleet pelting down on her.

The light had turned green, but there had been a car making a turn, a black Mercedes, and she'd desperately tried to get out of the way ...

It was inconceivable that the accident had been planned. She had decided on the spur of the moment to run to the drugstore, to alleviate her headache, to think a bit clearer ... it couldn't possibly have been deliberate. For all she knew, it could have been a different Mercedes altogether.

It had been an accident, truly. But when she'd materialized at Robert Miller's office, unannounced, he'd certainly been less than pleased to see her. A slick actor, he'd covered it well. Had his brother given him a share of the firm's money?

She could scarcely think. She placed the picture down, wanting nothing more than to flee. She had to get away from this place. She needed time to get her riotous thoughts in order, and she needed to do it in private. She turned to leave.

There, standing framed in the doorway to his office, was Michael Sloane, his mouth ajar.

Fear became a taste in her mouth.

For several seconds, neither of them spoke. He looked startled to see her, and Sarah realized that she'd left that morning before his brother had had the chance to drive past Anne's house. He'd had no warning that she would make an appearance.

What would he do? Sarah thought wildly. She heard a babble of voices in the reception area. No doubt the secretary had returned, perhaps with clients. They weren't alone, thankfully, and he surely couldn't harm her with others around.

He set his mouth in a grim line and entered the room. She could see the wheels turning in his mind, wondering how to proceed. She said nothing, since she couldn't muster the words if she'd tried. Although she felt on the verge of collapsing from the anxiety she was experiencing, she somehow still had the presence of mind to understand the importance of keeping a confident veneer.

He broke the silence by clearing his throat.

"Well, well … if it isn't the elusive Sarah Morgan. Nice of you to drop by."

He sat down behind the desk, seemingly unperturbed, as

if this was a normal, everyday occurrence. He wasn't as good an actor as his brother, however, for she saw beads of sweat glistening on his brow.

She sat down, as well, facing him. Her legs simply couldn't hold her any longer.

"Well?" he began.

She found her voice. "Well, what?"

"Why are you here? What do you want?" he challenged.

She thought hard. What was it that she wanted? If she'd said that she wanted her firm back, would he just snap his fingers and hand it back to her on a silver platter? It wasn't at all likely. Not when he'd planned the takeover so well, effectively ousting her from the very firm that she'd started four years earlier. No, these things just didn't work that way. There had been too much subterfuge, too much at stake. No doubt he'd covered his tracks well.

What could she say?

I know your brother, Robert, drives a black Mercedes. There was a black Mercedes that drove by the house the entire time I was in Chicago ....

It was absurd, total conjecture. She could prove nothing.

And even if she'd get the authorities involved, and went through all the proper channels, what then? It would likely cost her years of legal wrangling, tens of thousands of dollars ... and for what? Even if he would one day relinquish the firm, and it would be hers once more, would that make her happy? Is it what she truly wanted?

The words were out of her mouth before she could stop them, not that she wished to stop them. The words were truthfully simple.

"I don't want anything from you."

His eyebrows lifted in surprise. Evidently, that hadn't been what he'd expected her to say.

"You mean to tell me ..." he began.

"You can have it. All of it." Her voice started as a whisper, but got stronger with each breath. She finally knew what she'd wanted all along, and it had nothing to do with the firm of Morgan-Sloane.

She reached into her pocket and withdrew the diamond ring.

She thrust it onto the desk. "This is yours, as well."

He genuinely appeared baffled. It was apparent that he'd expected her to fight hard for her firm, the way she'd have battled before. He didn't realize that she was not the same person.

She was tired of fighting for things that caused her so much misery, as it was an exercise in futility. There were dreams in life worth struggling for, goals that had nothing to do with the firm or what it stood for.

She had aspirations that would provide her with the inner peace and happiness she'd craved since she was a child.

She stood up to leave, and she was almost out of the door when he called out, "That's it? You're leaving, just like that?"

"Yes, just like that," Sarah repeated.

And that was how she left, without so much as a backwards glance. With each step she took, she felt stronger and more confident.

She walked past the reception desk and out the door. Sprinting into the hallway, she took the steps two at a time, spiraling downwards, not stopping until she was outside, panting in the midday sun.

Remarkably, she felt reborn. Instead of feeling sadness at the thought of losing Morgan-Sloane, she knew she was free, no longer a slave to values that were warped and brought her nothing but despair. She walked to where her car was parked, opened the door and got in. She knew how much money she had in her account, and she knew how much her apartment and car were worth.

It would be enough to last her for quite some time.

But before she considered her future plans, she was eager to revisit her past, and she hurriedly started the car, excitedly driving down the street that would lead her to the freeway, to her grandmother ....

1:45 P.M. THE SAME DAY
BETH SHALOM HOME
FOR THE AGED

She walked into the cool, darkened lobby of the nursing home, where she wiped perspiration from her face with a tissue. It was warm outside, quite a contrast from Chicago, but all of her inner anticipation, fueled by sheer adrenaline, had left her feeling sweaty and breathless.

There was no one at the front desk, but she knew the directions to her grandmother's room, regardless. It was located down the long corridor, the very last room on the right.

As she walked down the hallway, she suddenly remembered the disturbing dream she'd had on the flight to Chicago, wondering how her grandmother would react ...

It no longer mattered now, and the thought put a spring in her step. A huge weight had been lifted from her shoulders, and she thought to herself, *Don't worry, Bubbie. I remember who I am now, and I won't ever forget again.*

The door was open and Sarah peeked in. There was an upholstered wing chair by the window, but her grandmother wasn't sitting in it. The bed was neatly made, but empty. She checked the bathroom, only to find it abandoned, as well.

She figured that perhaps her grandmother was outside on the covered veranda, recalling how she would oftentimes sit there in the afternoons with friends to enjoy the fine weather.

She walked back through the lobby, which was still deserted, and opened the door to the veranda. There were several people seated there on sturdy lawn chairs, but her grandmother was not one of them.

Her pulse began to quicken. *Where was her grandmother?*

She walked back to the front desk and pressed a little bell, hoping someone would come quickly. Sure enough, a door opened and an efficient-looking woman came to the desk briskly.

"Can I help you?"

"Yes, thank you," she said. "I'm here to see my grandmother, Pearl Morgenstern. I've been to her room and she wasn't there. Perhaps she switched rooms?"

"Morgenstern ... let's see," the woman said, looking at the computer screen. "Yes, I'm afraid she's not here."

"Where ... where is she?" Sarah asked, her voice rising in panic.

"I'm sorry, but it says here that she was experiencing some chest pains and had to be transferred to the hospital. Didn't someone notify you?"

Sarah could barely form the words. "I – I was away."

"Oh, I'm truly sorry about that. She's been taken to Cedars-Sinai."

"I'll go there right now. Thank you for your help," said Sarah.

She spun around and practically ran to her car, where she got in and turned on the ignition. Instead of backing out of her space, though, she wearily leaned forward, put her head on the steering wheel and let the tears flow unchecked.

It was too much.

How much anxiety could she tolerate? How much uncertainty and fear could she endure in the space of one day? She felt as if she was on some sort of macabre ride in an amusement park, and all she wanted to do was to get off. She was all alone, and it seemed like too much to bear ....

And that's when she remembered.

She was not alone. She had never truly been alone.

Hashem was watching over her, waiting to guide her through every step of the way. She took out her book of Psalms that Anne had given her, turned to Psalm 121 and murmured in English ...

A Song for the Degrees ... I lift up my eyes unto the mountains; whence shall come my help. My help is from the L-rd, the Maker of Heaven and Earth ...

She recited it quickly, knowing it practically by heart, having said it so many times. Although she wished she could read it in the original Hebrew, she still drew strength from the powerful, timeless words.

She then wiped her eyes with her hands, took a deep breath and backed out of the driveway, steering the car toward Cedars-Sinai Medical Center, which was a short distance away.

As she drove, she was consumed with thoughts of her grandmother, how kind she'd been to her as a child, how supportive she'd been to her as an adult. She had been so fortunate to have her in her life. Did her grandmother even know how much she'd meant to her? Had she ever told her?

Hang on tight, Bubbie, she thought. *I'm coming, I'm on my way ....*

Her head pounding, it was fortunate that she knew where the hospital was located, having passed by it so many times before.

Recent events had brought her to a crossroads, and she didn't know which way to turn. Her life, as she had known it, had disappeared, and her future was up in the air. But for now, it was her grandmother who had taken center stage, and it was her Bubbie's well-being that was first and foremost in her mind.

Please help me, Hashem, thought Sarah. *Please let Bubbie recognize me .... I need to let her know how much she means to me ....*

She turned her car into the busy parking lot, only narrowly avoiding a collision with a tow truck. The parking lot was so congested, she couldn't imagine how she'd ever find a spot in which to park, when miraculously a space became available right in front of her. She slid into it and exited the car, sprinting to the front lobby with surprising agility for someone who had been through so much in the past hour.

It was adrenaline that was fueling her now, plain and simple. That and the belief that soon she'd be reunited with her grandmother, and whatever happened, it was for the best.

She entered the lobby and was not prepared for the onslaught of emotions that overcame her. The information desk, the upholstered couches in the waiting area ... the interior design of the space so resembled the hospital in Chicago that she felt familiar feelings of panic bubble within her.

She could not ... would not ... allow her fears to overtake her. She was not here as a patient, she reasoned; she was here as a visitor, to see her beloved Bubbie. She needed to see her before it was too late.

And so it was with a sense of urgency that she marched over to the desk and asked for Pearl Morgenstern's room.

"Intensive Care Unit, eighth floor," she was told by the harried woman behind the desk, who didn't even look up. "Are you immediate family?"

"Yes, I am," she replied. "I'm her granddaughter."

"All right, then, go on up. Second elevator on the left. When you exit the elevators, make a sharp right at the nurses' station," she continued in the same bored monotone.

Sarah swallowed a sick feeling of revulsion as she walked toward the elevators, which reminded her of her own brief stay at Chicago's Northwestern Memorial. The experience had been so terrifying, so dreadful; she couldn't have imagined anything worse, and yet … and yet …

She never would have met Anne Lewis if she hadn't been brought there.

And she never would've been introduced to a different, and decidedly superior, path of life to follow had she not met Anne Lewis.

Everything was meant to be, was it not? It was food for thought, to be sure, but she didn't have the time to dwell on it just then, since the doors had closed around her and she was being rapidly transported to the eighth floor where her grandmother lay waiting … in what condition, she did not know.

The corridor opened to her, an antiseptically sterile, harsh environment, with glaring overhead lights and a nurses' station to her right. She ignored the hammering of her heart as she walked toward the nurses' station, her anticipation at seeing her grandmother far outweighing any reservations she possessed.

A young nurse asked, "Can I help you?"

"I'm here to see Pearl Morgenstern. I'm her granddaughter."

To her utter amazement, the nurse smiled. "Oh, I'm so glad. Sarah, isn't it? Your grandmother's been asking for you all week. We tried calling your home, but we haven't been able to reach you."

"I … I've been away," she murmured, lamely.

Guilt pierced at Sarah's heart like a knife. Her grandmother had been here for a week already. She was probably brought in around the same time that she'd begun to retrieve her memory.

Why had it taken so long for her to return? Why had she procrastinated so?

True, there had been travel arrangements to consider, and she hadn't wanted to leave Anne in an abrupt manner … she truly hadn't wanted to leave Anne at all ….

And so she'd stalled for the better part of a week, not wanting to return, not wanting to face what she'd needed to face.

And her grandmother had needed her.

"She's actually sleeping now," the nurse said kindly. "You can go in if you'd like. Twenty minutes, no more."

Sarah nodded and walked to the corner room just beyond the front desk, in the direction that the nurse had pointed.

She hesitated by the door and watched her elderly grandmother who was asleep, surrounded by machines that monitored her vital signs. An oxygen tube was snaked across her grandmother's delicate, frail features, and there were various tubes in her arm linking her to the machines next to the bed. Other than those telltale signs, it was a soothing scene, since her grandmother appeared to be sleeping soundly and not in any pain.

There was a small chair near the bed, and Sarah crossed over to it and sat down, content to be there, at long last.

I'm finally here, Bubbie, she thought. *And I'm not going to leave you. Not this time.*

Peter sat at his desk and tried to concentrate on his work. After twenty minutes or so, he realized that he couldn't recall a word of what he had been reading.

It was no use. Who was he fooling?

His mind was elsewhere as he glanced at the picture of Danielle that was on his desk.

All he wanted was to be with his daughter and experience more of the short-lived serenity he'd felt in her presence, and in the presence of the special people who lived in Israel.

His people.

He thought of the trip he'd taken and compared it to taking a small bite out of a succulent fruit, which he'd never before tried … and it had left him wanting more. He'd only gotten a brief, tantalizing taste, but it had been enough to whet his appetite.

What was he doing thousands of miles away in this office?

Like a man possessed, he got up from his chair and paced around the room like a caged bird, desperately wanting to be set free. His mind was made up, and so was his resolve … he was only waiting for the right moment, and soon he would spread his wings …

… and fly.

CHAPTER 17

Lee Ross was the last one to sit down in the conference room, her mug of steaming hot chocolate balanced precariously with an armful of papers that she placed on the table. Ray Adams was there already, as fidgety as ever, looking bored as he twirled a straw wrapper in his fingers, waiting for the meeting to begin.

Peter had called this impromptu meeting with the two of them. It wasn't truly impromptu, of course, since he'd planned this in his mind for the last several days. They needed to hear this from him, just as he needed their cooperation.

"Sorry I'm late," Lee said as she slid into a chair.

"That's all right," said Peter.

They both looked at him expectantly.

Peter rubbed his hands together. He had prepared what he'd wanted to say, going over the dialogue frame by frame in his mind. But now that the time had come, the words seemed stuck in his throat, unable to exit.

Ray broke the silence. "If this is about the Monagrane case, I think I might have thought of a way around it ...."

"It's not about the Monagrane case," he stated quietly.

Ray Adams and Lee Ross looked at each other questioningly.

"All right, Peet-O, you know I'm not big on mysteries. We're here, you're here ... what's the deal?" Ray wanted to know.

"It's just that, well, I wanted to run an idea by you, that's all." Lee raised the mug of hot cocoa to her lips and took a sip.

Ray looked at him curiously, something he'd been doing a lot lately, and waited.

Peter began. "You both know that I've recently spent some time in Israel with my daughter. And, Ray, you know more than anyone that I haven't been quite myself since I returned ...."

"That's the understatement of the century," quipped Ray.

Peter ignored this and continued. "In any case, I experienced a number of things there that gave me pause; ideas that started me thinking about elements of my life, the things I like, and the things I want to change."

"What do you mean?" Lee Ross asked.

"Well, I've been working here for, I don't know ... twenty years or so. I started as an associate before I was made partner, years ago. When Adam Heller passed away, I worked night and day to make this firm what it is today. Basically, what I'm trying to say is that this firm is all I know ... all I know is work, work and more work."

They stared at him disbelievingly.

"There is a whole world out there that I've never seen, never experienced," he said, his voice rising with emotion. "My entire life has been lived within the confines of these walls. I'm Jewish, as you both know. Do I even know anything about my heritage? Do I even have the vaguest understanding of what it all means?"

Lee Ross blanched, spilling her hot chocolate onto her lap. Ray handed her a handkerchief, muttering under his breath, "Oh, boy ... he's really flipped."

Lee Ross recovered first, protesting, "Think about what you're saying, Peter. You've built this firm from the ground up, in essence. We've enjoyed much success and will continue to enjoy more ... now isn't the time to have a mid-life crisis."

"This isn't a mid-life crisis," he responded simply. "It's a new outlook on life."

Lee turned to Ray challengingly. "You see what I always say about religion? It plays with people's minds ... it just ruins everything."

Peter said, "I'm not going to debate religion with you, Lee. There's too much you don't understand. But I am telling you both that there will be some changes around here."

"Changes?" asked Ray, blankly. "What sort of changes?"

"Well, let's see. I figured that I took a total of twenty days' vacation time in the twenty years that I've been working. That includes the week after my wife's passing, and the time I just spent in Israel. That would amount to one day per year ... I think it would be fair to say that I've accrued some time off."

They were both quiet. When put that way, the point was impossible to argue. Everyone knew that no one worked harder than Peter Strauss.

"How much time did you have in mind?" asked Ray.

"I'm not exactly sure, four or five months at least, maybe more."

"Starting when?"

"Starting now ... today. The world isn't as large as it once was, either. I have a PDA, a laptop ... don't worry, you'll still be able to reach me, should the need arise."

Ray nodded.

Peter continued, "I'm leaving things here in capable hands. Ray, as of today, I'm promoting you to full equity partner."

Ray's mouth dropped open in shock. For once, he was speechless.

"You've been my right hand man, Ray, and you've been here the longest. It's something I should've done long ago."

He turned to Lee Ross. "Your efforts haven't gone unnoticed, either. In my absence, it will mean more work for you, and you'll be compensated nicely, I assure you. You can expect a significant raise next paycheck."

Lee looked quite pleased at the news. Peter stood up, signaling that the meeting had come to a close. Lee thanked him, congratulated Ray and left the room, still mopping the chocolate stain from her skirt.

Ray was still silent, and the thought occurred to Peter that he'd never seen him go for so long without speaking.

Peter clapped him on the back. "Heller, Strauss and Adams has a nice ring, don't you think? We can work the details out later."

Ray found his voice. "Look, man, I really don't know what to say …."

"You don't have to say anything, Ray. Just keep things running smoothly, just like I know you will."

"You can count on me, buddy. I won't let you down."

Peter knew that he would keep his word, for behind all his bravado, Ray was an honest, decent man.

They shook hands, and Ray turned to leave. Before he left the conference room, he turned around.

"Just for the record, dude … I don't really think you're crazy. Actually, I think it takes a lot of courage to want to make changes this late in the game. You're not getting any younger, you know."

"I'm not that old, Ray. Now leave before I change my mind," said Peter, good-naturedly.

Ray saluted and left, closing the door behind him.

Peter leaned back in his chair and closed his eyes for a brief moment, savoring the solitude of his newfound freedom. He had accomplished exactly what he'd wanted to do, and it felt wonderful.

He opened his top drawer and withdrew the tickets that he'd purchased late the previous evening. The flight was to leave the following evening, and he had much to arrange in very little time.

It was time to go. He gathered his briefcase and looked around the office, wondering when he'd see it next. He then opened the door and walked through it without looking back.

TUESDAY, MARCH 17
5:15 A.M.
CEDARS-SINAI MEDICAL
CENTER
LOS ANGELES, CALIFORNIA

Sarah massaged her neck, her muscles knotted and tight. It had been a long night, and she'd slept badly on the hard chair in the hallway, more from sheer exhaustion than anything else. The day before, she'd been unable to see her grandmother for more than a few minutes at a time, and each time she had been soundly asleep, sedated from a procedure that had been done earlier.

In the middle of the night, she'd cornered a young intern who'd been making his rounds and questioned him about her grandmother.

"Congenital heart failure," he'd replied.

"Is there anything that can be done for her? Was the procedure a success?"

He shook his head. "I'm afraid not. Surgery would be most beneficial, but in a woman her age, surgery just isn't an option ... it's basically just a matter of time."

"How long?" she'd persisted.

"A few days, sometimes more ... sometimes less," he'd answered truthfully. "I'm sorry."

Sarah knew that her grandmother was ninety-eight years old, and she'd been relatively healthy for most of her life. Still, the thought did little to assuage the pain. Her grandmother was rapidly fading, and she was determined to be with her every precious moment in her final hours.

She groggily checked her watch, waiting for the nurse's signal that she could enter her grandmother's room. Sarah had been told earlier that she had awakened, and she was eager to see her, to talk with her, to be there for her.

The nurse soon gave the thumbs-up sign to Sarah, and she quickly got up and walked the short distance to her grandmother's room.

The curtains were open, and the dawn was about to break in the still-darkened sky. Sarah could see that her grandmother's eyes had opened, and she had been moved to a semi-sitting position in the bed.

"Bubbie?" she asked, tentatively, as she walked into the room.

"Sarah?" the older woman said softly. "My dear, is it really you?"

"Yes, Bubbie," she answered shakily, grasping her hand. "I'm here. I'm so, so sorry it took so long for me to get here."

Her grandmother smiled. "Sarala, dear, I've been so worried about you."

She swallowed. "Everything is fine, Bubbie, really. You don't need to worry about me."

The elderly woman gazed at Sarah pointedly.

"What time is it, dear?"

Sarah checked the clock on the wall. "It's after five in the morning, Bubbie. It's Tuesday morning."

"Tuesday already? I'm losing track of time ..." her voice trailed off.

"It's all right, Bubbie."

"Why don't you sit down, Sarala?" Her voice was thin and weak, but it didn't matter to Sarah. She was alive, she had recognized her; it was more than she'd dared to hope for.

Sarah obediently brought the chair close to the bed, sat down, and held her grandmother's hands in her own.

Her grandmother's eyes studied her closely, missing nothing.

"There's something you're not telling me, dear. Do you think you can fool your old Bubbie?" she asked, tenderly.

"Of course not. It's just — well, I was away in Chicago, Bubbie. I got ... delayed there, I guess you could say. But something wonderful came out of the whole experience, Bubbie."

"Oh, my ... and what is that?"

"I stayed at the home of the most remarkable woman, Bubbie. Her name is Anne Lewis, and she's Orthodox. She lit candles on *Shabbos* just like you did, remember, Bubbie?"

The cloudiness in the older woman's eyes seemed to lift as she murmured, "How well I remember, Sarala, dear. How well I remember, indeed."

"Bubbie, the whole experience changed me, somehow. I'm different now, Bubbie. Do you understand?"

For the first time since she'd entered the room, her grandmother noticed her long skirt and sleeves that somehow seemed incongruous with the California weather. Slowly, she nodded, her face breaking into a lovely smile. Her skin had such a dull, lifeless pallor, but now that she was smiling, she appeared lit from within.

"I believe I do, Sarala, dear."

Sarah leaned forward and said softly, "Bubbie, I'm going to learn all I can about becoming observant. I've already started, in fact. I want to lead a true Jewish life, a true Torah life …."

Was it her imagination, or did her grandmother seem to draw strength from her very words? Her voice sounded stronger as she said, "I am so proud of you, my dear child. This is the life you were meant to live, my Sarala. I always wanted this for you, but you were too young to understand, and I didn't have the knowledge to explain it to you. Times were different then, I didn't know enough … I never was taught. No, you needed to find it on your own … to become the person you were meant to be."

"I'm going to try very hard, Bubbie. It's what I want above all else."

"You know, Sarala, your father never much cared about these things, and I blamed myself … when he threw away his religion, I can't describe the anguish it caused me. I never spoke of it, of course; he was still your father. Unfortunately, he wasn't blessed with years, and the years he did have were wasted making terrible choices, terrible mistakes … but he did bring you into this world …."

She paused before continuing, as each word was an effort. "Sarala, my time in this world is nearly over, and long after I'm gone, you'll continue on … you'll bring religious observance back into our family, and my life will have meant something …."

"Don't talk like that, Bubbie."

In a rush, Sarah said the words she'd been longing to say for years, her voice thick with emotion. "Bubbie, those years I spent with you as a little girl were my happiest years … you treated me with such love, such compassion. You've accomplished so much …. I wouldn't be where I am today if it weren't for you."

Her grandmother grasped her hand tighter.

"And I wouldn't be here if it wasn't for you," murmured her grandmother. "You gave me a reason to go on, when there were times it felt like too much. When your father, my only child, passed away … I knew I had to be strong for you."

"You were strong, Bubbie," agreed Sarah. "You still are strong."

"No, my Sarala," she shook her head. "My time is drawing nearer …. I can feel it. No, don't look like that, Sarala, it's the natural way of things. I've led a long life, longer than most. I can't live forever … listen, my precious girl, you must promise me one thing."

"Anything." Sarah leaned forward.

"All of the arrangements are made," continued her grandmother. "I made them all myself years ago."

"What … what arrangements?" asked Sarah, tremulously.

"The burial arrangements, Sarala," she answered. "No, don't look like that. There's a piece of paper in the drawer, over there … go on …"

She pointed to a bedside table that held a single drawer. With shaking fingers, Sarah obediently went to the table, opened the drawer and withdrew the folded paper, her stomach tied in knots.

She sat down once more and offered the paper to her grandmother.

"No, dear child, you hold on to it. It's the Rabbi's name and number. He has made all the arrangements for a proper Jewish burial. And that's what I needed to discuss with you ... you must promise me that you'll make the final trip with me, that you'll make sure everything is done correctly."

"I ... I don't understand."

"Oh, dear, I haven't been explaining things well, have I?" her grandmother said, her breaths becoming shorter and more raspy.

"Maybe just rest a bit, Bubbie. You can tell me later."

"No, Sarala. I must tell you now .... I've had a lot of time to think when I was at the nursing home, all I had was time on my hands, after all ... and I realized that I've never been to the Holy Land. All of my life, I've wanted to go, of course. But, for one reason or another, the timing was never quite right ... and I never got the chance."

Sarah leaned forward, listening to each word.

"And then, one day it came to me .... I never had a chance to go there in life, but I could be buried there, and spend my rest in the land that G-d gave the Jewish people. You see, don't you, Sarala?"

Sarah nodded, tears flowing freely from her eyes, unable to speak.

"Don't look so sad, my dear child. Think of it as my last adventure. I want you to accompany me on my final journey, to make sure it all goes smoothly."

"I will," managed Sarah.

"I knew you would, Sarala." Her grandmother leaned back against the pillows, satisfied. "The Rabbi will take care of all the details, and everything is paid for. You just need to call him when I ..."

"Don't say it, Bubbie," she cried. "I can't take it."

"Sarala, listen to me. Don't be afraid. I'm not afraid, truly I'm not. I will be reunited with my dear parents … lately, when I sleep, I can almost see them … they're coming nearer and nearer …."

It gave Sarah a measure of comfort knowing that her grandmother had accepted her fate and was ready to meet her Creator. However, the void that she would feel upon her grandmother's death seemed overwhelming to her … she didn't know if she could bear it.

"But what about me?" she sobbed, anguished tears blinding her eyes. "You're the only relative I have left …. I'll be all alone!"

Her grandmother looked at her lovingly. There was deep understanding in her tired eyes as she said, "No, you'll never be alone, Sarala. You'll see … you'll go on, you'll marry … you'll have children who will cherish you. You'll have a wonderful, long life … goodness, I'm getting so sleepy again, my dear, I'm going to rest my eyes for a bit …."

The nurse then came to the room, signaling that Sarah's twenty minutes had come to a close.

Sarah squeezed her grandmother's hand once more whispered, "I love you, Bubbie."

And she left the room, her heart feeling as if it would shatter from grief. She sat on the hard chair in the hallway, her head in her hands, and waited ….

CHAPTER 18

"It's basically just a waiting game now," said Sarah morosely into the phone.

"They're saying it can be at any moment …."

"Have you eaten anything since yesterday?" Anne asked her in concern. "Have you been back at the apartment?"

"No," replied Sarah. "I couldn't eat anything if I tried. No, I came to the hospital right after – after –"

She didn't need to elaborate further. She'd been on the phone with Anne for nearly an hour, explaining in great detail everything that had happened since her return. From the shocking betrayal that she'd discovered at the office to the impending demise of her beloved grandmother … the dam had burst inside Sarah, and the words had gushed forth in a torrent of emotion.

It had been cathartic for Sarah to unburden herself to Anne, who had listened sympathetically throughout the entire exchange.

"You need to keep your strength up, Sarah," she persisted. "Why don't you go home and eat something, maybe lie down for a while?"

"I don't want to leave her, Anne," she answered. "I'm staying here as long as I can stand upright."

"From the sound of things, that doesn't seem like too much longer," remarked Anne.

"Don't worry about me, I'll be fine."

"All right," Anne said. "Listen, when the time comes, let me give you my son and daughter-in-law's phone number. You remember Aaron and Rachel, don't you?"

"Of course." Though she'd just seen them the week before, it seemed like ages ago. "Do they live in Jerusalem?"

"Yes, in a neighborhood called Bayit Vegan. I know that Rachel would be delighted to host you during your stay."

"Oh, I wouldn't want to be a bother ... I could always stay at a hotel," offered Sarah.

"Nonsense, I won't hear of it. We're your family now, Sarah, remember that. Really, I insist. Write down the number ...."

Sarah wrote the telephone number on the outside of the folded slip of paper that she'd held in her hand for the last two hours. She hadn't had the courage to open it, as of yet.

"You'll call Rachel, won't you, Sarah?"

"I'll call her."

"Good. Listen, Sarah, whatever happens ... remember, it's all meant to be. Stay strong."

"I'll try," whispered Sarah. "It's so hard, though."

"I know, dear ... I know how hard it is," agreed Anne. "But you'll see, in the days and weeks ahead, things will get better ... they always do. And don't forget to call Rachel."

"I'll call her," repeated Sarah.

They said good-bye, and Sarah was just about to put her cell phone into the pocket of her skirt when she saw two nurses, accompanied by a doctor, rushing toward her grandmother's room, the faint sound of an alarm wailing from somewhere in the room.

She remained where she was, steeling herself, scarcely able to breathe. Minutes ticked by … and then she saw a nurse leave the room and walk toward her.

"I'm sorry," she said, putting a hand gently on her arm. "She's passed on."

Sarah fought for composure, knowing that in her grandmother's final hours, she had had the privilege to tell her what she'd wanted to say, and that she'd given her grandmother satisfaction and joy. Oddly enough, there were no tears … she'd cried oceans of them all day, and now her eyes remained strangely dry.

There was one thing left to do. She slowly opened the folded piece of paper in her palm. There, in her grandmother's spidery handwriting, was a short message.

Sarah, my dear … call Rabbi Joseph Katz. His number is 555-6731. He'll know what to do.

She swallowed. If there was a call that she never wanted to make, this had to be it. Still, she had given her word and wouldn't let her Bubbie down.

She flipped open her cell phone and dialed the numbers, hoping it wasn't too early to call.

The phone was answered on the first ring by a man with a kindly voice.

"Hello?" he asked.

"Hello … Rabbi Katz? This is Sarah Morgenstern, Pearl Morgenstern's granddaughter …."

6:20 P.M. EASTERN TIME
CLEVELAND, OHIO
EN ROUTE TO TEL AVIV,
ISRAEL

Sarah leaned back in her seat and yawned, all the while rubbing her eyes out of sheer exhaustion. If it hadn't been for the wonderful, saintly Rabbi Katz, she doubted that all of the preparations would've gone as smoothly as they did. He had met her at the hospital literally fifteen minutes after she'd phoned him, emphasizing to her the necessity of speed in such cases.

"You'll need to catch the noon flight to Cleveland, and then non-stop to Israel," he'd informed her. "Because of the time difference, you'll arrive in Israel tomorrow afternoon."

He'd signed all of the necessary hospital paperwork and had her grandmother swiftly transferred to the Jewish funeral home, where she'd received a ritual purification to prepare her for her final rest.

Sarah had less than an hour to return to her apartment loft in order to make the flight. She was able to change her clothing, throw some personal items into a suitcase, grab her passport and leave. Rabbi Katz had even insisted on accompanying her to the airport, on the way briefly outlining to her what she could expect when she'd arrive in Tel Aviv.

"When you'll arrive, you'll be met by members of the *Chevra Kadisha,* and they will escort you, along with the deceased, to Jerusalem. There will be a *minyan* there of ten men, and they'll say the special *Kaddish* for your grandmother, of blessed memory."

"Is there anyone to call? How will they know to be there?" she'd asked.

He replied, "Don't worry. Everything will be taken care of."

He'd then handed her a copy of a pamphlet that described what would happen in greater detail, printed by the *Chevra Kadisha* organization. It was remarkable to Sarah that there were organizations that took care of such matters, that there were people such as Rabbi Katz, who graciously volunteered his time to help ease this difficult transition for her, with dignity.

It had all been so fast ... Sarah had hardly a moment to process it all. The four-hour flight to Cleveland had been a blur, and Sarah had just been grateful that there had been no need to change planes. Her entire being was so weary, so fatigued, she was content to stay in her seat. After an hour or so on the ground, the plane had gathered speed and lifted once more into the air. The next stop was Tel Aviv, and Sarah knew that she would finally get some sleep on the ten-hour flight. Her eyelids were already so heavy, she could barely keep them open.

Her last thought before drifting off was how pleased her grandmother would be to know that her dream of returning to Israel was becoming a reality, and that it was she who was accompanying her on her final journey ....

4:00 P.M.
BEN GURION AIRPORT
TEL AVIV, ISRAEL

Though the flight had seemed interminably long, Sarah was grateful that she had slept for several hours, uninterrupted. When the flight attendants had come by with her kosher meals, she had awakened, ravenous, and she tried not to wolf down the food. She then read through the pamphlet that Rabbi Katz had given her, preparing herself for what was to come.

When the plane touched down to a roar of applause, Sarah blinked back tears.

You did it, Bubbie! We're here ... we're in Israel, just as you wanted.

Somehow it all seemed so fitting, so absolutely right, and a feeling of calmness washed over her for the first time in ... well, longer than she cared to remember.

She followed the crowds of people off the plane, toward the long lines at the gates to have her passport stamped. It all seemed surreal.

Was it only the day before that she'd been in L.A.? It seemed inconceivable, but here she was on the other side of the world, with only her small suitcase. She didn't know the language, where to go, or what to do ....

And yet, she wasn't worried.

Somehow, she knew that it would all work out well.

And, sure enough, after she'd had her passport stamped and found her suitcase, two men approached her.

Both of them were dressed in traditional Chassidic garb, with long side curls on either side of their faces.

They seemed genuinely concerned, eager to be of help.

"Morgenstern?" one of them asked.

She nodded.

"It's arranged," he said in halting English. "Please ... follow us."

They wordlessly led her outside where a white van had pulled up. A lump formed in her throat and hot tears scalded her eyes as she saw the wooden coffin that had been placed in the back.

Bubbie ... Bubbie ... see? All of the plans you arranged ... it's all coming to fruition ... we'll be there soon, Bubbie ....

She got into the van, and as it pulled away from the curb, the men began to recite special prayers. There was a card on the seat that had the prayers written in Hebrew and English. She began to read …

The first prayer was from Psalms, Chapter 91.

Whoever sits in the refuge of the Most High, he shall dwell in the shadow of the Almighty. I will say of Hashem, "He is my refuge and my fortress, My G-d, and I will trust in Him …."

She recited the meaningful prayer in its entirety. The next prayer she recognized was the beautiful song that had been sung on Friday nights at Anne's home, the song from Proverbs, *Aishes Chayil*.

An accomplished woman, who can find?
Far beyond pearls is her value …

As she read through the beautiful prose, she tasted her salty tears …

False is grace and vain is beauty.
A G-d-fearing woman – she should be praised.
Give her the fruits of her hand,
And let her be praised in the gates by her very own deeds.

The men continued to intone the same prayers over and over again, and so Sarah did the same. They drove that way until they had climbed into the majestic mountains of Jerusalem.

As they climbed ever higher, a heightened sense of awe gripped Sarah.

They were on their way to the holy city of Jerusalem, the place that Jews had struggled to reach throughout history, the place that was mentioned so often in the prayers she had learned, and Sarah felt humbled beyond measure.

6:20 P.M.
HAR HAMENUCHOS
JERUSALEM

It was late in the day, and brilliant streaks of fuchsia and violet lit up the sky as the sun began to set over the Jerusalem hills.

It was a breathtaking scene, one that Sarah realized would remain etched in her memory forever.

It was exactly as her grandmother would have wanted it to be, and it had all happened exactly as Rabbi Katz had said. There were ten men assembled at the gravesite, and they had said the appropriate prayers and the holy *Kaddish*.

After the short funeral was over, and the few people gathered had dispersed, she walked down the path of the cemetery, alone.

It was the end of an era, she knew. Her grandmother had been the only relative she'd had left. A terrible feeling of melancholy settled over her.

What would she do now? Where would she go?

She suddenly remembered Anne's words.

We're your family now, Sarah, remember that. Call Rachel.

She reached into her bag and found the piece of paper, the same piece of paper with her grandmother's handwriting on it.

Anne had given her so much already, how could she impose on her children? Yet, she had told Anne that she would, and she yearned to see a familiar face.

She made the call.

One year later ...

EPILOGUE

As Sarah walked in the direction of the *Kosel,* she once again felt the pure serenity that permeated her very soul each time she went there. The sun was high in the blue Jerusalem sky and the birds fluttered about, singing songs only they could understand. No doubt their Creator knew the meanings.

As she walked ever closer to the *Kosel,* she reflected back on the past year, and her gratefulness knew no bounds.

Aaron and Rachel had opened their home to her, and she boarded in a small, back bedroom for a modest rent. Initially, they'd refused her offer of payment, but she'd been adamant. She could well afford her room and board, she'd reasoned, and she also insisted on paying full tuition for her courses at the women's seminary for *baalos teshuva* at which Rachel taught.

She'd actually been a student in one of Rachel's classes, and she'd enjoyed every moment immensely. Rachel was a dynamic teacher, and Sarah had found herself enthralled with the *Chumash* that they were learning together. It was amazing how far she had come, how quickly she had learned. A whole new world had been opened to her, and it had come to her so naturally, as if she'd been waiting for it her entire life.

The seminary was in Bayit Vegan, the same neighborhood in which they lived, and Sarah had enjoyed her daily stroll to her school just down the block from the apartment. The classes had been wonderfully stimulating, and though Sarah had been a quick, eager learner, she couldn't help but notice that she was one of the older women in her classes, if not the oldest. Most of the students were much younger, young enough to be her daughter.

She thought of Daniella Strauss, a girl of nineteen, who had been the most outstanding student in the class. She was so bright, in fact, that Rachel had paired them up in class to learn together. Sarah had felt sorry for the young girl, being saddled with her as a study partner. She had been nothing but kind, however, and she'd tutored her quite expertly for someone so young.

Everyone at the school had been so welcoming, so supportive. Now the school was on a break to gear up for the approaching Pesach holiday, and Sarah was secretly counting the days until she could go back and resume her learning.

As the *Kosel* came into view, she reminded herself of the conversation that had been held two months prior. It had been that exchange that had propelled her to come to the *Kosel* on this special quest, these past forty days in a row.

She had been in Rachel's kitchen, and Anne had been there, as well. She had been visiting more frequently as of late since she was house hunting. Anne was on the verge of retirement, and she was looking for an apartment closer to her children. As always, it had been a treat to spend catch-up time with her.

They'd sat together in the sunny kitchen for hours talking over glasses of iced tea, with little Eli playing with a friend on the floor. They hadn't been discussing anything in particular. No, it had just come out of the blue, so to speak.

"You've come such a long way," remarked Anne. "It's almost as if you were a different person."

"It's true," agreed Sarah. "I've learned so much from Rachel, from you ...."

"You're an extraordinary person, Sarah. You deserve to have happiness," stated Anne gently.

"I'm very happy, Anne," she replied honestly. "I'm happier than I've ever been in my life."

Anne was quiet for a moment, as if debating with herself how to proceed.

"I know you are, Sarah, but you're all alone. You would make the most wonderful wife, the most wonderful mother. Surely, you've thought about it, no?"

Of course she had, more times than she cared to count. While it was wonderful living at Rachel's house, she inwardly yearned for a home of her own. She actually found herself dreaming quite often of how it would feel to have a Torah home, how divine it would be to raise children with a partner who shared the same values she did.

Still, Sarah was plagued by uncertainties.

"But my past ..." she said to Anne.

Anne shook her head. "Sarah, one day you'll learn to leave your past where it belongs ... in the past."

"But what respectable person would want me?" insisted Sarah.

"That's a question only *Hashem* knows the answer to, and I have little doubt that He has wonderful plans for you. You just have to do your part, and let *Hashem* take care of the rest."

"I guess I don't know what my part is."

Anne appeared thoughtful. "You know, Sarah, I have an idea. It's widely known that there is a tremendous *segula* to find one's *bashert*. Would you be willing to try it?"

She did not hesitate. "Yes."

"Good. Go to the *Kosel* and *daven* for forty days in a row. Ask *Hashem* to send the one who's destined to be your partner in life. Don't skip a day."

It had certainly sounded straightforward enough. She'd given Anne her word, and even long after she'd returned to the States, Sarah had dutifully gone each day to the *Kosel*. True to her word, she had not missed a single day.

She now stood in front of the *Kosel*, each crack in the smooth stones stuffed with so many tear-stained scraps of paper. The poignant sight never failed to move her.

Today was like no other day. It was a culmination of sorts, for it was the very last day of the forty-day quest. Though she felt sorry that her daily trek had come to an end, there was a heady, intoxicating feeling lifting her spirits.

She felt quite ready for her life to begin.

She *davened* to *Hashem* from the depths of her soul, holding the small sheet of paper on which she'd written her deepest thoughts and dreams. She recited her words silently, but her purpose was clear. Afterwards, she lingered at the Wall, her hands touching the smooth stones, not wanting to leave.

After much time had elapsed, she reluctantly walked backwards until she reached the plaza area in front of the *Kosel*, and wondered if she would find an available cab to take her back to Bayit Vegan. Just then, she spied Daniella Strauss who stood close by, not seeing her.

She walked over to her.

"Daniella?" she asked.

The young girl turned to her.

"Oh, hi, Sarah, how are you? Enjoying time off from school?"

"Not really," confessed Sarah. "I enjoy the seminary so much, I can hardly wait to resume classes after *Pesach*."

"I know what you mean," she answered understandingly.

"Are you heading back to Bayit Vegan? Would you like to share a taxi?"

"Actually, my father's here," she replied. "Oh … there he is now. Dad! Over here!"

Sarah stared in astonishment as Peter Strauss, the very same attorney that she'd met in Chicago a year earlier, strode over to where his daughter was standing. He looked the way she remembered, except … except …

There was a black velvet *yarmulka* on his head. He was dressed in a white shirt and black pants, and his entire demeanor seemed somehow changed, altered.

Could this possibly mean … ?

"Daddy, I'd like to introduce you to a classmate of mine. This is Sarah Morgenstern."

It was only then that Peter shifted his gaze from his daughter and saw Sarah for the first time.

For several seconds, neither of them spoke.

Peter found his voice first.

"A classmate?" he asked softly.

She nodded and looked down. The sincerity in his gaze was too intense.

"So it's Morgenstern, then?"

She nodded again. "My father changed it to Morgan, years ago. I … I changed it back to the original. It's a long story, I guess."

"I'm in no rush," he offered.

Daniella looked in confusion from her father to Sarah, and back again. They seemed to have forgotten that she was there.

"Do you two know each other?"

They nodded.

Sarah's face flushed crimson as she thought of their dinner meeting a year earlier, recalling what they'd said … what they'd eaten ….

It was totally obvious that they had each been different

people at the time. She was curious about Peter's remarkable transformation, and from the look on his face, he was just as curious about hers. She found herself wondering if she'd ever learn the answer, but somehow she knew that she would indeed become privy to that information, and soon.

As if on cue, Peter said, "You know, there's a nice little bagel shop just a few steps from here. Would you like to join us for lunch? It has a good *hechsher*, I understand."

"That's very kind of you, I'd like that," she replied with a smile.

And so it was that the three of them walked together, just steps away from the holiest site on Earth, their footsteps quietly echoing on the cobbled stones that had been tread upon by the Jewish people for generations. As they walked together, surrounded by the sun-drenched hills of Jerusalem, where *Hashem*'s presence hovers close and where dreams are realized, Sarah felt her past begin to fade into oblivion.

It was true that they had met each other under quite different circumstances. Yet her initial embarrassment soon yielded to a sense of soaring hope and joy. The tremendous obstacles that they had each overcome only served as a reminder of how much more there was still left to experience … to accomplish …

They'd only just begun.

All at once, Sarah felt that she was finally free to leave her past behind her, and begin to imagine …

The future.

GLOSSARY

AISHES CHAYIL – the last chapter of Proverbs, traditionally sung on Friday night in praise of both one's wife and the Sabbath

AUFRUF (Yidd.) – celebration for the groom, held on the Sabbath before his wedding, at which he is called up to recite the blessings on the Torah reading

BAALAS TESHUVA – a woman who has returned to Torah observance

BADEKEN (Yidd.) – part of the Jewish wedding ceremony in which the groom covers the bride's face with a veil and blesses her

BAR MITZVAH – coming of age for a thirteen-year-old Jewish male, at which point he assumes the responsibilities of an adult to fulfill the Torah's commandments. It is usually accompanied by a party.

BASHERT (Yidd.) – destined marriage partner

BAT MITZVAH – coming of age for a twelve-year-old Jewish female, at which point she assumes the responsibilities of an adult to fulfill the Torah's commandments. It is sometimes accompanied by a party.

BENTCHER (Yidd.)– booklet containing the text of Grace After Meals

BRACHOS – blessings

BUBBIE (Yidd.) – grandmother

CHALLAH – special bread used for the Sabbath and holidays

CHEVRA KADISHA – burial society

CHUPPAH – wedding canopy

DAVEN (Yidd.) – pray

KADDISH – prayer that expresses hope for the ultimate Redemption, customarily recited during the eleven months following the death of a parent and on the anniversary of a parent's death.

KALLAH – bride

KIDDUSH – blessing that sanctifies the Sabbath

KOSEL – the Western Wall, a remnant of the containing wall from the Second Temple

HAVDALA – blessing made at the conclusion of the Sabbath, which separates between the Sabbath and the weekdays

HECHSHER – kosher certification

MAGEN DAVID – Star of David, a traditional Jewish symbol

MAZEL TOV – good luck

MINYAN – quorum of ten adult Jewish males necessary for public prayer

MITZVAH – Torah commandment

ROSH CHODESH – the beginning of a new month in the Jewish calendar

SHABBAT – the Sabbath; Sephardic pronunciation

SHABBOS – the Sabbath; Ashkenazic pronunciation

SHALOM ALEICHEM – lit., "peace be upon you"; traditonal Jewish greeting

SHEVA BRACHOS – blessings recited at the wedding and following the newlywed couple's meals during the seven days after the wedding

SHIDDUCH – potential marriage partner

SHTETL (Yidd.) – traditional Jewish village

SIDDUR – prayer book

TESHUVA – repentance

YARMULKA (Yidd.) – skullcap

YESHIVA – school that teaches Torah